A Close En[...] Mushrooms

M000309989

(A second case for Commissario Beppe Stancato)

Richard Walmsley

By the same author
The 'Puglia' series of novels
Dancing to the Pizzica (2012)
The Demise of Judge Grassi (2013)
Leonardo's Trouble with Molecules (2014)
+
Long Shorts
(A collection of fifteen unusual and amusing stories – updated 2015)
+
The Commissario Stancato novels – set in Abruzzo
The Case of the Sleeping Beauty (2015)
A Close Encounter with Mushrooms (2016)
The Vanishing Physicist (2017)

+
The Curse of Collemaga (A novel 2019)
+
Puglia with the Gloves Off - Book 1 Salento
(A travelogue – 2019)

Cover design by Esther Kezia Thorpe

esther.k.thorpe@gmail.com

(The cover image depicts the town of Loreto Aprutino, in Abruzzo, based on a photo taken by the author and adapted by EKT)

Published by nonno-riccardo-publications

richard_s_walmsley@hotmail.com

Introduction

It is a fact that hundreds of Italians indulge in the nation's passion for mushroom picking every year. Poisonous mushrooms are all too frequently mistaken for their edible counterparts – with occasionally fatal consequences. This simple starting point gave me the idea of writing a mystery novel about how a man with murder in his heart uses his knowledge of poisonous mushrooms to take his revenge on the man whom he believes to be responsible for his wife's death.

This is the second novel in the Commissario Beppe Stancato series, set in that unspoilt and little-known region of La Bella Italia – Abruzzo. Although there are a few references to the previous novel, 'The Case of the Sleeping Beauty', this story is entirely free-standing.

There is a glossary of the very limited number of Italian expressions used - intended purely to add local colour - plus some interesting cultural notes at the end of the book.

Buona lettura!

August 2016

Prologue

Do you realise these are worth upwards of €50 per kilo? Where on earth did you find them, Salvatore?

No more than three kilometres away. I was out with the dogs. I went up the mountains towards that waterfall, you know, the one just outside Farindola. I came across them by chance in the woods nearby. I'll take you to the spot if you like.

I know where the *Vitello d'Oro* waterfall is – and even what it is called. By the way, I hope you have a licence for picking mushrooms, Salvatore. May I call you Salvo? You could get yourself into big trouble with the *Guardia Forestale.* If I had a grudge against you, heaven forbid, I could simply report my suspicions to them – or to the Chamber of Commerce in Pescara. I've known a number of amateur mushroom-pickers who have been shopped to the authorities in this manner – often with the simple motive of ensuring that as few people as possible can legally forage for our precious mushrooms. So have a care, Salvo! The fines can be hefty and you can make enemies all too easily. The rivalry between mushroom pickers is fierce. *È la guerra* – and not always a cold war either.

Oh, I doubt whether I shall make a habit of it. But I would like to make a risotto out of these – if you are certain they are edible, of course.

Edible! They are fit for a king - or, as a good Republican, maybe I should say fit for a president. Just don't share your risotto with anyone else, though. It will be wasted on ordinary mortals. Besides which, you only picked enough for one generous serving.

So what kind of mushrooms are they? I suppose they have some exotic-sounding name that only you would know?

You flatter me, Salvo. I can assure you there are a number of mushroom experts in these parts – not to mention restaurant owners - who would pay double their worth just to create a risotto or serve them up with a plate of *pappardelle.* You have just picked the choicest possible examples of a mushroom whose official name is *Ovolo dei Cesari.*

I am none the wiser, but thank you for reassuring me as to their edibility.

It's a pleasure, Salvo. But I must castigate you, *amico mio.* Should you ever go foraging for mushrooms again, please take a proper knife with you. You have tugged this rare species out of the ground. Always cut mushrooms low down on their stem. That way, they will grow again.

Of course! How remiss of me! I'm sorry, er... Damiano. I realise I've just committed a mortal sin in the eyes of the mushroom fraternity. Don't worry. I doubt I shall go mushroom-picking again – not on my own at any rate.

Then I merely wish you a rewarding culinary experience, Salvo.

Are you sure you won't share them with me?

Next time, maybe. Someday soon, we'll go mushroom-hunting together. Then you can show me exactly where you found these - how shall I put it? - quite *exceptional* specimens! On this occasion, just enjoy them all on your own. I would feel guilty if I deprived you of even one single mouthful. In fact, why don't you let me give you a handful of extra mushrooms to add to your recipe? Some local *Gallinacci* mushrooms, which I collected only this morning; they'll enrich the flavour of your sauce. *(Gallinacci = Chanterelles)*

You are very generous. Grazie mille! They told me you would be very helpful.

Don't mention it, Salvo. *Buon appetito!*

* * *

The man, whom everybody in this mountain village of just 1500 inhabitants, knew simply as Damiano, wore a secret smile as he shut the main door behind his visitor's departing figure.

"Strange how things work out so perfectly sometimes," he thought as he pictured the outcome of Salvatore's culinary experiment. "It couldn't have worked out better if I'd been planning it for years," he thought with a profound sense of ironic satisfaction that justice would finally be meted out – as if by the hand of God. That, at least, was how Damiano chose to interpret his deadly sin of omission. "And to think he didn't even recognise me!" he muttered in disbelief. "It was only five years ago, after all. I suppose I must have aged more rapidly than I care to admit after what happened. But, more likely than not, he never really took the trouble to notice who I was," he concluded bitterly. But the name of the man who had condemned his lifelong partner to an agonising end was permanently etched in his memory.

His revenge would have been so much sweeter had Salvatore Carlettini fully appreciated the reason why he was suffering so much pain – in the same measure that his beloved wife, Renata, had had to endure for hours on end before death mercifully gave her eternal peace.

1: Beppe Stancato's self-fulfilling prophecies...

"The trouble with you, *amore*," said Sonia smiling across the breakfast table at her fiancé, Beppe Stancato, "is that you are far too complex a person for your own peace of mind. You have a secure job which you are brilliant at, a doting partner who can't get enough of you - and your own boat just a couple of paces away from this apartment. What more could a man wish for in this life?" she added mischievously, knowing full well what had provoked the unwittingly revealing sigh as he pulled his croissant apart and dunked bits of it aggressively into his cup of black coffee.

It had been over three months since *Commissario* Stancato and his team had dramatically rescued Serena Vacri from the clutches of the Mafioso *boss,* during the latter's seventieth birthday party.

In the course of that three month lull, the most demanding investigation the team had had to contend with was that of a covert group of reactionary eccentrics who had set fire to an old, petrol-filled Renault on a stretch of waste ground outside Pescara, where it was planned to build a new transmitter mast to improve mobile phone reception in the area. It had taken three days to identify the culprits, who had graced themselves with the ingeniously enigmatic codename of *Kay Tee* – designed to sound like an English girl's name.

It had been Sonia herself with the help of Pippo Cafarelli, Oriana Salvati, Danilo Simone and Gino Martelli who had done the leg work and the detection leading to the arrest of three sets of parents living near the proposed site of the new transmitter. They had acted decisively, they explained, because they believed firmly that the electro-magnetic waves would harm their children's brain cells. The ring-leader was indeed an English mother called Katie, married to an Italian husband. The "K", she explained, stood for KILL and the "T" for TRALICCIO – a transmitter mast. Thus, 'Katie' had a double sense.

Commissario Stancato had left the whole task to his team and they had successfully tracked down the "telephone terrorists", as the media had nicknamed them, entirely without his intervention. It had left him feeling like a desk-bound bureaucrat, good only for putting his signature to bits of pointless paper. With the *Questore's* consent, Beppe had not pressed charges against the culprits. The couples had paid a fine to cover the cost of cleaning up the damaged site and were warned not to attempt any more protests with potential risk to human lives.

"Please try some more conventional form of protest in future," he had caustically advised them.

Sonia had correctly interpreted his deep sigh at the breakfast table as that of a man used to a challenge, whose life had become too easy. She said so to Beppe in as many words.

"You should be proud of yourself that you have inspired so many of us to work together as a team. You have earned the undying loyalty of everyone in that police station," Sonia stated earnestly. "Your trouble is that you are suffering from guilt because you are enjoying life too much. I've always said you are a complex man, Beppe Stancato. To think you always tried to convince everybody how shallow you were..." she concluded smiling at the memory.

Beppe sat looking intently at his *fidanzata* from the other side of the breakfast table for a disconcerting fifteen seconds. Sonia did not flinch. She knew he was turning over her words in his mind before coming to terms with the truth they contained.

Somewhat to her astonishment, however, the wordless reaction of her lover was to stand up and walk round to her side of the table. He had *that look* in his eyes which meant they were about to return to their recently vacated bed.

Sonia found her arms being held firmly just above her elbows by Beppe's hands. She was being propelled backwards with a momentum she did not try to resist. The intensity of the expression in his eyes held her spellbound. She felt a deep sense of carnal excitement as she was robbed of any power to control what was happening to her. She collapsed onto the unmade bed.

Her climax was rapid as she felt every part of her body alive and vibrant. She felt something stir deep inside her. Some girlfriend of hers had once confided in her that she had registered the moment of conception of her first child. Sonia had been sceptical about the likelihood of such a thing. Now she was not so certain. Something out of the ordinary had just taken place in the mysterious workings of her womanhood.

A few timeless minutes later, Beppe was lying breathless beside her. He had a self-satisfied grin on his face born out of the mutual release of their pent up energies. A good job it was Sunday, thought Beppe. The distant chiming of church bells echoed round the city, calling the faithful to early mass.

When the power of speech returned, Beppe spoke to his partner calmly.

"I want you to know that I love you more than words can say, Sonia Leardi. My present *ennui* at work has nothing to do with what we mean to each other. That is as solid as a rock on the ocean floor..."

Sonia felt a flood of warmth spreading throughout her body at his words but she did not say anything - not wishing to trivialise the moment.

"What I wish for most is to have children with you and, preferably, to have some compellingly engaging investigation land on my desk by tomorrow," continued Beppe as if talking to himself.

Without a word, Sonia shifted her position. She lay on top of him and cupped his head between her palms, partly covering his ears. He was aroused by the sensation of her breasts, stomach and thighs pressed against the length of his body.

"You should be careful what you wish for, *amore mio*," she whispered fiercely.

* * *

The main reason Sonia and Beppe attended mass on alternate Sundays at 11 o'clock was out of respect for the Archbishop of Pescara, Don Emanuele, whose quasi-paranormal intervention had enabled Beppe to force the Mafioso *boss* Don Alfieri to confess his guilt, thereby saving police time and bringing the case of the 'Sleeping Beauty' to a satisfactory conclusion.

Sonia pointed out that they might well end up getting married in the cathedral of *San Cetteo* and it was therefore a sound gesture of ecclesiastical diplomacy to be seen to attend mass regularly there. She was hoping that Don Emanuele would be the one to tie the knot for them when the appointed day arrived. The Archbishop preached a sermon in the cathedral on a fortnightly basis. It was as well to turn up early on those Sundays because it was obvious that the faithful – and even the disbelievers - of Pescara all thought the same way when it came to being inspired by Don Emanuele's sermons. His famous sermon just after the earthquake in L'Aquila had passed into the realms of urban legend; he had been reduced to tears of grief in the middle of his own homily. The population of Pescara had found this far more comforting and convincing than all the pious words of the other clerics put together.

Thus began the phenomenon of a cathedral filled to bursting point on the Sundays when he was due to give his sermon. Latecomers were obliged to stand up during the whole of the service filling up the spaces at the back and the sides of the wide nave. The parish priest had proposed selling tickets at €5 a time on the Sundays when the Archbishop was due to preach, to help with the upkeep of the cathedral. But the scheme had been instantly quashed - by the Archbishop himself, who believed unshakeably that God always provided for just sufficient financial support to be on hand at any given time.

On this particular Sunday, Beppe and Sonia had decided to walk to the cathedral on such a sunny autumn day and, consequently, were obliged to stand in the side aisle of the church in the company of the other latecomers who had been unable to find seats.

They had crept in unobtrusively just as the Archbishop was about to begin his sermon. He always preached standing on the lowest of the steps leading up to the altar – an unconscious act of humility maybe. "I am one of you," he had replied simply when a member of the congregation had asked why he never preached from the lectern. His voice was always calm and crystal clear and the silence in the cathedral was such that his words filled the spacious nave without the help of the loudspeakers. "Did Jesus need a microphone when he spoke to the crowds on Mount Eremos?" he was purported to have exclaimed on one occasion.

Sonia was quite convinced that Don Emanuele had noticed their late arrival. She was equally convinced that his brief smile was directed straight at them as they tried to mingle with the people nearest the door without being spotted.

*When I was a teenager in Naples, **I** always tried to arrive at mass after the sermon was **over**!* Don Emanuele said emitting a chuckle.

There were ripples of subdued laughter from the congregation, who swivelled their heads round to see who the latecomers were. Beppe and Sonia merged with the crowd, trying to look inconspicuous. Now the whole congregation was looking expectantly at the Archbishop - curious to know what spiritual path he would lead them along on this particular occasion.

"In the name of the Father and of the Son and of the Holy Spirit," he began, making the sign of the cross.

*In today's gospel, we heard about the miracle of the feeding of the five thousand. An atheist friend of mine told me a few days ago what he thought had **really** happened before all those people suddenly discovered there was food to go round. "Jesus must have been a great psychologist," my disbelieving friend told me. "**He** knew that every family had secretly brought food with them but they had kept it hidden because they were afraid they would have to share theirs with their neighbours. As soon as they saw the disciples coming round with pieces of bread and a few fish, they decided it was safe to delve into their own food baskets and surreptitiously tuck in. That's why there was enough food to go round!"*

Some of the congregation found this interpretation amusing – especially the younger ones. Others sat in frozen shock that the Archbishop had seemed to be casting doubts on the veracity of what was one of Jesus's most memorable miracles. Don Emanuele continued unperturbed.

My very disbelieving friend, Sebastiano, went on to tell me that there is no such thing as miracles - that there is always a simple, logical explanation.

The Archbishop paused with perfectly timed dramatic effect as the rays of the sun, transformed by the stained glass windows into warm autumn colours, lit up the crown of his shaved head. His ascetic looking figure seemed to have grown in stature. His piercing grey eyes encompassed the whole congregation sitting or standing under the gentle arch of the curved wooden vault high above their heads. The feeling of expectant anticipation was tangible as the whole congregation waited to see how this man of God would cope with his atheist friend's cynicism.

Oh Sebastiano, I said, open your eyes and see God's creation as it really is. Every single day, every single breath we take is a miracle in itself. For all the evil in this world - which I cannot begin to comprehend - there is a sense of mystery in everything we do. This week, I met a young priest from Città Sant'Angelo who came to see me with the sole purpose of sharing with me his soul-changing experience of a few days previously.

"Monsignore," he began – before I begged him to call me padre, *telling him I was an ordinary priest like him.*

"Thank you, father," he said. "I have to tell you about a little six-year-old boy called Lorenzo in my parish. He is an only child and he was taken to our hospital here in Pescara suffering from some rare strain of nephritis, which was attacking his kidneys. His parents came to mass on Sunday and I asked them after mass why they hadn't got their little boy with them. The mother burst into uncontrollable tears. It was Lorenzo's father who managed to tell me what had happened. What could I do, father? I said the first thing that occurred to me. 'Come back inside the church and let us pray together at the altar,' I suggested to them. Honestly, father, I felt a bit stupid but Lorenzo's parents would have clutched at any straw at that moment. They nodded and followed me back into the church."

I hope you're concentrating on this, Sebastiano, I told my atheist friend, because he had a scornful smile on his face while I was telling him about this priest's experience.

"Well," continued my humble parish priest. "We were all three kneeling at the altar with the mother between me and her husband, when I blurted it out!"

I had to wait a minute or so before the priest could find the courage to carry on.

"I don't know to this minute what made me do it, father. After we had been praying in silence for some time, I stood up and I found I was saying the words: 'Don't worry anymore. Your little boy Lorenzo will be fine.' The parents looked at me as if I had taken leave of my senses. At that moment, the mother's mobile phone began vibrating. She apologised for it being on in church. I waved my hand to say it didn't matter. A look of sheer dread passed over her face. 'It's the hospital,' she said.

"Father," continued my priest almost in tears. "I could clearly hear the words of the doctor over the phone. He was saying: 'Signora, I think you and your husband should come to the hospital at once.' The mother was looking at me with a look of such deep resentment that I wanted the floor to open and swallow me up. I tried to apologise to her for raising false hopes but the words stuck in my throat. Then I heard the doctor say: 'And bring some clothes with you for Lorenzo. It would appear that he has made a complete recovery.'

The Archbishop paused as if he had finished all he had to say. There was total silence in the cathedral. Beppe found that Sonia's hand was gripping his own hand tightly. Everybody was waiting for the Archbishop to continue. After a few minutes the Archbishop made the sign of the cross saying the words: *In the name of the Father...* as if that was the end of the sermon.

"NO!" cried out a woman's voice from the seated congregation. After being briefly startled by this unexpected interruption, a wave of laughter broke out, as people realised that the woman was expressing the same sense of frustrated anticipation which they all shared. Don Emanuele, who had not quite got to the "and of the son" part of his cross, had a smirk on his face.

"He's enjoying himself," thought Beppe.

The young woman who had called out rose sheepishly to her feet.

"Father, please! You can't leave it like that! Was it a miracle – or not?"

"What do YOU think, signorina?"

"I... I don't know. I think so. Can't you tell us, please?" she said pleadingly.

"What I say to you all is this: Blessed are those of you who have heard only my words – and yet believe," said Don Emanuele, misquoting the words of the Bible when Jesus chided his disciple Thomas for not believing he was resurrected – even though the other disciples had told him so repeatedly.

The woman sat down again, still blushing at her own impetuous outburst.

The Archbishop smiled kindly at her and let out a sigh of mock despair at her seeming lack of faith.

Just remember that miracles occur every day. Think of a baby being born. Nine months before this event, there was no baby. He or she has been miraculously created out of almost nothing – exactly like our own universe.

Sonia held Beppe's hand even tighter as she was reminded of her powerful sensations earlier on that morning. Don Emanuele let out another sigh of feigned resignation. The congregation stirred at his next words. He had been leading them on intentionally.

"Fortunately for you all, there is someone present here today who can put all your doubts to rest. Dottore Esposito – can you please come and tell these good people about little Lorenzo?"

The well-known figure of the hospital's chief toxicologist arose from the congregation and came and stood next to Don Emanuele. In a quiet and dignified voice, he uttered the words:

"I can confirm that Lorenzo was discharged from our hospital. All traces of his nephritis had disappeared – overnight. I can offer you no medical explanation as to why this should be so."

The doctor sat down again.

"Now, does anybody want to ask me a question?" said Don Emanuele with a broad smile on his face.

"What about the priest, father? What has happened to him?" asked someone out of genuine curiosity.

"Oh, I packed him off to the Vatican to talk to the Pope," answered the Archbishop, who then completed making the sign of the cross from where he had left off, signalling to the whole congregation that he had nothing to add.

* * *

After the mass was over, Don Emanuele, in his immaculate white alb, was standing outside the cathedral saying goodbye to his congregation or blessing the occasional toddler when requested by the parents. Beppe and Sonia headed purposefully in his direction. He seemed to be expecting them. Beppe apologised for arriving late but the Archbishop merely shrugged and said: "It's alright, Beppe and Sonia. You didn't miss much."

Sonia was looking meaningfully at Don Emanuele.

"You want to ask me if I will marry you both don't you, Sonia?" he stated simply.

Sonia's mouth dropped open in astonishment. The Archbishop's steely grey eyes held hers. She felt mesmerised.

"It will give me great joy to unite you two in marriage, Sonia. And..." he paused for a few seconds, "... I think that this happy event will have to take place sooner rather than later, don't you?" he added looking meaningfully at Sonia, who continued to gaze at the Archbishop with her mouth agape.

"How did you know...?" she finally managed to stutter. She left the sentence unfinished, quite bemused by his apparently uncanny insight.

"Is there something you ought to have told me?" asked Beppe on the way home. Despite himself, he felt piqued that the archbishop seemed to have spotted something that he hadn't. He had also been shaken out of his habitual procrastination when it came to resolving issues in his personal life.

The presence of the inexplicable still clung to them both after the extraordinary revelation during Don Emanuele's sermon. It prompted Sonia to blurt out:

"I'm expecting our first child," she said. "Or, at least, I think I am..."

"But how long have you known this?" asked Beppe, secretly filled with joy, tempered by a hint of resentment that Don Emanuele seemed to have known about it before he did.

"Oh, about two hours," replied Sonia as nonchalantly as possible.

Beppe walked home with his arm round Sonia's waist. He had a dreamy, smug grin on his face. Was he finally going to be a father?

"No more red wine for us from now on," he said with barely a note of regret in his voice.

* * *

Such was the impact of the events of that Sunday that Beppe and Sonia barely registered any surprise when, walking into the police station in Via Pesaro the following day, *Agente* Remo Mastrodicasa, on duty at the reception desk, informed him that the *Questore* needed to see him urgently.

"He's got a rather unusual assignment for you, *capo* – he told me to tell you."

Sonia smiled broadly at Beppe as he set foot on the first step of the stairs which led to the upper reaches of the police station.

"I told you to be careful what you wished for, *amore,*" she said.

2: The dogs that wouldn't stop barking...

"Ah, *buongiorno, commissario,*" said the *Questore,* Dante Di Pasquale, dressed in full regalia. He got up from his swivel chair and walked round to the front of his desk to greet Beppe, his hand outstretched. The two men shook hands warmly, the *Questore* cupping Beppe's right hand in both of his. Disarmed by the warmth of his chief's gesture, Beppe did not have time to be taken unawares by the direction that the conversation took.

"I understand you've been getting a little bit bored over the last few weeks, Beppe. They tell me you haven't had enough to occupy your mind," began the *Questore,* smiling at his second-in-command. "I think I might have found something worthy of your attention," he continued, sitting down on one of the padded chairs in front of his desk whilst gesturing for Beppe to occupy the second one.

Beppe smiled wryly at his chief.

"I thank you for bearing me in mind, *capo.* I am always full of admiration as to how well-informed you manage to be about what is happening down below you. On occasions, I even suspect that you may possess some uncanny powers of clairvoyance..."

"You mean, like our Archbishop, Don Emanuele," interjected the *Questore* to Beppe's further astonishment. "I was at that mass too yesterday, Beppe – out of uniform, of course. I saw you and Sonia sneaking in late. Quite a remarkable sermon wouldn't you say?" continued the *Questore,* ignoring the look on his senior officer's face. "And do you know? The newspapers are already trying desperately to find some rational explanation for that little boy's recovery. There is a disturbing lack of faith in our modern-day society, wouldn't you agree?"

The thought was going through Beppe's mind that his chief was an adept at the art of maintaining the respect of his team by knowing exactly what was going on while appearing never to interfere in everyday matters. It was an impressive gift, he thought.

He acknowledged both his respect for the man and agreement with the sentiment expressed by his chief, inclining his head and spreading out his arms, palms upwards, in a gesture that was intended to indicate that there was little else he could meaningfully add.

"Now, wouldn't you like to know what I have in store for you, Beppe?" continued the *Questore* with a grin.

"Of course, I would *capo,*" replied Beppe, stifling the desire to ask how on earth the *Questore* had found out about his state of restless dissatisfaction.

His chief sensed what he was thinking and merely added diplomatically:

"I think you'll find that your team are genuinely concerned about your lack of a motivating case to investigate, Beppe."

Beppe was looking expectantly at his chief.

"*Dunque,*" continued the *Questore.* "I had an unexpected phone call from our *Carabiniere* colleague, *Il Colonnello* Riccardo Grimaldi."

"Don't tell me he needs the help of the humble State Police!" exclaimed Beppe with mock irony.

"You know what the *Carabinieri* are like, Beppe. It might be they are happy for us ordinary policeman to deal with what they consider a minor investigation. But the *Colonnello,* Riccardo Grimaldi, isn't tarred with the same brush as the majority of his colleagues – as we know from his recent willingness to cooperate with us. Apparently, he has been contacted by a young officer of his called Enrico Nardini, from Loreto Aprutino. You most certainly remember him from when he was a simple *tenente* in Sulmona."

"I remember him well, *capo*, during the hunt for our Sleeping Beauty. He made a very good impression on both me and Sonia. But what's he doing in Loreto Aprutino?"

"He's been promoted to *capitano* and was transferred to Loreto Aprutino, as far away as possible from that somewhat ineffectual captain in Sulmona, who is now, mercifully, only three months away from retirement."

"Enrico Nardini deserved the promotion. I'm happy for him," commented Beppe. "But how come he's asking for *our* help?"

"There's an unlikely – but healthy – network of friendships between Enrico, Giovanni Palena and his partner – our very own Oriana Salvati. Oriana and her partner, Giovanni Palena – you remember, the officer from L'Aquila – live in Loreto Aprutino too. Apparently, Oriana and Giovanni considered it fairer to live halfway between their respective places of work. To cut a long story short, it was Oriana who suggested to Enrico that he should contact the *Colonnello* here in Pescara to see if they could enlist your help, Beppe."

So, thought Beppe, he had Oriana to thank for his unexpected reprieve from inactivity. Not exactly the hand of God but, these days, the Good Lord seemed to be working very hard through human agents on his behalf, considered the *commissario*.

"So," continued Beppe, coming back down to earth, "what seems to be the problem?"

"I gather Enrico Nardini has landed up with a case that he is finding somewhat baffling. I'm told he isn't sure how to proceed. They were wondering if I could spare you for a couple of days to go up to Loreto Aprutino to give him some inspiration. Naturally, I said I would have to ask you first."

"But what makes this case so problematic, *capo?*" Beppe asked, puzzled by the request.

"Well, I'll let Enrico fill you in as to the details – should you decide to follow it up, of course. On the surface, it appears to be an accidental death by food poisoning – some guy with two dogs. The neighbours were alerted because the animals wouldn't stop howling. I gather he consumed some deadly concoction of mushrooms – apparently made into a pasta sauce. By the time the ambulance got him to the hospital in Penne, it was too late to save him."

"So why does Enrico need *my* help?" asked Beppe, still perplexed.

"He can't quite put his finger on it, Beppe, but he strongly suspects that the death wasn't a simple case of accidental poisoning. He's not sure how to set about proving his suspicions are justified."

The *Questore* had stopped talking and was looking expectantly at his second-in-command, who appeared to be plunged into deep thought.

To his own bewilderment, Beppe was less overjoyed at the prospect of a challenging investigation than he had imagined. He quickly identified the reason for this reaction at the same moment as he realised that he could not allow his personal feelings to interfere with his professional life. He simply felt he could not abandon Sonia at this crucial point in their relationship. He countered the argument by reasoning with himself that they were not officially certain about her expecting a child at this point in time. No, there was no logical reason why he should not leave her for a couple of days to go and give a helping hand to a colleague.

The *Questore,* sensing the reason for Beppe's hesitation, said quietly:

"Don't worry, Beppe. We'll keep an eye on Sonia for you."

At least, thought Beppe, his chief's insight hadn't led him to the same conclusions as Don Emanuele, the Archbishop of Pescara, outside the cathedral the day before.

"Yes, of course I'll go to Loreto Aprutino and see what I can do to help *Capitano* Nardini," he said finally.

"Get one of the team to drive you there, Beppe," suggested the *Questore.* "If you've never been to Loreto Aprutino - or its near neighbour, Penne - then you are in for a treat. They are both beautiful medieval hilltop towns. In fact, Penne has the privilege of being officially designated as one of "The Most Beautiful Towns in Italy".

"Exactly the right setting for a case of good old-fashioned poisoning!" muttered Beppe as if to himself.

* * *

Later that morning, Beppe and his colleague, Pippo Cafarelli, were driving at a steady pace towards Loreto Aprutino – no more than half an hour's journey from Pescara along the provincial road. Pippo was at the wheel, driving unusually slowly for him, thought Beppe, leaving him time to reflect on his unexpected break from bureaucratic monotony.

Before leaving the police station, Beppe had taken Sonia to one side while he explained to his *fidanzata* what their chief had in mind for him. Was it his imagination or did Sonia give the impression that the news was not as totally unexpected as it might have been? If Oriana had been the instigator behind his reprieve from boredom, it was quite probable that she had already talked to Sonia about Enrico Nardini's request. Beppe looked suspiciously at Sonia, who kissed him on the mouth and added:

"I shall miss you, *amore.* Make sure you keep out of trouble, won't you!"

"I'll phone you later on," he promised, thinking it was unnecessary to delve into the matter of what steps had led to his release from routine. After all, it had all been with his best interests in mind. Nevertheless, wasn't he supposed to be in charge of his own professional life?

He had passed Oriana Salvati in the corridor. He had wanted to reprimand her mildly but she flashed an engaging smile in his direction and hurried on towards the entrance to the police headquarters in the company of the two male officers, Danilo Simone and Gino Martelli.

"Sorry, *capo.* I can't stop. There's a tobacconist in town who's just been held up by two helmeted gunmen... *In bocca al lupo,"* she had added before disappearing.

She wished me luck, thought Beppe. The benign conspiracy theory held good.

On the road to Loreto Aprutino, Beppe had expected to pass a restaurant called *La Bilancia,* where they had once been treated to a much-needed lunch by Oriana's uncle, the proprietor of the restaurant. On that occasion too, Beppe had had the distinct impression that Sonia and Oriana had colluded to engineer the visit to this restaurant. His tendency to skip lunchtimes when engrossed in a case was legendary at Pescara's police headquarters. To his surprise, Pippo took a right-hand turn well before they reached *La Bilancia.* Beppe commented on the route they were taking.

"This is the quickest route into Loreto Aprutino, *capo.* We're about to pass a famous old church called *La Chiesa di Santa Maria in Piano.* When you're not so busy, you and Sonia should go and have a look inside it. It's got some of the best-preserved frescos in the whole of Italy. They are truly breathtaking to behold."

"I'm sure Sonia already knows all about the frescos," said Beppe sullenly - the shadows of his conspiracy theory still niggling away despite his efforts to dispel them.

"We *all* know about these frescos, *capo*," said Pippo, who merely reinforced the *commissario's* sense of his team's collusion by the unintentional ambiguity of his observation.

Like his own very circumspect father, Beppe found it very hard to express his innermost feelings – especially when he acknowledged that they were negative. Yet he knew that if he had shared his misgivings with Sonia, she would simply have replied:

"But surely you can see that it's because everybody loves and respects you, Beppe? Everyone wants the best for you."

He sighed with a mixture of resignation and self-satisfaction as the police car pulled into the small car park behind the local *Carabinieri* station.

"Do you want me to stay with you, *capo?*" asked Pippo. "In case you need a lift back later?"

"Thanks Pippo. Yes, stay with me and see what Enrico Nardini has to say. I would value your company and your opinion."

"*Grazie, capo,*" replied Pippo gratefully, thereby dispelling the last vestige of resentment that Beppe had been harbouring that he had been manoeuvred into this investigation. *Capitano* Enrico Nardini came out into the car park smiling broadly at the two police officers as they stepped out of the car. He wore a look of relief on his face.

"Thank you so much for taking the trouble to come here, *commissario*," he said, shaking Beppe and Pippo by the hand.

* * *

Enrico Nardini had assumed that, since it was lunchtime, both his visitors would be in need of food. He drove them quickly across the hillside on a minor road towards Penne. At one point, the surface of the road seemed to have a gash in it like an open wound.

"As you can see, they haven't quite got round to repairing the road after the earthquake," Enrico explained with more than a touch of bitterness in his voice. Beppe was having his first glimpse of Penne. He caught sight of the magnificent round red-brick tower and its archway that led into the old city, whose streets were all cobbled. Enrico, however, continued to skirt round the old city. On the left, they passed a modern Conad supermarket.

"That's the road that leads down to Penne's lake," he pointed out a minute later. "It's a WWF nature reserve," he said with some surprise in his voice that such a place could exist in a country where the freedom to hunt wildlife was considered a birthright. Very soon afterwards, they pulled up outside a restaurant called *La Vestina,* Enrico parking the police car in *La Piazza XX Settembre* – officially reserved for residents only.

"Parking in Penne can be a bit of a problem, *commissario!*" he explained in all innocence. "Everybody for miles around comes to eat here," he explained to Beppe and Pippo as they entered the crowded restaurant. His guests were eyeing a whole hog supported on metal stands behind the counter from which several slices of meat had already been skilfully carved. The presence of two uniformed police officers and a third man who looked as if he meant business magically cleared a table in the restaurant area beyond the counter.

A girl in her twenties came over immediately to take their order. Enrico addressed her by her first name, Mariangela.

"She's the owner's daughter," he explained after he had ordered on their behalf. "You usually just order a cut of *porchetta* and a selection of side dishes. I hope that's alright for your two? You won't be disappointed."

Beppe had missed this kind of family run eating place since he had arrived in Pescara and was delighted to find such a restaurant where you simply ate what arrived in front of you. It was proof that the traditional Italy still survived as soon as you drove out of the city centres. He did not utter a word of protest when a litre carafe of red wine arrived with a bottle of spring water straight from the tap. He mentally raised his wine tumbler in respect for his absent partner, who had vowed to give up wine altogether. He would allow himself one glass, he thought to himself guiltily. The meat was accompanied by three varieties of carefully prepared side dishes, which complemented the tasty roast pork to perfection.

Viva l'Italia! Viva gli Abruzzesi!" said Beppe, as he toasted the occasion with the local wine.

"The wine is only 11 degrees of alcohol," said Enrico. "It's quite harmless! The owner makes it out of his own grapes."

Observing the proper Italian procedures, the business in hand was not mentioned until their appetites had been satisfied. Only then did Beppe look at Enrico Nardini, inviting him to begin telling them about his troublesome investigation. Pippo signalled to the waitress to bring them three coffees. They arrived with three small glasses of the local liqueur – *genziana.*

"Offre la casa," said the waitress, Mariangela, with a smile. "My dad's orders!"

"Thank your father very much," said Pippo, who managed to wrench his eyes away from the waitress and turn his attention to what Enrico was saying.

"The victim's name is Carlettini, Salvatore. He was forty-nine years old. He lived on his own with his two

Labradors in a country house just outside Montebello di Bertona – that's a village about ten kilometres from here as you begin to climb up towards the Gran Sasso," explained Enrico. "It was Salvatore Carlettini's neighbour who first raised the alarm almost two weeks ago. She told me the two Labradors had been barking all day. Of course, like most ordinary people, she didn't want to 'make a fuss' as she said. She just assumed her neighbour had gone out and left the dogs on guard, but added: 'He never leaves those animals alone normally'. It was only when the dogs started howling at night time that she decided to call us…"

"The general public never want to believe that something bad has happened on their own doorstep, do they?" said Beppe.

"That's right, *commissario,*" agreed Enrico. "So we lost a vital twelve hours before we broke into the house – after dark. I won't go into the details of the state we found the place in – not so soon after eating. But you can imagine it for yourselves. The dogs hadn't been let out all day…"

"*Che schifo!*" muttered Pippo, who was always sickened by the ease with which human and animal life could degrade into a state of putrefaction.

Enrico hurriedly continued with his narrative, avoiding the more gruesome physical aspects:

"Anyway, to cut a long story short we found Salvatore Carlettini barely conscious, lying on his bed. He was rushed to the hospital in Penne, where he was diagnosed with a massive failure of his kidneys and liver. They had him transferred overnight to the *Santo Spirito* hospital in Pescara. But they're not equipped to do liver and kidney transplants – he would have to have been transferred to Milano or Roma. Sadly, he passed away the following day…"

"So, *capitano*, we come to the big question," said Beppe. "What makes you think it was not simply a case of poisoning?"

"The autopsy quickly revealed the presence of poisonous mushrooms when they carried out an examination of his stomach contents... Sorry, *ragazzi,*" said Enrico as he noticed Pippo instinctively pushing his coffee cup away. "I contacted Salvatore's next of kin. He has a brother who lives with his wife and son in Città Sant'Angelo and a sister who lives here in Penne. It was the sister who first led me to believe that it might not have been a simple case of mistaken mushrooms. She rejected the notion outright that her brother would ever have run the risk of eating *anything* which he wasn't certain of. 'My brother was a hygiene *maniac,'* she told me. 'He cooked his chicken dishes until the bird was hardly recognisable. He washed his hands about a hundred times while he was preparing a meal. There is simply *no way* he'd have eaten mushrooms without being two-hundred per cent certain they were edible.' That's what makes me suspicious, *commissario.*"

Enrico Nardini paused for breath.

"That is about as much as I have to go on," he confessed sheepishly. "I merely had a gut feeling..."

"Well, Salvatore Carlettini certainly had that as well," muttered Pippo as if to himself.

"Sorry, I wasn't thinking. I'm waiting now to have a final report from the toxicologist in Pescara..."

"Are we talking about Doctor Bruno Esposito, by any chance?" asked Beppe, whose ears had pricked up.

"Yes, that's right, *commissario.* Do you know him?"

"Come on, *capitano.* Let's get back to the police station. I'll give Bruno Esposito a call from your office. He may well be able to shed some further light on your investigation. By the way, 'gut feelings' as you so aptly put it, are never to be dismissed in our profession."

Enrico did not ask for a bill, but went straight to the counter where the owner, Mariangela's father, was manning the cash register. The two 'strangers' in town complimented him on the food, the wine and the ambience. His gruff face was transformed by a beatific smile. Enrico looked at the bill and handed the proprietor a twenty euro note. Beppe and Pippo had automatically reached for their wallets and fished out the same amount of money. Enrico looked amused.

"The twenty euros was for all three of us," he said. "I'll treat you today."

"Non ci posso credere!" said Beppe outside the restaurant. "I can't believe how cheap that was."

"Antonio makes up the prices depending on how he feels about you on that particular day," explained Enrico with a grin. "But he always gives everyone a till receipt."

* * *

Back at the *Carabinieri* station, Beppe finally managed to track down his toxicologist friend, Doctor Bruno Esposito. He put the phone on loudspeaker mode as soon as he had got through.

"Ah, *Commissario* Stancato!" he said, agreeably surprised. "What can I do for you?"

Beppe explained why he was sitting in the police station in Loreto Aprutino in the company of an inquisitive *capitano* called Enrico Nardini.

Bruno Esposito had fallen silent for the space of ten seconds – which feels a long time when one is on the phone, thought Pippo. Finally, he began speaking:

"All I can say to your *capitano* is that Salvatore Carlettini ate some *very* toxic mushrooms and died a painful death all on his own. For reasons which we cannot speculate upon, he failed to call an ambulance in time to save his own life..."

Enrico's face had fallen on hearing these words. He sighed in resignation.

"The only aspect of this case which might be of some help to him..." continued Bruno Esposito after another significant pause, "...is that the two varieties of highly toxic mushrooms which I found in that poor man's stomach both have a *sosia* – an exact double – in the world of edible mushrooms."

All three police officers instantly looked alert at the doctor's words.

"We're all agog, Bruno," said Beppe.

"*Dunque...* Salvatore Carlettini had eaten **two** distinct types of poisonous mushrooms – that in itself is very unusual, Beppe. The first type was a species called Amanita Muscaria – very nasty, attacks the liver and kidneys within hours. But it has a highly prized and very edible 'double' called Ovolo dei Cesari. The second one is called Cortinarius Speciosissimus, and guess what? It can easily be mistaken for the eminently edible Gallinacci mushroom – Chanterelles as the French call them."

There was another long pause, so Beppe tried to pre-guess the direction that his friend's thought processes were taking.

"You mean that, given the victim's allegedly fastidious character, it is very unlikely that he didn't consult an expert before cooking them – am I right, Bruno?"

"Yes, that's precisely what I was thinking – but I don't want to put fanciful notions into your heads."

"Thank you, Bruno. You've given us a lot of food for thought," said Enrico Nardini, only recognising - for the second time - his hapless choice of words.

"Yes, thank you Bruno. You've been a great help. Could I possibly come and see you…?" Beppe began.

"By the way, Beppe – there *is* just one more peculiar aspect to this case," interrupted the toxicologist. "I'm sure this must be purely coincidental, but you remember the Archbishop's sermon yesterday, don't you? Yes, of course you do! Well, Salvatore Carlettini's brother, whose name is Ernesto, happens to be the father of the little boy who was inexplicably cured of nephritis."

3: Commissario Stancato's views on coincidences…

"Of course, I believe in coincidences, Pippo," said Beppe in answer to his junior officer's question, as they drove back to Pescara at a leisurely pace. Beppe had promised Enrico Nardini that he would return in a couple of days' time with a view to staying for as long as the investigation lasted.

Beppe had decided that it would be worth his while to have a longer talk with his friend the toxicologist as well as paying a visit to Ernesto Carlettini, the victim's younger brother. It was, Beppe considered, stretching coincidence too far that Salvatore Carlettini should die of failed kidneys and liver whilst his nephew should contract an illness related to his kidneys. He wanted to ask his friend, Bruno Esposito, whether the two events could possibly be connected. For the life of him, he could not see a connection. But the chain of events of the last two days had rendered him far more receptive to the notion that seemingly random occurrences appeared to be linked by invisible strands.

"For example," continued Beppe dutifully wishing to do justice to Pippo's query, "it was a coincidence that the Mafioso boss, Gianluca Alfieri, should have a birthday party on the day when we needed to raid his house to rescue Serena Vacri. All too often, coincidences appear to us mortals to be guided by providence. But the chances of two members of the same family independently suffering from kidney failure, seems to be stretching coincidence just a bit too far."

"I agree with you, *capo*," said Pippo.

"In any case, a visit to Ernesto Carlettini might well shed some light on the fate of his brother. I am also very curious to know more about their son, Lorenzo. I want to know whether the little boy's father believes his son was miraculously cured."

"Do you mean, *capo,* that you think there might be a rational explanation for the boy's cure?" asked Pippo, wanting to probe the strength of his senior officer's belief in a story which was rapidly circulating round the town of Pescara since the Archbishop's sermon of the previous day.

The police car had travelled a further two kilometres before Beppe answered his colleague. Pippo was regretting having asked the question at all. He was about to apologise for his lack of discretion as the heavy silence became increasingly embarrassing.

"No, I believe it was a miracle, or something very close to one," replied Beppe finally. "I cannot accept that the Archbishop on the one hand and Doctor Esposito on the other would have announced such a thing in church unless they considered that the boy's cure was not entirely explicable in medical terms."

Beppe wanted to tell Pippo about Don Emanuele's uncanny revelation outside the cathedral but he decided that his junior officer would be unable to keep the news to himself. In any case, Beppe reminded himself forcibly, there was no certainty as yet that he was about to become a father.

* * *

Back at the police headquarters in via Pesaro, the *commissario* was greeted with surprised delight by Sonia who had not expected him to return that day. He was simultaneously assailed by the three officers whom he had met heading for the exit that morning on their way to investigate the tobacconist who had been held up at pistol point.

"We need to have a word with you about this hold-up, *capo.* In our opinion, there is something about this incident that doesn't quite add up," said Gino.

"And it's the second such hold-up in the space of three days," added Oriana. "The first hold-up was a bit odd too."

Danilo merely nodded in agreement. The three officers followed their chief to his office. Beppe was thinking that their period of relative calm had come to an abrupt end.

"Right, *ragazzi* - so tell me what's bothering you," said Beppe, who had an inner dread that he knew precisely what his three team members were about to reveal.

Each of the officers looked at the two others in mute invitation, not wishing to be the first to express their suspicions.

Beppe took a silent bet with himself during the expectant lull. He reckoned that it would be Oriana who would take the initiative. He guessed correctly.

"There was the tobacconist today and a *salumiere* nearby a couple of days ago, *capo,*" she began. "You know – he runs that little delicatessen shop in *Viale Torrevecchia.* He seems determined to defy the supermarkets."

"These two thugs burst into the tobacconist's today," said Gino, taking up the narrative. "One of them was wielding a revolver. The tobacconist is a young guy and pretty solidly built – obviously not too easily scared. He told us his attackers were only teenagers – or at most in their early twenties."

"The tobacconist – he's called Luciano Quadri – told us he had the impression the youths just wanted to scare him - you know, as if it was some kind of teenage prank," continued Danilo. "They had motor-cycle helmets on and the one with the gun waved it about in the air demanding that the shopkeeper should empty his till. When Luciano refused, the other one came round and took a swipe at the cigarettes on display, scattering them all over the floor. He shouted insults and threats at the tobacconist. Luciano just went to pick up his telephone saying he was going to phone the police if they didn't clear off immediately..."

"Then a couple of customers entered the shop and the two thugs simply ran away," said Oriana.

"What about the *salumiere*?" asked Beppe, not yet wanting to ask the question which he feared would confirm his suspicions.

"He's a much older man and he was too scared to stand up to them, *capo*," said Gino. "He thought it would be safer to hand over the two hundred or so euros that he had in his till – it was only about nine o'clock in the morning so he didn't have a lot of cash anyway. But his description of these hoodlums exactly matched the one given by Luciano, the tobacconist..."

"Anything else unusual?" asked Beppe, tentatively.

The three officers looked at each other, silently waiting to see who would pluck up the courage to deliver the inevitable *coup de grâce*. Once again, it was Oriana who spoke up.

"Both Luciano Quadri and the *salumiere* told us the youths didn't have local accents. Luciano said it was quite distinctly a *pugliese* accent. He was very categorical; he told us that they came from Foggia..." Oriana paused, noticing the expression of resigned despair on their chief's face.

Commissario Stancato let out an audible sigh. It was exactly as he had feared.

"We thought the Puglian mafia might be endeavouring to expand their territory up here in Abruzzo," added Gino reluctantly.

"I wish I could tell you all that I don't agree with your interpretation, Gino," said Beppe after a brief pause. "But, I can't. I had an intuitive feeling about this almost before you began telling me about the hold-ups."

"So it's the *Sacra Corona Unita* on the move, is it?" stated Danilo quietly.

"It looks like it, *ragazzi.* I'm very familiar with the pattern. They start off by intimidating shop-keepers, restaurant owners, coffee-bars – often prostitutes too. They create a sense of fear in a particular neighbourhood by using unemployed teenagers and aspiring gangsters right down at the bottom of the clan's hierarchy – they are disposable items in the eyes of the clans. The mafia bosses know that their victims will become uneasy and talk to all the others just to reassure themselves they are not isolated. The fearful ones spread panic quickly."

Beppe looked at his team to gauge their reaction before continuing.

"When the management rank, within the clans, judge the time is ripe, they send the "negotiators" in. These individuals – always respectably dressed and sporting designer sunglasses and Rolex watches – do the rounds of all the establishments in the area. Increasingly - I hate to say this - the clans are using women. Many people running shops, restaurants, coffee bars and so on, find the presence of a woman beguilingly reassuring..."

"That would work very well when dealing with *le ragazze squillo* too, I imagine," observed Oriana Salvati thoughtfully.

"*Brava,* Oriana. You are absolutely right. Call girls are very vulnerable – and a lucrative source of income. Nobody – no man at least – wishes to believe that women are capable of being ruthless members of the mafia clans," Beppe added.

"Oh, we are a dangerous breed, *capo* – never to be underestimated."

Oriana was smiling impudently as she spoke these words, looking challengingly at her three male companions.

Beppe acknowledged the received message with a rueful smile, adding pointedly:

"Well, I guess there *are* times when we have to thank you women for your intervention in our lives – wouldn't you say so, Oriana?"

To his surprise, his junior female officer blushed whilst valiantly refusing to abandon her smile. She's really very sensitive beneath the tough exterior, thought the *commissario.*

"Anyway, getting back to the matter in hand..." he continued.

"So what form does the second visit by these so-called 'negotiators' take on, *capo?*" asked Danilo.

"Well... they like to appear as normal clients and ask for cigarettes, or to see a menu. Then one of them will broach the subject of the threats. You can imagine how they start off: "We've heard you've been having a bit of trouble in this area recently... very disturbing for you, I imagine." All said with great concern, of course. They will then explain that they are in a position to help protect the interests of local businesses, often saying they work for a specialised security company - or something of the kind – conveniently based far away in one of the big northern cities like Milan or Turin," explained Beppe.

His team members were listening with rapt attention to their chief's explanation of this new aspect of the underworld; Pescara had so far been relatively free from the tentacle-like grip of the mafia clans.

"It's an easy step from that point," continued their chief, "to persuade them to part with a small 'premium', along with the promise that there will be twenty-four-hour protection from the intrusion of hoodlums into their daily lives. If the 'persuaders' succeed, all they do is to tell the minor gangsters not to attack those particular premises again. This softening-up process often happens before the shopkeepers or restaurant owners realise who is behind the scam. Their 'premium', paid via an electronic transfer into a 'legitimate' bank account up north, becomes a fully-fledged *pizzo*." *(pizzo – protection money paid to the mafia clans)*

"But what can we do to prevent this happening, *capo?*" asked Gino.

"For the next day or so, *ragazzi,* I shall be involved in another case," said Beppe, looking meaningfully at Oriana Salvati – the instigator behind his new investigation. This time, however, she convinced herself there was a glint of humour in his eyes. "But you can organise yourselves during my absence. Take as many of the team as you can. It will involve a lot of footwork but well worth the effort, I'm sure you will all agree..."

"I guess we should do the rounds of every business in the neighbourhood and warn them of what is happening, *capo,"* said Oriana.

"*Appunto,* Oriana! Make sure you stress that, at this stage, there is little personal danger involved. If they feel intimidated, then tell them not to give way immediately to any threats. If they are anxious about their safety, they should part with as little cash or goods as possible. Just point out that, if they fall for the scam, they will be parting with a *minimum* of ten per cent of their takings for the rest of their lives!"

Gino and Danilo gasped in astonishment.

"It's outrageous!" they said in chorus.

"And what about the prostitutes?" asked Oriana with her usual openness. "Should we worry about them too?"

"I'll talk to Sonia about that tonight," said Beppe after a pause. "It might be a good idea to take precautionary measures. Maybe you and Sonia could spend a bit of time on that side of things, Oriana. It needs a sympathetic approach. It shouldn't prove too onerous a task - these ladies have the knack of passing on information amongst themselves faster than it takes a mobile phone signal to go up to a satellite and back. The main thing is to persuade them to stay with their regular customers. They should try to avoid clients they don't recognise. But by the nature of things, that is a significant problem – as you can imagine. The girls are sometimes run by local 'protectors' – who are no match for the clans who would be usurping their position..."

"What about the male prostitutes – not to mention the transsexuals?" asked Gino with a hint of a malicious grin on his face.

The *commissario* looked hard at his junior officer until the facetious leer on his junior officer's face dissolved.

"I don't think you need to treat them any differently to the others, do you Gino?"

"No, *capo*. I apologise," said Gino contritely.

"You'll all manage fine! Just remember, as you spend hours plodding around Pescara, repeating the same formula to every shopkeeper, restaurant owner – and don't forget the hotels – that we simply have to stamp out this threat before it takes root. You might want to look into installing miniature video cameras in the threatened premises too..."

"Pippo Caferelli isn't going to be pleased when he finds out that the Foggia *mafiosi* have followed him up to Pescara, chief," said Gino.

"That's true, Gino, but his experience of the *Sacra Corona Unita* will prove invaluable. Each clan employs a different gamut of techniques. Just remember, *ragazzi*, they are totally single-minded and ruthless. I don't reckon I'll be away for more than two or three days. But phone me whenever you need to. I'm sure Sonia will keep me posted," he added.

"But surely, by mafia standards, exerting all this pressure just to extricate protection money can't be all that lucrative, *capo?*" asked Danilo thoughtfully.

"Oh, you'd be surprised," said Beppe. "But this kind of activity enables the clans to get to know a neighbourhood well. This can lead on to other more profitable activities...such as drugs."

The meeting broke up and the team went their separate ways, each one preoccupied by their own thoughts. Yet again - as with the search for the Sleeping Beauty - the comfortable routine of the police station had been disrupted.

Before searching out Sonia, Beppe decided to talk to his colleague, Pippo Cafarelli. He brought him up to date with the potential invasion of Pescara by Pippo's old enemy – the Foggia based *SCU* clans. Pippo turned very pale during the account.

"Coincidence or fate, *capo?*" Pippo asked his chief with a quizzical eyebrow raised.

Beppe sighed.

"It feels more like fate, doesn't it?" replied the *commissario* resignedly.

4: The strangeness of the family Carlettini...

Before Beppe and Sonia left the police station together later that evening, he had made an appointment to meet his toxicologist friend, Bruno Esposito, at the hospital at nine o'clock the following morning. He had also phoned the dead man's brother, Ernesto Carlettini, and arranged to call on them at eleven o'clock at their home in Città Sant'Angelo – a short drive northwards out of Pescara. Beppe had sensed more than a hint of reluctance to meet him on the part of Salvatore's brother – an unwillingness which he could not define. Ernesto had tried his best to postpone – or avoid - the meeting with the words: "But surely the reasons for my brother's tragic demise are already clear cut, *commissario.* What do you hope to learn by...?

Beppe cut into his protest in an unequivocal manner:

"We have grounds for believing that there are suspicious elements surrounding your brother's death, *signore.* Besides which, I would welcome the opportunity to share your joy that your son, Lorenzo, has been spared a similar fate to his uncle..."

Beppe's shot in the dark struck home. He could not imagine why his words should unnerve Ernesto Carlettini. But it was immediately apparent that Ernesto had temporarily lost the power of speech. And why, thought Beppe, had Ernesto used the word 'demise'? It was a euphemism for the word 'death' that you would never use for a close relative, surely?

"*A domani, alle undici,*" said Beppe in a tone of voice that brooked no argument.

"Very well, *commissario* - we'll be expecting you at eleven," the brother finally managed to articulate as if he was about to choke on a crumb stuck in his throat.

* * *

Sonia and Beppe were lying drowsily in bed that evening in the darkened bedroom. They had discussed in great detail every aspect of the day's events until Beppe was satisfied that his brief absence from his place at the helm would not jeopardise the outcome of their 'anti-mafia' campaign in Pescara.

"Don't worry, Beppe," Sonia reassured him. "I have some very good contacts with the girls in the sex trade. And I am sure that Pippo and company will be able to cover the shops, bars, restaurants and hotels very competently. You just concentrate on finding your mushroom poisoner and get back here safely as soon as you can."

Beppe was gently stroking his partner's stomach as if the action of his hands would stimulate into existence the tiny life-form that he hoped was secreted in her belly.

"I still think he or she is inside there, *amore,*" said Sonia drowsily in response to his caresses.

Quite unbidden, there came to Beppe's weary mind a random memory from that long day. He felt irrationally bound to ask his partner a question:

"Did you know about the frescos in a church called *Santa Maria in Piano?*" He spoke in a tone of contrived nonchalance.

"Of course, I do. *Everybody* in Abruzzo knows about those frescos. What made you think of such a thing...?

Sonia's voice trailed off as sleep got the better of her.

* * *

Beppe and Doctor Esposito shook hands warmly and chatted about inconsequential matters for a few minutes before they broached the subject uppermost in Beppe's mind.

"Could you tell me a little bit more about the little boy, Lorenzo?" asked Beppe. "I suppose I am curious to know how he contracted a kidney disease at the same time as his uncle Salvatore died from kidney and liver failure."

"Ah, you think it must be more than a simple coincidence," replied the doctor as if he had come to the same conclusion.

"Yes, Bruno - I tend to be suspicious of coincidences. Plus, I understand, Salvatore's sister seems to be convinced that her brother was simply not the kind of person to run the risk of eating mushrooms unless he had been reassured as to their edibility."

Bruno Esposito remained thoughtful for several more seconds before he spoke.

"So... you are looking for some person, purporting to be a mushroom expert, who had a serious grudge against Salvatore Carlettini?"

"Something of the sort, Bruno. I was wondering if the boy, Lorenzo, could somehow have ingested the same mushrooms."

Bruno Esposito did not hesitate before stating:

"Nephritis is an unusual illness which can have a number of causes – I won't bother you with the medical details. But it certainly *is* a fact that the illness can be triggered by eating poisonous mushrooms."

Beppe's eyes were alert with interest.

"Bruno, may I ask you why you were so convinced that little Lorenzo was miraculously cured?"

"I'm sure I did not use exactly those words in church the other day, Beppe," said the doctor, with a wry smile. "But the fact remains that we diagnosed nephritis and did the only thing possible; we began to administer the appropriate medication. It would have required at least half a dozen doses before we could tell whether the little boy was going to respond to the treatment. There are no guarantees of recovery with kidney and liver problems once their degeneration has begun. Lorenzo recovered – completely – after only one 'dose', so to speak."

Bruno Esposito looked at Beppe and added with a broad grin:

"As to whether his nephritis was brought about by eating mushrooms, I'm sorry I can't tell you – an autopsy didn't seem appropriate in the circumstances. If that *was* the case, either his parents did not know – or they failed to tell us."

Beppe was looking very thoughtful as he shook his friend's hand and took his leave. He thanked the doctor profusely, explaining that he was about to go and visit the Carlettini family.

"I am so much better prepared to deal with them thanks to your clear explanation, Bruno. *Di nuovo, grazie.*"

"*In bocca al lupo,* Beppe," said Bruno Esposito as they went their separate ways.

(Di nuovo grazie = Thanks again) (In bocca al lupo = Good luck. Literal translation: 'In the mouth of the wolf')

* * *

It was Ernesto's wife who opened the door to Beppe, ushering him into the spacious modern flat just outside the historic town centre of Città Sant'Angelo.

"I'm Luisa Arielli," she said with a smile which, whilst not relaxed, seemed to Beppe to be sincere. "My husband will be here in a few minutes," she added with a note of apology in her voice. Please sit down, *commissario*. I'll go and make us some coffee."

There was no apparent sign of Lorenzo, their six year old son. Instead of remaining seated as he had been told, Beppe got up and walked around the room. He headed for the family photographs. It was rare for him not to glean some titbit of information from this source. There were a number of photos showing the Carlettini couple with their son at various stages of his development. He had almost abandoned the task when he came across an old, faded colour photo of two young men standing either side of an elderly woman, each with an arm round her shoulder. None of the three people in the photo was smiling. The two men looked so alike that they could easily have been twins.

When Ernesto Carlettini's wife, Luisa, came in carrying a tray containing a Moka pot and three small espresso coffee cups, she found the *commissario* studying the photo closely.

"Is this a photo of your husband and...." began Beppe with a reassuring smile on his face.

"... and his brother, Salvatore, yes - with their mum," said Luisa, whose face was suffused with a slight blush.

"They look so alike, don't they, *signora?*" said Beppe with his brightest and most reassuring smile.

"Yes – they are often mistaken for twins, *commissario.* But, in fact, there is eighteen months difference between them..." Her voice trailed off.

"What about their sister?" asked Beppe pressing home his tactical advantage.

"She doesn't look like them at all," replied Luisa abruptly. "She has a dark complexion..."

No photo fitting her description was anywhere to be seen in the room.

The sound of a door closing down the corridor could be heard. A few seconds later, Ernesto Carlettini entered the sitting room. Beppe was still clutching the photograph in his hand. There was no doubt about it, thought Beppe - the momentary flash of anxiety, or anger, was apparent on the younger brother's face, quickly replaced by an attempt at a welcoming smile. He walked towards Beppe, abruptly took the photo away from him before shaking his hand perfunctorily. The photo was replaced meticulously where it had been before Beppe had picked it up. "It's not just Salvatore Carlettini who is pernickety," thought the *commissario*. But he sensed that Ernesto's reaction in snatching away the photo concealed some darker motive. Beppe decided to capitalise on this couple's evident discomfort at his line of enquiry.

"You and your late brother can hardly be told apart, *signore.* The likeness is striking," he began. "I'm very sorry about your loss – especially as the poor man must have suffered greatly." Beppe had spoken in a quiet, respectful tone, whilst looking directly at Ernesto. Beppe's unwavering stare was disconcerting. Ernesto Carlettini was finding it difficult to look at this police inspector straight in the eyes.

"Yes, it was most… unfortunate," he muttered finally. Ernesto rallied his strength for a moment or two. "But you implied, *commissario,* that there were suspicious circumstances surrounding his death. I wonder what you can possibly be thinking of."

"Your sister believes that Salvatore would *never* have eaten mushrooms unless he had been doubly certain about their edibility…"

"My sister has an over active imagination, *commissario.* I can assure you that she…"

"When did you last see Salvatore?" interjected Beppe brusquely, with a just a hint of aggression in his voice.

For the first time since Ernesto entered the room, he looked wildly at his wife. The look on their faces clearly indicated to Beppe that they were regretting not having anticipated that particular question. Luisa covered up as best she could by pouring out three cups of coffee.

"It must have been a few days before he...became sick," she said, concentrating hard on not missing the little coffee cups as she poured out the steaming black liquid. "Do you take sugar, *commissario?*"

"*No, grazie, signora.*"

Beppe was sure that her hand was shaking despite the nonchalance of her voice. "Won't you sit down?" she invited. Beppe sat down in the chair she had indicated and accepted the proffered cup. He had not quite finished his first skirmish with this inexplicably diffident couple.

"Was that here – or at your brother's house in Montebello?" he asked Ernesto pointedly.

"At *his* house, *commissario,*" replied Ernesto with obvious reluctance and with just a suggestion of resentment maybe, observed the *commissario* privately. *Basta!* It was time to change tack.

"Thank you both for your cooperation – you've been most helpful," he said, relishing the ironic ambiguity of the words. He smiled at them both. "There, I have no more questions, *signori.* Let's just enjoy our coffees."

He clearly detected a relaxing of tensed up shoulders as the couple fondly imagined that the *commissario's* suspicions had been allayed. Beppe did not give them more than a couple of seconds to enjoy their sense of relief before launching into his second attack – accompanied by an angelic smile.

"I was present at mass on Sunday at the cathedral. I heard Don Emanuele's remarkable sermon. You must be overjoyed at Lorenzo's recovery..."

"Oh, *commissario,* overjoyed is an understatement," replied Luisa with a radiant smile. She was on home territory again and her reaction was uninhibited.

"I suppose Lorenzo is at home?" asked Beppe.

By an unusual juxtaposition of mirrors in their hallway, the couple had been quite unaware that, from where the *commissario* was sitting, he could see through a half-open bedroom door, the figure of a boy sitting playing with his Lego on the floor.

"Yes, he's sleeping at the moment," Ernesto Carlettini lied.

So, thought Beppe, they don't want me to talk to him. He let the matter go and soon stood up as if ready to leave. The couple ushered him out of the apartment, being careful to make sure he didn't have a chance to look back down the hallway.

"I'll keep you posted as to any progress in my investigations," he said tantalisingly, as he shook hands with the couple. "We may have to talk to you again," he added. He went down to where his car was parked.

As soon as he was in the car, he phoned Sonia and told her about his visit to the Carlettini family. He then explained in detail what he wanted her to do.

"Take one of the others with you, Sonia – just in case you need official corroboration," he added, before sending a loud *bacio* down the phone.

"*A presto, amore,*" she said. "Take care of yourself – for my sake…"

Beppe started up his car and headed towards Loreto Aprutino. His *Carabiniere* colleague, Enrico Nardini, would be delighted to know that his suspicions about the death of Salvatore Carlettini would almost certainly turn out to be well-founded.

He was sure the Carlettini family's evasiveness was hiding some complex issues. It was pure intuition at this stage. "A gut feeling, as Enrico Nardini would put it," he thought.

***

As soon as *Capitano* Nardini and Beppe stepped into the Carlettini sister's home in Penne, the *commissario* was struck by the tangible difference between her and her brother, Ernesto. Enrico Nardini had, of course, met the sister before. He introduced her formally to Beppe.

"This is *Commissario* Stancato, *signora*," explained Enrico. "He has come up from Pescara to help us with our enquiries."

"*Piacere, commissario!* My name is Ludovica Carlettini – just call me Ludovica, please."

"Certainly, Ludovica – thank you," said Beppe. "I'm sure you must be busy, so we won't keep you too long."

"Well, my daughter will need picking up from nursery school in a few minutes, but it's just round the corner..."

"Would you mind repeating to me, Ludovica, what you told *Capitano* Nardini the other day? I'm sure you appreciate that, if what you say is true, it sheds a very different light on the events surrounding your brother's death..."

"*Commissario*, Salvatore would *never* have dared to eat mushrooms without verifying their edibility. In fact, I am astonished that he ate them at all. He must have consulted someone who totally convinced him they weren't poisonous. It means you are looking for a mushroom expert who has cause to hate my brother to the extent that he was willing to condemn him to a lingering, painful death. That's how it seems to *me*," she concluded.

Beppe looked at this vivacious woman in her thirties who was returning his look unwaveringly, without a vestige of doubt about her opinion.

Beppe smiled at her warmly.

48

"What would you say if I told you your brother Ernesto thinks you suffer from an overly vivid imagination, Ludovica?"

Ludovica let out an unrestrained guffaw.

"Ernesto would accuse me of frivolity if I suggested he take his wife out to the cinema on a Saturday evening," she said scornfully.

"*Allora*...would it be true to say that your two brothers were very similar in nature? A trifle unadventurous and over-cautious...?"

"To say the least, *commissario!* They were always very pale in complexion and had mousey coloured hair. If you saw them together, you might have mistaken them for twins. Their childhood fragility was to do with a low red blood cell count, or something like that. As kids, they were always scared of falling over and bleeding to death."

"You don't mean they were haemophiliac, do you?" asked Enrico.

"No, no, nothing as serious as that. They suffered more from a hypochondriac mother who wouldn't let them be normal boys, I would say. They inherited their character – and maybe their blood cell deficiencies too for all I know – from their mother."

The obvious suspicion became a certainty in the *commissario's* mind:

"So, Ludovica, Ernesto and Salvatore are not, genetically speaking..." he began.

"You've got it, *commissario.* They are – or were - my half-brothers. I was always something akin to the black sheep of the family as far as Ernesto and Salvatore were concerned."

There was a silence during which Beppe and Enrico looked at each other knowingly – as if this revelation explained everything.

"Yes, I am the result of a rash moment of passion on the part of my father," she added. *"Povero papà!"*

Hearing the words 'poor daddy', Beppe looked at Ludovica and felt compelled to comment:

"It seems to me that he made a very fortuitous mistake, *signora,*" he said with absolute sincerity.

Ludovica Carlettini blushed but looked at Beppe with a radiant smile on her face.

"Grazie commissario! That's the nicest compliment I have ever had - from a policeman," she said mischievously.

"May we talk again if we feel you can help us with any other aspect of this affair, Ludovica?" asked Beppe.

"Of course, you can. Just give me a call beforehand to make sure I am in. I'll come downstairs with you now and pick up my daughter."

Beppe had wanted to ask her about the house in Montebello. He was curious to know whether there might be contentious issues over the inheritance. But that could wait for another day. He had the sensation that some element of this case had clicked into place – even if he had not quite identified what this 'element' was.

* * *

Having taken their leave of Ludovica, Beppe and Enrico walked back to the police car through the ancient, cobbled streets of Penne. Beppe's chief had been right; Penne's medieval buildings, with their turrets and pink tiled roofs exuded a sense of the past at every turn. In the upper reaches of the town, the streets were too narrow to allow easy access by car – adding intensity to the feeling of times gone by.

"Now we can begin our investigation in earnest," said *Commissario* Stancato. "I would like to go and see the house where Salvatore Carlettini lived. It would seem to be a good starting point…"

"Only after we have had lunch, *caro commissario,*" said Enrico decisively.

He had been warned by Oriana Salvati about Beppe's habit of skipping lunch whenever he got his teeth into a new investigation. He frequently forgot that other people required a regular intake of food at midday. It was already well past one o'clock.

Beppe smiled and gave in with a good grace.

"Back to *La Vestina,* in that case," he suggested. "If that's alright with you, *capitano?*"

"It's where I usually end up for lunch, *commissario.*"

On the way to the *osteria*, Beppe was already turning over in his mind how he should set about the task of unearthing the names of all the mushroom experts in the vicinity of Penne. Quite a tall order, he imagined – especially as there would be enthusiastic amateurs mixed in with the professionals. Maybe *Agente* Remo Mastrodicasa could help him. Yes, he would ask Remo to do the research for him on his computer. More likely than not, Remo would welcome the chance to work on the computer rather than pursuing the *Sacra Corona Unita* and their cronies round the streets of Pescara.

5: In a cold dark place...

The sound of water cascading down the sheer vertical drop was deafening. Adolfo D'Angelo – middle name Damiano – welcomed the constant drumming vibration inside his head. It was the torrent that washed away the insidious onset of guilt which had assailed him over the last few days. He no longer had to think whilst he remained close to this powerful and bewitching manifestation of Mother Nature.

"Oh, Madonna mia! What have I done?" The words reverberated in his head over and over again. If he simply kept on repeating the question, he never had to worry about the answer; it was a sublimely comforting sensation. Perhaps it would be simpler if he threw himself headlong into the thundering wall of water and allowed himself to be washed away for ever? If the worst came to the worst, this was exactly what he would do. But would he be reunited with his beloved Renata if he took that path? His deep-rooted adherence to the teachings of the Catholic Church informed him otherwise. But surely, he had already elected to follow the road to perdition by his rash act of revenge? More questions! He remained rooted to the spot and let the hypnotic sound of the cascading water hold him in its spell.

He had experienced a fleeting sense of satisfaction when, days ago, he had closed the door on the man who had killed his wife through one single act of culpable negligence. He had watched the brief report of Salvatore's death on TV-Tavo, the local TV station, cleverly named by its founder after the river Tavo which flowed down from the mountains before amalgamating its waters with the Adriatic Sea.

"A warning to all Italians to be wary of eating wild mushrooms without first consulting the experts," concluded the newsreader. The report gave the startling national statistics for the annual death toll of the victims of mushroom

poisoning – as well as the number of patients who required liver or kidney transplants. They were the lucky ones, concluded the reporter. Damiano had smiled knowingly – lucky, that is, if you happen to live in Rome or the prosperous north of Italy and have access to hospitals able to carry out such operations.

Even at that stage, he had not felt particularly remorseful; after all, justice had been meted out. But he no longer felt that this act of retribution had been executed by the hand of God. He alone was responsible for the death of Salvatore Carlettini. He confessed to himself that it was the fear of being found out which terrified him most.

What was it that Salvatore had said when he – and his dogs – had visited his house? *'They told me you would be very helpful'.* Who were these people? How had Salvatore Carlettini found out about him before he appeared on his doorstep? He feared Salvatore must have enquired at his local bar – where *everybody* in Farindola went to catch up on the village gossip. He had not dared to show his face there since that day. He needed to decide how he should react when the owner of the bar challenged him.

"Ehi, Damiano! What about that guy with the two Labradors who came in asking if there was anyone who was knowledgeable about mushrooms? He's died from eating his own pasta dish. We sent him down to see you! What on earth did you tell him?"

Should he deny that the man had ever come to see him? A bit risky in a village like Farindola where everybody knew what everybody else was doing. Or should he just look tragic and tell them simply: "Yeah, there *was* this guy who came to see me but I told him the mushrooms he had picked weren't edible."

He had so far been unable to resolve this dilemma.

But the dilemma had become an absolute crisis when, two days previously, he had been distractedly watching the local evening news. His horrified glance at the screen showed him the image of the man he thought he had dispatched into eternity, in the company of his wife and a six-year-old boy. They were claiming the boy had been miraculously cured of some kidney disease. They had called the man Ernesto Carlettini. Damiano had only known his wife's executioner by his surname - *Carlettini.* A shocking explanation to this seemingly supernatural coincidence struck him like a lightning bolt from the heavens.

"Oh, Madonna mia! What have you done, Adolfo Damiano d'Angelo?"

He closed his eyes and allowed the torrent to wash through his body and mind. He might have cast himself off the ledge at the top of the precarious stone steps with its dangerously insecure railing there and then, but he heard voices which barely managed to penetrate the deafening sound of falling water.

Merda! There was a group of trekkers walking along the lower woodland trail that led to the *Cascata del Vitello d'Oro.* Mechanically, Damiano clung on to the railing, hoping the trekkers would not spot him high up at the top of the falls. They were chatting animatedly – two young couples laughing and joking together. But then, inevitably, one of the group looked upwards and pointed an alarmed finger at the middle-aged man poised in frozen stillness at the summit of the falls. Four scared faces were staring upwards. There was nothing for it. He climbed back down the rickety stairway leading to the river bed. He began to trudge back towards the village along the narrow gorge at the foot of the rocky cliffs – finally out of sight of those irritatingly intrusive tourists.

"I thought just for a minute that he was going to leap off the platform," said one of the girls with obvious relief.

"Well," replied her partner with deliberate cynical humour, "it would certainly have been a spectacular way to end it all!"

"And where did he just disappear to?" said the other girl.

The sight of this strange figure, which had seemingly vanished into thin air, added a sinister sense of mystery to this enchanted place, where blackbirds and thrushes continued to sing invisibly - oblivious to the vagaries of mankind.

6: Following the scent...

The house was a two-storey, detached building made of stone. The roof was traditionally constructed with pink tiles that looked as if they had been skilfully cut into sections from a rounded chimney pot and laid, one tile abutting the next one, to form an undulating pattern across the width of the roof. The slatted wooden shutters, painted light blue, appeared to have been installed recently. The garden, surrounding the whole house, was well cared for.

"A beautiful, spacious house," observed Enrico. "A bit of a waste since apparently only one person was living here."

Beppe and Enrico ducked under the red and white crime scene tape, with the word CARABINIERI printed across it in black letters. They entered the late Salvatore Carlettini's house in Montebello almost reverently. Enrico observed that the locksmith had fitted a new lock after the *Carabinieri* had forced the door open – and, as requested, had left the new key hidden on a concealed hook.

Beppe's first unpleasant sensation was that the inside of the house smelt strongly of dogs. His nose wrinkled up in disgust. His colleague seemed less troubled by the pungent odour which pervaded the place.

"I've been here already, *commissario*. It was much worse than this when we first broke in."

"That's good to know," said Beppe ironically, trying his best to breathe through his mouth.

"Excuse me asking, Enrico – but why has someone put crime scene tapes across the porch? Was that you, by any chance?"

Enrico Nardini was surprised that he had been addressed by his first name. He considered whether he should reply in like manner. After all, his rank as a *capitano* was roughly the equivalent of that of *commissario.* Maybe the military status of being an officer belonging to the *Carabinieri* deterred him from being familiar with an 'ordinary' police inspector.

"It was partly intended as a deterrent, *commissario,*" he replied automatically. "You'd be amazed at the number of empty houses which get broken into at night time – especially in the country. It's usually teenage drug addicts hoping to fund their habit by stealing anything they can lay their hands on – or sometimes because they just want somewhere to smoke without being disturbed."

"Nothing is sacred anymore, is it?"

"It's tempting to believe that, yes," replied Enrico. "But I have to say, too, that I felt from the outset that we might have to do a proper search of the house at some stage."

"*Bravo, capitano!* Let's get started then," said Beppe.

"Are we looking for anything specific?" asked Enrico.

"Not really. But I can't help wondering why Salvatore Carlettini seemed to do *nothing* to notify the outside world that he was in trouble. For example, did he call his brother in Città Sant'Angelo? And why did he not call the emergency number 118 for an ambulance? Or maybe he wrote something down or left a message on a computer. So we are looking for *anything* that might give us a lead..."

"Oddly enough, *commissario,* we didn't find a mobile phone on him and the land line didn't have a dialling tone. I suspect that Salvatore Carlettini was a bit of a recluse – or hadn't kept up to date with his phone bills."

Beppe forgot to breathe in through his mouth and discovered that the air was still laden with the smell of distressed dogs.

"Crime scene or not, *capitano*, let's open a few windows and let some fresh air in," Beppe pleaded.

The *Carabiniere* captain smiled.

"*D'accordo* - permission granted."

After one hour's diligent searching, Beppe had come up with very little of real substance.

They met outside the house under a long veranda which ran along the front of the building. Beppe had found the victim's lap-top computer and an old Nokia mobile phone. He would get the technical team in Pescara to examine these items. He had also found a sheet of paper which he had come across in Salvatore's study. It looked like the beginnings of a shopping list. There were only two items on the list which appeared to have been written in the victim's own shorthand. He showed it to Enrico. The words *Farin* and *Demi* were written in almost illegible letters with a thick felt tipped pen.

"*Farina?*" suggested Enrico. "Maybe he needed to buy some flour? He probably made his own pasta like a lot of locals do out in the countryside. Some people even take their own grain to be milled privately. And *demi* must mean he wanted half..." His voice trailed off as he realised that something from his French lessons at school must have stuck.

"The only thing beginning with *Demi* that you might want to buy in a shop is a *demi-sec* wine – otherwise, we Italians always say *mezzo*-something for a half quantity," Beppe reminded his colleague.

It did not seem to the police officers that the hastily scribbled words on this very short list could mean anything useful. And yet, a dying man had written them to be seen by whoever found him. Beppe folded up the piece of paper and put it in an inside pocket of his jacket.

"It's odd though, Enrico," continued Beppe. "Apart from an unmade bed and a toilet that needs cleaning, the rest of the upstairs is neat and tidy. There's one room which is locked and I can't find a key to it."

"It's the same with the downstairs, *capo* – all very orderly. Perhaps Salvatore employed a house-keeper."

"We should go and ask the neighbour who raised the alarm about the barking dogs. She is bound to know if he employed a local woman to clean his house."

After a pause, Beppe asked Enrico in a voice that assumed he had had the same lack of success as himself: "How about you, Enrico? Anything?"

The *Carabiniere* captain fished around in his pocket.

"I found these… in the fridge of all places, *capo…*"

He was holding two pieces of Lego in his hand, a blue brick and a yellow flag pole with the Italian flag on top of it. Enrico quite failed to understand why his senior colleague had a beatific smile on his face. Beppe took the trophies with glee and slipped them into his pocket.

"Bravo, Enrico… That is *most* interesting!" was all he said, failing completely to enlighten his colleague.

"Excuse me, *commissario…"* began Enrico. "Could you possibly tell me why you think…?"

The thoughtful frown on Beppe's face stopped Enrico in his tracks. He had yet to learn that this unusual *commissario* had to digest information, sometimes for several hours, before he would ever commit himself to any conjecture – let alone a firm opinion.

"Let's take a look round the garden," Beppe suggested. "You never know…"

As they had noticed on coming in, the garden was cared for. Salvatore obviously employed a regular gardener judging by the well-tended lawn and flower beds.

At the back of the house, they were surprised to find a rabbit hutch with a big white rabbit inside, its pink nose quivering suspiciously. It had water to drink and a mixture of parsley and sorrel leaves to eat. It disappeared from sight in a compartment behind its cage as soon as the two police officers approached.

Beppe's hand slapped his forehead, startling his companion.

"Of course!" exclaimed Beppe, once again failing to convey his mental processes to Enrico.

"Commissario...?" he asked, hoping for an explanation.

"Have you ever read *Alice nel paese delle meraviglie,* Enrico?" asked Beppe enigmatically.

"Of course I've read *Alice in Wonderland* - when I was a child. But what on earth has that got to do with this case?"

"Nothing directly concerned with Salvatore's murder, I suspect. But it has just helped me understand something about the brother, Ernesto Carlettini, and his family. I know they are somehow crucial to this case; even though, as you said, it's just a gut feeling at present."

No other explanation was forthcoming.

Beppe apologised for his reticence. He was already thinking about other things.

"A bit of lateral thinking, *capitano!* You'll get there in the end," was all Beppe had to offer his colleague by way of consolation. "By the way, do you know what job Salvatore Carlettini did?"

"Yes, I do, as it happens. He worked for *Trenitalia* – he was a train driver on the *Freccia Bianca.* A well-paid job – with a good state pension at the end of his career..." Enrico's voice trailed off as he realised the irrelevance of this advantage to the victim.

"Come on, *capitano*, we've spent enough time here. Let's go and see the neighbour who alerted you about the barking dogs. Where are the dogs, by the way?"

"In kennels for now - until they find a home for them. Otherwise..."

Enrico passed the fingers of his right hand across his throat in a gesture whose meaning was all too clear.

The two officers walked round to the front of the house. A man was standing in the street. He was peering at the house through the ornate wrought-iron gates. He was wearing a worried frown on seeing a police car outside the house. The frown was replaced by a look of embarrassment and guilt when he saw the two officers coming round the corner of the house. He recognised the police inspector who had been to his house that morning. He looked as if he wanted to turn tail and flee. But he realised just in time that such a gesture would compromise his position utterly in the eyes of the *commissario* with the penetrating stare.

"I'll give you one guess as to who *that* is!" said Beppe to his companion.

"The ghost of Salvatore Carlettini – or his brother," replied the *capitano.*

Beppe put on his sincerest smile as he opened the wrought iron gate and held out an amicable hand to Ernesto Carlettini.

"What a surprise, *dottore,* to meet you again so soon!" he began. Beppe noted with satisfaction that Ernesto had winced at his choice of title. Addressing a person as *dottore,* Beppe knew, covered a multitude of professions – not exclusively people in the medical world. But it was a significant reaction on Ernesto's part and fitted in with the as yet ill-defined theory that had been evolving in his mind.

"How can we help you?" Beppe asked Ernesto Carlettini sweetly.

"Oh… oh… nothing really, *commissario* - I came up on the off-chance to make sure my brother's house was… euh… locked up and everything," stammered Ernesto unconvincingly.

"Quite natural of course, *dottore,* but as you can see, we are treating this as a crime scene."

"But the windows are all wide open," the fastidious brother protested.

"We shall secure the house before we leave, *dottore*. Rest assured. The house was a little airless." It was *Capitano* Nardini who had spoken this time.

"We have already found some very interesting bits of evidence," Beppe said tantalisingly, "his mobile phone, for example."

"Salvatore was not a great communicator, *commissario*," said brother Ernesto shiftily.

Ernesto Carlettini realised there was little point in hanging around.

"Have you any idea how long it will be before...?" he began lamely.

"We will inform you as soon as our enquiries are completed, *dottore*," interjected Enrico Nardini. "Rest assured."

"He's *dying* to get his hands on that property," observed Beppe as soon as the brother had driven away.

"You don't think *he* was the one who fed Salvatore those mushrooms, do you, *commissario?*"

For once, *Commissario* Stancato did not hesitate before replying.

"No, I don't. Not for a minute! This affair is far more complex than a simple family feud. But I have the strong impression that Ernesto is not too upset by his brother's death..."

Enrico Nardini nodded his head in agreement.

"*Capitano*, would you mind having a talk with the neighbour and see what you can find out? I need to contact Sonia and see if she has already paid a visit to the Carlettini household in Città Sant'Angelo."

Beppe phoned Sonia to see whether she had had time to visit the mother, Luisa Arielli, and her son Lorenzo. It would be good if she could get there before Ernesto got home from Montebello.

"Pippo and I are right outside their *palazzo* now, Beppe."

"That's brilliant, Sonia." Beppe filled his partner in rapidly on the discovery of the pieces of Lego found in the fridge. She cottoned on immediately to the significance of this seemingly trivial discovery.

"I'll phone you later on this evening, *amore,*" said Beppe.

"Where will you be staying?" Sonia asked her partner.

"I have no idea. I haven't broached the subject with Enrico Nardini yet."

"Let me know as soon as you can, please," said Sonia with womanly concern.

* * *

A breathless Enrico Nardini rejoined Beppe some fifteen minutes later. He had a gleam in his eye which told Beppe that he had found out something unexpected from the neighbour.

"Salvatore Carlettini *did* employ a gardener, *commissario* - a local man from Montebello who came once or twice a week. I've got his name. It *was* the neighbour – Cinzia, she's called - who's been feeding the rabbit – she said she felt sorry for it and didn't want to let it loose in the garden because a fox, or a wolf, might eat it. But you'll never guess what! Salvatore also had a semi-permanent, live-in housekeeper. He tried to keep her a close secret from the rest of the village. But in a place this size, he didn't stand a chance. She was very dark skinned. The neighbour said she once overheard Salvatore calling her *Dinusha.* She's disappeared, *capo...*"

"Dinusha is an Indian or a Sri Lankan name," said Beppe thoughtfully. "That might explain why there are so many photos of some exotic Asian country on his bedroom walls. It might explain the locked bedroom, too. I think our Salvatore must have travelled round the world – at least once. Maybe he found himself an exotic partner too."

"The neighbour told me this woman, Dinusha, often went away for days at a time – with a small trolley suitcase. I suppose we shall have to try and track her down," said Enrico.

Beppe nodded distractedly. He was surprised by this discovery, but despite the zeal of his companion, he did not believe for a second that this Dinusha was guilty of poisoning her Italian employer with mushrooms.

"She might go up north to Milan or somewhere. She probably has a family up there. She might well prove to be a legitimate asylum seeker. But you are right, Enrico, we should follow it up – she is almost certainly unaware that Salvatore is dead," added Beppe.

"Where to now, *commissario?*" Enrico asked after a pause. He was hoping that Beppe was ready to give up for the day; a forlorn hope.

"One quick visit to the half-sister in Penne, please. I want to ask our Ludovica a couple more questions - without raising the suspicions of Ernesto Carlettini and his wife. After that, I think we might call it a day."

Beppe noticed a look of relief pass across his colleague's face.

"I'm sure you must have other things to do, Enrico," said Beppe kindly.

The *Carabiniere* captain blushed.

"Ah!" said Beppe with a smile. "You have a *fidanzata* you've been neglecting because of me, I see."

"It's hard to find time for one's private life in this job, *commissario*. She's a primary school teacher whom I met a few months ago. She's called Alessia."

"We shan't spend long with Ludovica, I promise. Then you can leave me to my own devices. Where am I staying, by the way? Sonia seems anxious to be reassured I won't be a prey to temptation!"

"Oh, we're putting you up in a modest little hotel in Loreto Aprutino. You'll like it – and Sonia need have no qualms, *commissario*."

Enrico Nardini enjoyed the sensation of withholding further information from the *commissario* – for the first and possibly last time during their investigation.

* * *

"You can't seriously be telling me that I'm staying in *this* place?" said an incredulous *commissario*, after they had driven up the steep hill leading to the highest point in Loreto Aprutino. They passed through a pair of double gates and were instantly faced with an imposing old building which looked like a cross between a castle and a palace towering over them.

"Welcome to the Hotel Castello Chiolo, *commissario*."

"But a simple bed-and-breakfast place would have been fine!"

"Oh, I know it looks fit for royalty, but the prices are quite modest. Besides, we have special rates for our visiting celebrities – and it is off-season," said Enrico reassuringly. "And the restaurant does excellent local dishes. You'll be fine. You'll only have to put up with it for a week…"

"I am flattered by your faith in me, *capitano*. I hope your trust in my abilities is not misplaced."

"You have managed to achieve more in one day, *commissario,* than we achieved in a week of dead-end enquiries," admitted the *Carabinieri* officer with a tinge of envy.

Beppe, having showered for fifteen minutes, was lying on the bed in the sumptuous surroundings of one of the hotel's smaller rooms at the top of the hotel, going over in his mind the events of the day.

He had quizzed Ludovica about her half-brother Ernesto's profession.

"I believe he works as a dental technician, *commissario.* You know, he makes tailor-made crowns and dentures in a small workshop near the hospital in Pescara. I get the impression he has only been doing that for a relatively short time. I don't know what he did before that – something medical, I believe. But you must understand that I have only lived here myself for two years. I lived with my mum in Teramo before moving here to Penne – where my current partner lives..."

"What about Salvatore's house in Montebello, Ludovica? Do you have any claim on that?"

"I haven't a clue – but I doubt it, knowing Ernesto. In any case, I'm happy where I am, *commissario.* I have no desire to get embroiled in some legal wrangle as to my rights over Salvatore's property. I always had the impression that Ernesto was a bit jealous of his brother's stable, well-paid job and his big country house."

"Your directness is very refreshing, *cara* Ludovica," said Beppe with a warm smile. "By the way, did you know that Salvatore Carlettini had a live-in maid called Dinusha – from Sri Lanka, we believe?"

Once again, Ludovica had burst into unrestrained laughter.

"No, I didn't – what a dark old horse!" she said gleefully. "I bet that must have put the wind up his brother's sails! Come to think of it, it is quite probable that Salvatore never mentioned her existence."

Beppe and the *Carabiniere* captain had taken their leave of Ludovica and her little three-year-old daughter.

"Any time you want to come round, officers, I am at your disposal. I am becoming quite intrigued by what has been going on without my knowing."

Beppe thought it was high time he called his partner, Sonia.

She was astounded to learn where he was staying – paid for by the State. She promised to come up and join him if time allowed.

"I hope I shall be back in Pescara sooner rather than later, Sonia," he said.

Intimate preliminaries over, it was quite obvious that she was eager to tell Beppe what had transpired at the Carlettini house that afternoon. Her account of her informal meeting with the six-year-old Lorenzo had entirely justified the risk of interviewing such a young child. But Beppe knew from experience that Sonia was a 'natural' when it came to putting people of all ages at their ease.

"He's actually a lovely, normal little boy – although I had the impression he is a bit isolated, being an only child. I think he takes after his mother. But he was chatty and responsive with me. He was almost certainly unaware that he had been at death's door – let alone being miraculously cured! It was obvious that the mother was very reluctant to let me talk to Lorenzo. She tried to insist that we wait for her husband to return. In the end, it was Pippo who began – very tactfully - to interrogate her about her husband's job. She became so involved in avoiding giving precise details that I just slipped out of the room without her noticing."

"Really?" interposed Beppe. "It's just as I figured…"

He did not enlighten Sonia as to the direction of his thoughts, so she continued talking.

"Lorenzo opened up to me immediately. I asked him what he liked doing best. He told me he loved playing with Lego and watching DVDs. And guess what his favourite DVD is, Beppe?"

"Alice in Wonderland?" suggested Beppe.

"*Appunto,* Beppe! It took me some time to get him to admit that he had looked inside the fridge at "*zio* Salvatore's" house and seen those big yellow mushrooms on a plate. I had difficulty in getting him to confess he had even opened the fridge door. I had to tell him we found his Lego pieces in the fridge before he gave up."

"I was looking for a yogurt," he told me. "*Zio* Salvo always gets yogurts in for me when we go and see him. But then I saw those mushrooms. They seemed to be saying *EAT ME…* Lorenzo had been threatened by both his parents not to talk about the mushrooms to anyone else."

"Daddy was quite angry – he said someone might come and take me away from home if I told them I had eaten those mushrooms."

"His very words! Incredible, that man! And do you know why Lorenzo felt compelled to take a nibble, Beppe?"

"I think I can guess, Sonia, but tell me anyway." Her words confirmed exactly what he had worked out while he had been in Salvatore's house.

"He is very small for his age – he must be self-conscious about his height at school. And of course, he remembered that nibbling a bit of mushroom had made Alice grow much taller."

"Alice grew tall enough to see over the treetops," he confided in me. "Now, I know it was very stupid of me, Sonia," he told me, "because I became very ill for a few days!"

Beppe let out a sigh of self-satisfaction.

"You'd worked that out already, hadn't you? You're really quite bright, aren't you, *commissario?*" Sonia said with mock sarcasm.

"I had help, I have to confess."

"You mean our *capitano* Nardini?"

"No, Sonia – I had help from the White Rabbit," he explained enigmatically.

Sonia remained in the dark.

"I'll be back home tomorrow night or the day afterwards," he promised. "How's the anti-mafia campaign going?"

"Just routine so far, Beppe. Yes, please come back soon... *Mi manchi tanto!*"

"I miss you too," he said.

No wonder the Carlettini parents had tried to hide what had happened to their son, thought Beppe as he lay on his bed. They must have been scared stiff that they would be blamed for a total lack of supervision of their six-year-old son.

He must compliment *Capitano* Nardini on his choice of hotel, he thought before falling asleep. He had eaten just a first course - a *pappardelle con salsa di cinghiale;* the best he had ever tasted – even though he had hated eating on his own in the spacious, immaculate restaurant.

(cinghiale = wild boar. A speciality in Central Italy – often served as a pasta sauce with pappardelle)

* * *

Capitano Nardini quizzed his primary school teacher-girlfriend about that forgotten story from his childhood. She had told him how Alice had followed the White Rabbit down the burrow and how she had eaten substances that made her grow taller – and then shorter by turns.

"I heard a lecture on the author, Lewis Caroll, when I was studying in London," Alessia said. "The professor giving the talk told us he was probably influenced by hallucinatory drugs which were able to alter ones perception of reality. I think magic mushrooms were mentioned."

"Ah, so *that's* what the *commissario* worked out," he said, belatedly enlightened as to his temporary chief's elaborate thought processes.

7: Beppe's obsession with frescos...

Remo Mastrodicasa was delighted when his chief had phoned him just as he was about to set off with his colleagues to do the rounds of all the local shops, bars and hotels in Pescara to warn the owners of the attempted take-over by the *SCU* mafia clan from Puglia.

After his encounter with the Naples clan a few months previously, during which they had rescued the young woman whom they had nicknamed the 'Sleeping Beauty', Remo had sworn to himself and promised his *fidanzata,* Marta, that he would never shoot a bullet at another living soul – even if it meant saving an innocent person's life.

It mattered deeply to this gentle, considerate ex-waiter that his shot had saved the life of his fellow officer, Oriana Salvati. But the fact that it had been this single act of aggression which had given him heroic status in the eyes of his predominantly male colleagues left him feeling uncomfortable. He would much rather be appreciated for being the person he really was. Only his exceptionally *simpatico* chief, *Commissario* Stancato, made him feel valued as a member of this team of police officers for all the right reasons. The *commissario* had been the one who had chivvied the police clothing suppliers to exchange his ill-fitting uniform for a slimmer one, which had enhanced his self-respect instantly.

Thus, his feeling of gratitude was considerable when the *commissario* called him from Loreto Aprutino and gave him a specific task that required him to exercise his hidden analytical skills.

"What exactly do you want me to do, *capo?*" asked Remo.

"It should be straightforward enough, Remo," began Beppe, who had the distinct feeling that the task might prove to be anything but straightforward. "I need you to compile a list of names of all the people in the area of Penne who have an expertise in every kind of mushroom to be found in Abruzzo. One of them is almost certainly guilty of murder."

"I'll get started at once, *capo,*" said Remo, who was thinking that his chief had overlooked a very obvious source of information. Good! He would be able to furnish the list which his chief required with the alacrity of a conjuror producing a white rabbit from a hat, thought Remo, unaware that white rabbits had already assumed a significant role in this investigation.

"Thanks, Remo. I've said it before – you're a real star!"

"*La ringrazio, capo.* Leave it to me."

* * *

As soon as he had made the phone call to Remo Mastrodicasa back in Pescara, Beppe realised several things in the same instant of time: firstly, he was missing Sonia and feeling guilty that he was not there by her side; secondly, there was little else he could do until he had that list of the names of mushroom experts in or around Penne; and thirdly, it still niggled him that everybody who mattered in his life knew about the frescos in the church of *Santa Maria in Piano* except him.

He accused himself roundly of suffering from the southern Italian vice of irrational jealousy. He tried – and failed - to convince himself that the emotion was simply engendered by his desire to be a true *Abruzzese* like his partner and all those whom he worked with. But he knew deep down inside he was suffering from ignoble feelings of envy that he was not privy to the same knowledge as the others. It was all to do with those damned frescos! They had come to assume an importance that was totally out of all proportion.

"I think I should go back to Pescara today, Enrico," Beppe explained to the *capitano.* "I want that list of names and I also need to find out more about Ernesto Carlettini's previous career. Can you do without me for a day or two?"

The *Carabiniere* captain replied that he had plenty of other routine things to keep him busy for at least a week – including tracking down Salvatore's missing Sri Lankan housekeeper. He could not resist asking the *commissario* why he was so interested in the surviving brother's career history. What possible connection could there be between that and the poisoning of his brother, Salvatore?

"Just the usual intuitive feeling, Enrico! Just think about it for a moment or two..." was all Enrico managed to elicit from his elusive colleague. "I'll see you tomorrow, or the day after at the very latest."

As soon as the conversation was over, Beppe dressed, showered and went down to breakfast. He handed his electronic key card in at the reception and explained he had to return urgently to Pescara.

"We hope to see you again soon, *commissario,*" smiled the lady receptionist with what appeared to be total sincerity.

Beppe remembered only then that he had left his own car at the *Carabiniere* station and had to ask the hotel staff to call him a taxi to take him down to the town. The receptionist arranged for one of the staff to run him downhill.

"No need to waste money on a taxi, *commissario,*" said the receptionist. "We have our own taxi service here for emergencies like this."

As soon as Beppe was inside his own car, he headed back towards Pescara – via the minor road that would take him past *that* church. If it was locked, he would use his authority – or misuse it if necessary – to get the parish priest to let him inside.

"You are still a shallow man at heart," he roundly accused himself. But the desire to share the secret of those frescos had become a major obsession.

He found the church open and the priest saying mass. He had no alternative but to join the congregation and wait until mass was over. He had plenty of time to stare at the frescos. He finished up by being spellbound by their intricate and ornate beauty. Their brilliant colours seemed as vivid as on the day they had been painted. It was, fairly obviously, meant to depict The Last Judgement –Beppe managed to work out that much for himself. The figures of Jesus and – was it St Francis? – were dressed in coloured robes. The ordinary mortals were depicted as hopeless, asexual, naked, white figures scampering like albino primates clinging on to anything they could. Some of the figures were climbing up trees. Lower down, they were attempting to cross a flimsy bridge which threatened to cast them into the darkly flowing waters beneath them. The effect was overwhelming and disturbing.

It was the priest, noticing with cautious joy a newcomer to his congregation, who sped out of the vestry at the end of mass and quietly accosted this dark-skinned man in his forties whom he found standing transfixed by the paintings.

Beppe was treated to a thirty-minute account of the history of this wondrous work of art. He made no attempt to halt the priest's enthusiastic narrative – even asking questions for his own clarification.

"Can you tell me, father, the meaning of the figures crossing that flimsy looking bridge?"

The priest laughed. "It's called *Il ponte dei capelli* – The Bridge of Hairs. Some people have named it *Il ponte della prova* – The Bridge of Trials. It's a kind of obstacle course to test the strength of purpose of those crossing the bridge. Those found lacking in faith are cast into the river below."

"Sometimes I see myself as one of those lizard-like human figures attempting to get to the other side," said Beppe to the priest.

"Don't we all, *signor...?*" asked the priest, wondering how he should address this stranger with an accent which was obviously from the deep south.

Beppe told the priest who he was. To his surprise, the priest's face lit up with recognition.

"Ah, *commissario!* The archbishop has talked to me about you. He holds you in high regard, you know."

After over half an hour of further conversation, the *commissario* reluctantly took his leave of the priest and walked out through the main door of the church – to be confronted with a grey police car with the distinctive yellow stripe down the side, which marked it out clearly as belonging to the *Guardia di Finanza.* The car was blocking his exit. Inside, the two Finance Police were eyeing him suspiciously. Beppe put on his smiley face and showed them his *commissario's* badge. The two officers returned his smile with some relief.

"Good," said the elder of the two men, "we can stop playing at being traffic cops."

They asked him, more out of curiosity than suspicion, what he was doing inside the church. Beppe saw no reason not to give them a potted version of his visit to Loreto Aprutino.

"Ah, you're investigating the death of Salvatore Carlettini, are you, *commissario?* Interesting, we wondered if it might have been something more than simple mushroom poisoning!"

"So, you knew Salvatore Carlettini, did you?" asked Beppe.

"Not really," the Finance policeman chuckled. He looked at his colleague as if asking for his indulgence to let him relate a much-repeated joke. "We had some dealings with his brother. He makes dental apparatus. He made a set of dentures for my colleague's mother – and they didn't fit! Isn't that right, Matteo? His companion nodded. "According to our colleagues in Pescara, the Carlettini brother is about to be investigated over some financial irregularity. Nothing serious, mind you – probably just a VAT matter.

After banal pleasantries, the three policemen shook hands and went their separate ways. Beppe was amused at the coincidence but dismissed the conversation from his head as he headed back towards Pescara.

To his astonishment, Remo Mastrodicasa handed him his list of names in a neat plastic folder almost as soon as he arrived.

"You can't have managed to sort that out already, Remo!" said Beppe in astonishment.

"I got the Chamber of Commerce to supply me with a list of names of all those who have a licence to pick mushrooms in the Province of Pescara, *capo*. But there are over a hundred names on that list. They suggested you might want to contact the Mushroom Police in Pescara – they might be able to help you narrow down your search a bit..."

Beppe looked at his junior colleague in admiration.

"Don't dream of leaving the police force, Remo. Not while I am *commissario*, at any rate."

Remo blushed with pleasure at the praise. He shrugged his shoulders modestly.

"It was no trouble, *capo*. Tomorrow, if you like, we can try eliminating some of those names."

"*Di nuovo, mille grazie,* Remo," said Beppe, holding his colleague's elbow affectionately.

* * *

Later that evening, as they were lying in bed in each other's arms as if they had been apart for months, Beppe asked Sonia a question:

"What can you tell me about *Il ponte dei capelli, amore?* It's part of the frescos in the *Chiesa di Santa Maria in Piano* – you know."

"I have no idea, Beppe," she replied taken aback by such an unlikely question. Knowing her partner well, she suspected she was being quizzed rather than being asked for enlightenment.

Beppe felt unashamedly smug as he explained all about the human figures trying to reach paradise over the insubstantial 'Bridge of Hairs'.

Sonia was impressed. "I don't believe I've ever noticed *that* detail," she admitted reluctantly.

His detour to visit the church of *Santa Maria in Piano* had been well worth the effort, the *commissario* considered. His bruised ego had recovered some of its lost ground.

Beppe and Sonia's deep sleep was shattered at about six o'clock the following morning by a phone call from the police station in Via Pesaro. It was the night officer on duty, Danilo Simone. He spoke breathlessly – wanting to impart the disagreeable news as rapidly as possible:

"*Capo,* I am so sorry to disturb you at this hour. But I thought you would want to know. One of the barkeepers has just phoned in, very distraught. She's called Monica Barone. She opened a new bar in Via Foscolo called *Il Bar Galileo* about three months ago. She was one of those whom we had already warned about possible mafia activities in the area.

She wanted to report that someone has set fire to the entrance door of her bar during the night. Not much damage but... she's very scared, *capo.* She was close to tears..."

8: Gathering pace...

Beppe, accompanied by Sonia, was already in Via Foscolo by quarter to seven. The early morning clientele, drinking their coffees and eating their *cornetti* were subdued. The threat from the underworld had suddenly become a tangible reality, in the form of a charred wooden door.

"Maybe it was a simple act of vandalism," one of the customers was saying to the *padrona*, Monica Barone, in an attempt to minimise the impact of the crime.

"A false hope, I'm sorry to tell you, *signore*," said the *commissario* to the man in question. Turning back to the *padrona*, he said:

"Can we go and sit round one of your tables, *Signora* Monica?" he suggested.

The bar owner looked at the young man who was behind the bar. He merely nodded as if to reassure Monica he was quite capable of holding the fort. Barely had they sat down when he brought over three coffees and three glasses of water on a tray which he set down in front of them without a word.

"*Grazie,* Carlo," said Monica with an appreciative smile.

"Can you tell us exactly what happened, Monica?" began Sonia Leardi in a gentle voice. "We don't imagine this just happened out of the blue..."

Monica nodded.

"It happened exactly as your colleagues said it would when they came round to warn us about a possible visit from *those people* earlier on in the day," began Monica looking at both the police officers in turn. "Just before we were closing up last night at around, half past ten, this man and woman arrived and asked for a late-night drink. I knew they were trouble because they were wearing sunglasses. They were smartly dressed and were trying too hard to sound casual.

79

They began talking to me about the town of Pescara and asked how long this 'smart new bar' had been open. Then, as if it was an afterthought, the woman mentioned they were in Pescara on business. They began talking about taking out an insurance policy with them – 'to cover eventualities like this'. She claimed they were from a company in Milano... just as your officers said they would."

Monica was obviously becoming upset again as she related these events.

"I expect they handed you a business card at this point, didn't they Monica?" said Beppe brusquely. His harsh tone of voice took both Sonia and Monica by surprise. But it had the desired effect on Monica. A look of anger replaced the onset of tears.

"Yeah, exactly like that. But it had the minimum information on the card. There was some company name in tiny letters. The woman's name was clearly written but only the telephone number was in big, bold type."

"Did you take the card?" asked Sonia.

"No, I did exactly as your officers instructed us. I told them categorically that I was not interested in their proposal."

Beppe was puzzled by the fact that the clan members – he was convinced they were dealing with the mafia – had acted so precipitously in setting fire to the door. They usually waited until the first two or three 'warnings' had been ignored before showing their hand.

"Monica," he asked in a voice that had become gentle and persuasive, "did you say anything else to them?"

Monica Barone blushed and said, with a mixture of embarrassment and defiance:

"Yes, *commissario* - I told them I did not believe they were who they claimed to be and that I had no intention of paying money to a criminal organisation."

The *commissario* had fixed her with a stare that was so disconcerting that she was on the point of blurting out an apology. Without thinking, Sonia placed a hand on Beppe's arm to remind him that he was probably terrifying the barkeeper – a lady who was roughly Sonia's age. But after ten eternal seconds, Beppe smiled broadly at Monica.

"Well, you've certainly given them a good idea of what to expect from the inhabitants of Abruzzo. *Brava...bravissima,* Monica! You are a very courageous woman."

"He means it, Monica. The *commissario* is always sincere in his praise," explained Sonia, seeing that Monica suspected this senior police officer of being sarcastic.

"*I* mean it too, officers. I refuse to be intimidated by this incident," replied Monica defiantly. She was, nevertheless, relieved that she had not made a huge gaffe in the eyes of these two *simpatici* police officers.

"Would your courage extend to being interviewed on TV-Tavo, Monica?" asked Beppe who realised that the time had come to mount a public media campaign.

She nodded. At a sign from Beppe, Sonia outlined the procedure to Monica. Sonia went on to tell her how she would be getting extra support from the police over the next few weeks.

"We won't let you face all this on your own, Monica," Sonia concluded.

Whilst Sonia was talking, Beppe was thinking he would have to pay another visit to his own chief, the *Questore,* who would be sure to enlist the help of the *Carabinieri.* Sonia was completely engrossed in talking to the bar owner.

As usual when his partner was engaged in conversation with a third party, a feeling of profound sensuality stole over him. He found himself surreptitiously watching the movement of her lips and the warmth of expression on her face. Unbidden, there came into his mind the overwhelming desire to ask her how long it would be before the monthly workings of her body would tell them whether or not she was going to be a mother. He shook his head imperceptibly to expel the images provoked by his momentary lapse of concentration. This was not the right moment to become distracted by extraneous thoughts. He had already overindulged his curiosity the previous morning by doggedly pursuing the matter of the frescos.

Beppe and Sonia left the bar owner ten or so minutes later with further reassurances that she would not have to fend for herself.

"We'll install a miniature video camera behind the bar, Monica – and somebody will constantly be monitoring it," promised Beppe.

"We'll be in touch soon about a TV interview," said Sonia.

They shook hands with Monica – and her *barista*, Carlo, who seemed totally unruffled by events. He was just the right person for Monica to have around for the next few days, thought Beppe.

* * *

"We should know one way or the other in the next couple of days or so, *amore,*" said Sonia, as they were driving back to Via Pesaro.

"Are you a mind-reader as well as being a man's perfect partner?" replied Beppe, startled by Sonia's words, which had been spoken as if in answer to a direct question.

"Only if the man happens to be *you!* I saw the way you were looking at me back there, Beppe. I nearly lost my train of thought," she said scoldingly. "And don't you remember the time we were both about to say the word 'telepathy' at exactly the same moment?"

Beppe smiled at the memory of the incident at the very outset of their relationship. After an unexpected lull in the conversation, they had both simultaneously begun asking the question: "Do you believe in ...?" Only the following day had they discovered they had both been thinking of the word *telepathy.*

Beppe remained silent until they reached the police station car park. A rapid *bacio* followed by a brief discussion about what they each had to do before the day was out.

"I hope you are not going back to Loreto Aprutino tonight, *amore,*" said Sonia, trying hard to suppress the pleading note in her voice.

"I hope so too," were the only words of reassurance Beppe had to offer. There were so many hidden aspects to this case still to be unearthed before he would see light at the end of the tunnel. He kept reminding himself there was still scant proof that Salvatore Carlettini had been deliberately poisoned. 'Gut feelings' were all very well, but there was a risk he was pursuing this investigation merely to satisfy his own insatiable curiosity. He thought about the frescos again – and let out a long sigh.

Sonia placed a hand on his knee before they got out of the car.

"Be careful, *amore,*" she whispered with an edge of anxiety in her voice provoked by a fleeting image of impending danger.

* * *

As Beppe stepped into the *Questore's* office, Dante Di Pasquale's desk phone began to ring. His uniformed chief held up a hand to excuse the interruption. After listening to his interlocutor for no more than ten seconds, the *Questore* put the phone into loud speaker mode and gestured with his free hand for Beppe to sit down.

Beppe soon understood the motive behind Di Pasquale's reaction. He recognised the peeved tones of Ernesto Carlettini. Beppe listened attentively to the ensuing dialogue:

And what exactly is the nature of your complaint, *Signor* Carlettini?

Two of your officers arrived at my home yesterday afternoon while I was out of the house and proceeded to interrogate my wife and my six-year-old son, who has recently been very ill...

I understand your son has made a complete and very unusual recovery, *signore*. I am very happy for you and your wife. Do you have the names of the two officers who came to your house?

There was a man and a lady police officer – who interrogated my son without my wife being present...

I apologise for interrupting you, *Signor* Carlettini. When the police officers arrived at your front door, did they state the reason for their visit? I presume it was your wife who let them in?

Yes, of course!

Did the two officers force their way into your home?

No... my wife let them in. But my complaint is that...

Again, I apologise for cutting in, *signore*. Did my officers say why they wanted to question your wife – and your little boy?

Yes, they said they were investigating the death of my brother. But that is not the point I am trying to make...

So, your wife let them into your home of her own free will at that point?
(Pause while Carlettini searches for words)

Yes, I believe so.

You say that one of the officers – I imagine we are talking about *Agente* Leardi... *(Beppe nodded in confirmation)* ...interrogated your son while   your wife was not present. Is that correct?

Yes, precisely, signor Questore.

Where was your wife at that moment?

In the living room talking to the male officer.

And your son and *Agente* Leardi?

In Lori's bedroom. That's why I object...

Did Officer Leardi close the bedroom door, *signore?*

No, it was left open. But I...

Did you get the impression that your son was being coerced into talking to Officer Leardi?

No, of course not - but he is a young and impressionable boy. He might quite unintentionally have said something which wasn't true, or even said...

Something that *was* true, were you about to say? I would stop there, if I were you, *Signor* Carlettini, before you say something *you* might regret. If I understand you correctly, two officers arrived at your front door. They clearly stated the reasons for their visit before being ushered inside your home by your own wife. They then proceeded to do exactly what they had told her *before* they had been invited inside. Does that seem to sum up fairly what happened?

Yes, yes, Signor Questore. But I still believe your officers acted...

Try to remember the fact that we are investigating the death of your own brother, who died in very suspicious circumstances. If you wish to make a formal complaint about either of the two officers who visited you, may I suggest you come to the *Questura* in person? Meanwhile, I will make enquiries to ascertain whether my officers' conduct was in any way inappropriate. I thank you for your call, *Signor* Carlettini. We shall keep you informed as to any developments regarding your brother's death. Oh, and by the way, our conversation has been recorded – just for your peace of mind. *Arrivederla signore.*

The *Questore* hung up and looked quizzically at the *commissario*, who was soundlessly applauding his chief's handling of Ernesto Carlettini's pernickety complaint.

"I just *know* that man is anxious to conceal something," commented Beppe.

"I think you are right, Beppe. Now, do you want to fill me in on everything else?" invited the *Questore*.

Beppe launched into a very full account of events since his journey to Loreto Aprutino – omitting nothing except his unscheduled stop at the church of *Santa Maria in Piano.*

"So you see, *capo,*" concluded Beppe, "we have established that Ernesto Carlettini and his family *did* go to Montebello just before his brother's death. We have discovered, incidentally, how Lorenzo contracted nephritis. I am convinced – although I have no proof as yet – that there is some incidental link between Ernesto Carlettini and his brother Salvatore's death."

"What makes you think that, Beppe?"

"A hunch – based on the simple fact that the two brothers look almost identical."

The *Questore* looked astutely at his senior officer for fifteen seconds before saying quietly:

"Do you mean that the intended victim was not Salvatore Carlettini, but his younger brother?"

"Yes, I do. But I still have to be certain," said Beppe.

"But it *is* a case of murder, isn't it?" asked the *Questore.*

"Oh, yes, there is no doubt about *that,*" Beppe assured his chief.

Beppe and his chief then spent another hour talking about the invasion of the Pugliese mafia. He told his chief about Monica Barone and the recent attack on her bar.

"Leave everything to me, Beppe. I'll contact the *Carabinieri* – we shall need their cooperation from now on. As to the TV interview with Monica Barone, I'll set that up immediately. We can't afford to hang about. Once again, Beppe, you have amazed me as to how much you have achieved in such a short space of time. But please have a word with Sonia, just to make sure she is doubly careful in future. Knowing her, I am quite certain that she did nothing improper. But you know what some members of the public are like..."

The two men shook hands warmly and Beppe turned his attention to the next steps he needed to take to get to the bottom of the mystery of the poisonous mushrooms. He went back down to the ground floor. The police station seemed empty. Of course - it was nearly lunchtime! If he was lucky, he might catch the technical duo before they too disappeared for lunch. He prayed that they had managed to glean some information from Salvatore's computer and his mobile phone which might shed light on the final hours of Salvatore Carlettini's life.

He descended to the basement where the technicians' laboratory was situated. He was not surprised to find the place deserted. There was a note attached to the door which said simply: *Back at 14.00h.* He trudged upstairs again and went to see if Sonia was on the premises. Sonia was nowhere to be seen either. He headed for the reception desk and was pleased to find his longest serving officer, Giacomo D'Amico on duty.

"Any idea where I might find Sonia?" he asked casually.

"Sonia and Oriana are out, *commissario.* I understand they are visiting our fellow citizens who work in the 'hospitality industry' – and their so-called protectors," said Giacomo with a humorous glint in his eye. "Under your orders, I believe, *commissario.*"

"Thanks, Giacomo. By the way, I think it's time we had a briefing meeting. Can you get everybody together for six o'clock this evening?"

"No problem, *capo.*"

Beppe did not feel like having lunch - and especially not on his own. He sloped off in desultory mood and sat behind his desk, brooding on how he could find out what he wanted to know about Ernesto Carlettini, without having to alert the man that he was delving into his past life. He was convinced that the key to the death of Salvatore lay in whatever it was that the Carlettini couple were at pains to conceal. His suspicions were tenuous, he admitted. He was driven by intuition and curiosity alone.

It was at that precise moment that an idea sprang all unbidden into his mind. His brain was in 'play-back' mode; he found himself recalling the conversation he had had with the two Finance Police outside the church in Loreto Aprutino. It occurred to Beppe that the chance encounter might inadvertently have provided him with a way forward. Once again, he found himself debating the difference between coincidence and... yes, he forced himself to say the word out loud: 'Fate.' It would be ironic, he thought, if his gratuitous visit to see the frescos might actually have provided him with a way forward in this difficult investigation.

He would have to go back to see the *Questore* again to put his idea to his chief and enlist his help. But when he reached the upper floors of the police station once again, he was greeted by Dante Di Pasquale's secretary.

"I'm sorry, *commissario*," she said with an apologetic smile. "The *Questore* has just gone to lunch."

9: The deviousness of Commissario Stancato…

Beppe was sitting in a cramped office somewhere in the back streets of Pescara. The room smelt of stale coffee mixed in with an unpleasant hint of domestic bleach. The frosted glass window behind the desk was impossible to open since the handle had seized up years ago. Beppe had been deposited on the 'client' side of a large desk by a nervous officer wearing the official uniform of the Mushroom Police.

"My chief will be back from lunch in a couple of minutes," he was assured. However, the chair on the 'official' side of the desk remained stubbornly empty for a lapse of time that extended well beyond twenty minutes.

Commissario Stancato was becoming impatient. Italian officials' extended lunchtimes had a significantly adverse effect on the country's ability to solve its deep-rooted problems, he thought crossly. In the end, he stood up and went in search of the pale young man. He found him cowering behind a smaller desk in a cubby hole next to the main office.

The junior mushroom officer looked apologetically at this *commissario* with the off-putting stare. Beppe's reputation in Pescara had become legendary and the man, barely more than a teenager, was in awe of him.

"Surely, you must be as qualified as your senior officer to answer a simple enquiry?" snapped Beppe.

"My chief prefers to deal with queries himself, *commissario.* He gives me a hard time if I…"

"*Coraggio giovanotto!* Let's buck the trend shall we? *You* are here and your chief is not! Now, will you at least try to answer my query?"

The mushroom policeman nodded fearfully. Beppe proceeded to give him a brief account of the investigation – enough to impress the importance of the matter on his reluctant interlocutor.

"Do you know what species of mushroom was involved, *commissario?*"

"Two kinds, *agente* – Amanita Muscaria and Cortinarius Speciosissimus," replied Beppe without hesitation.

The officer looked at the *commissario* with eyebrows raised. His whole aspect changed. He obviously felt on home territory.

"Poor man! He must have suffered an excruciatingly agonising death! But those species are certainly not to be found near the coastal zones, *commissario.* You would have to be in the foothills of the Gran Sasso itself – possibly in the forests in the vicinity of the *Cascata del Vitello d'Oro...*"

"The Golden Calf Waterfall - where on earth is *that?*"

"Oh, *commissario* – everybody knows where that waterfall is! It's just beyond a mountain village called F..."

At that moment, they heard the sound of the main door opening and a bulky man in his sixties with a greying, ferocious-looking moustache entered the cramped space and glared at both his junior colleague and the *commissario.* The youth, who had almost managed to give him some piece of vital information, was looking cowed again.

Beppe reacted quickly. He held out his hand to the young policeman and said smilingly:

"You have been very helpful, officer...?

"Davide Bianco," he replied supplying his name.

Beppe turned to the chief of Mushroom Police and flashed his identity badge in the man's unsmiling face.

"Congratulations, *capitano.* You have trained your colleague admirably. He has been most helpful to us in our enquiry. I apologise for the fact that I was unable to wait for you to finish your leisurely lunch."

Without waiting for a reply, the *commissario* headed for the exit without a backward glance.

Inside the police car, he pressed his foot down on the accelerator and shot off angrily in the direction of the police headquarters.

He had only just satisfied himself about those frescos and just a few hours later, he had heard those cursed words again:

Oh, commissario – EVERYBODY knows where the Cascata del Vitello d'Oro is!

Everybody except him, apparently! He sighed resignedly as he parked his car at the police headquarters.

At least his chief, the Questore, would have had ample time to finish *his* lunch...

* * *

Beppe was feeling considerably happier one hour later as he shook his chief by the hand and thanked him yet again for his support and help.

The *Questore* was phoning his opposite number in the *Guardia di Finanza* and briefly outlined Beppe's unusual request. It was gratifying to note the *Guardia di Finanza's* willingness to cooperate as soon as they realised the request had emanated from Beppe.

"Your *commissario* made our task so much simpler when we were sorting out the finances of that *Mafioso*, Don Alfieri, earlier on this year," said the *Guardia* Colonel appreciatively. "We would be delighted to help if we can."

"Maybe I should let our *commissario* himself explain what he has in mind, *Colonnello*," he said handing the phone over to Beppe.

Beppe outlined the details of the investigation as succinctly as he could.

"By a happy coincidence, Beppe, we do have the dental studio of Ernesto Carlettini in our sights. As it wasn't urgent –

just a VAT issue - it was put on hold for a week or so. But now you've given us an extra motive for going to see this gentleman sooner rather than later; a fortunate coincidence, wouldn't you say?"

Beppe repressed the temptation to enlighten the *Guardia di Finanza* officer as to his personal views on coincidences.

"What exactly would you like to know about *Signor* Carlettini, Beppe?" he was being asked.

"What jobs he has had before he opened his dental studio, if you could, *Colonnello.* Both he and his wife have been uncommonly reticent about this aspect of their lives."

"That's not a problem. We usually go into the career history of people we're investigating - as a matter of routine. Strange though that Ernesto Carlettini's name should come up again - one of my junior colleague's mother had a set of false teeth supplied by the Carlettini studio. It had to be sent back because it was too big for her mouth."

Beppe refrained from telling him about his encounter with his two *Guardia* officers outside the church in Loreto Aprutino. The *Colonnello* might have assumed it was yet another coincidence.

* * *

Now, finally, he could go down to the basement and see if the technicians had unearthed anything of interest from the victim's mobile phone and his antiquated lap-top.

He was greeted by the effusive and well-rounded personage of Bianca Bomba.

"On your own today, Bianca?" Beppe asked, surprised not to find the playful duo together. The two technicians enjoyed making the most of their superior knowledge to keep Beppe on tenterhooks if they suspected he was impatient to pick their brains.

"Marco is out installing a video camera in a local bar, *commissario*. So you are in the fortunate position of commanding my undivided attention."

It was obvious that Bianca had no intention of relinquishing the pleasure of milking the situation as much as she could. Beppe summoned up his store of patience and good humour, sighing with mock resignation. It would be quicker in the long run, he reasoned.

"Not a very communicative individual, this Salvatore Carlettini, *commissario*," she began.

"He's certainly not very forthcoming now, Bianca," replied Beppe without a hint of a smile.

Bianca Bomba let out a cheerful ripple of laughter – which could only emanate from a person who is at ease in her skin, thought Beppe.

"We like you, *commissario*," Bianca said playfully. "I wish I could tell you something that might help you solve your case with a single click on an icon. But what this Salvatore actually managed to communicate is very scant. I have a feeling he might have been in considerable pain. Just look at this single e-mail he sent – to a family member, Ernesto Carlettini. His brother, I suppose?"

Beppe nodded and looked at the brief attempt at communication.

Son stato venelato. Ho magniato qualche fugno. Mi ha consilgiato un esperto... Lui mi ha mentito... *(I've been poisoned. I ate some mushrooms. An expert told me they were alright... He lied to me... The Italian version contains a number of significant misspellings. Author's note)*

Beppe read the words and looked quizzically at the technician.

"It looks as if he just gave up," observed Beppe.

"My impression too, *commissario* – it was all too much effort for him. But you notice the strangeness of his spelling, don't you?"

"Yes – he keeps reversing letters in some of the words. He can't seem to concentrate... Or else he can't spell!"

"You know what *I* think, *commissario?*"

Beppe looked at Bianca expectantly. He had recognised the familiar signs; the lady technician was keeping him waiting, which meant she wanted to impart something of significance. Beppe played the game. He stared intensely at her until she relented after a record pause of only five seconds.

"I would say your victim was dyslexic," she said triumphantly.

Beppe's brain cells had gone into overdrive. Some thought he had been harbouring in the backwaters of his mind clicked into place.

He hardly dared formulate his next question.

"Bianca, you know more about this than I do, I am sure. But can you tell me, please – does dyslexia run in families? Can a brother also inherit the same... defect?"

"Absolutely, yes, *commissario.* It's very common."

"But Salvatore Carlettini was a *Freccia Bianca* train driver, Bianca. Surely such a problem would prevent him from becoming...?"

"Not necessarily, *commissario,*" interrupted Bianca. "He might have only had mild dyslexia – if I can put it that way. And don't forget, seeing his age, he must have been driving trains before the authorities recognised dyslexia as a problem – especially if he was never involved in any incident while driving his trains. Besides which, colour-blindness is a more serious problem than dyslexia for a train driver."

Beppe had fallen into a state of deep meditation. So much so, that Bianca thought it wise to alert him as to her continued presence.

"I don't suppose you are still interested to know if I discovered anything from his mobile phone?" she asked impudently.

Beppe merely looked at her again – having immediately understood that she had something else to say.

"Well, Bianca? What did you find out," he asked in the end.

"Nothing at all, *commissario.*"

Beppe gave her his sternest look.

"Except that his last call was made to this number just before he must have succumbed to the last throes of agony. The number is 349 88 66 627."

Beppe had not come across this mobile phone number before, but he would bet that it belonged to Ernesto Carlettini. Up until that moment, he had always contacted Ernesto on his land line.

"Bianca," he said, cupping her face gently between his hands, "you are a star that shines on its own in the night sky. *Grazie mille!*"

He kissed her noisily on the forehead. She barely blushed but looked at him with a gleam in her eyes.

"So glad to have been of service," she said ironically.

Beppe left Bianca to her isolated post in the basement and skipped upstairs. His predominant thought was that at no point had Ernesto told them about either the e-mail or his brother's final phone call. He wondered whether Ernesto would have even bothered answering the call. There was a simple way to confirm whether the final number really did belong to brother Ernesto, although he had no doubt that this was the case. Beppe had conceived a dislike for this shifty individual, who seemed so indifferent to the reality of his brother's death. He decided he would allow himself the luxury of being just a tad unprofessional; he would check that it was Ernesto's number, of course, but make out the call was from someone else. One of his less acclaimed talents was an ability to mimic various regional accents. He would take a perverse delight in putting the wind up Ernesto Carlettini.

* * *

18.00h – Meeting

There was one vital member who was not present. Beppe instinctively cast his eyes round the expectant gathering of uniformed police officers. A sudden pang of anxiety shot through his whole body like a shockwave of fear.

"Where's Sonia?" he asked not bothering to conceal his concern from the team.

Oriana Salvati spoke up from the front row:

"Sorry, *capo,* I thought you would have been told. Sonia is at the TV-Tavo studio, with the lady who runs the *Bar Galileo.* They are preparing an interview with the *Questore* which will go out this evening at peak viewing time..."

Beppe was shocked at how efficiently and rapidly his suggestion had been taken up and turned into a media reality. He hoped Sonia was not going to appear on the live broadcast. He was fearful that any public exposure could make her more vulnerable to reprisals from the *mafia* clan which was attempting to infiltrate the town of Pescara. His fear must have shown on his usually passive face.

"Don't be anxious, *capo,*" said Oriana with an unaccustomed tone of sympathy and kindness in her voice, "I'm sure she won't do anything rash."

"Especially now she's bearing our child," Beppe was briefly tempted to reveal.

The meeting continued normally for a further fifteen minutes. There had, during the course of the day, been two more attempts to spread alarm amongst the shop-keepers. A jeweller's shop and a men's hairdressing parlour had been 'visited' by the two youths in an attempt to intimidate the local *commercianti*.

"Apparently, the jeweller remained very cool, *capo*. The two thugs made a mistake too," said Officer Danilo Simone. "They had to take their helmets off to get past the security door, since the jeweller would never have opened the door to them otherwise. He pointed out the video camera above their heads. That was enough. They scarpered in a hurry. So now we've got a picture of their faces. We're intending to go round the cheap hotels and find out where they're holed up, *capo*."

"Save yourself the effort and wasted time, *ragazzi*. Those two hoodlums will have rented a cheap apartment somewhere in down-town Pescara – or they'll be with someone who has already begun the process of infiltration and be at a private address. You'd be better employed going round all the estate agents. Ask if any of them have recently rented out a flat to anyone with a Pugliese accent. In all probability, the Foggia clan has already taken over the running of one of the smaller estate agents in town. The clans know how much money can be made by controlling property sales…"

"This has become a major issue, hasn't it *capo?*" said Giacomo D'Amico. "I've never heard of the mafia clans taking over the property market before."

"In one town outside Lecce," began Pippo, who had come up to Abruzzo to escape from the *Sacra Corona Unita,* "the local clan has taken over property sales completely. I was told about a lady doctor from Bologna, who wanted to buy a holiday home in Salento. She had agreed a price with the estate agent and was about to sign the property documents. At the last moment, a deeply embarrassed estate agent told her the sale had been blocked. He refused to give a reason. He was too scared to tell her the truth; the local clan had found a buyer who was prepared to pay a much higher price."

"That's how they work, *ragazzi.* So if you want to do a bit of *real* investigating, do the rounds of the smaller estate agents and see which one of them is only playing at selling houses. You can tell by the shifty look in their eyes, as if they are scared of making a decision on their own. They will always have to 'consult' their boss. What about the hairdresser's parlour?" asked Beppe.

"That was almost comical, chief," said another officer. "The hair-dresser is...eh... how can I put it? A bit *effeminate...*"

His delicate choice of words produced a wave of ribald mirth round the room.

"He was shaking so much he had to stop work. He was in the middle of shaving the foam off his client's neck with a cut-throat razor."

More laughter, but Beppe did not attempt to admonish his team. They had yet to learn how little there was to be amused about when a mafia take-over was in progress.

"There were half a dozen other clients waiting their turn – including a couple of builders," continued the officer. "They were magnificent – they all stood up as if to go for the two thugs. They just ran out of the shop, hopped on a Vespa scooter and shot off."

"The trouble is, of course," Beppe pointed out, "as far as the two yobs are concerned, they had already achieved their main purpose – intimidation. We shall have to be doubly vigilant from now on."

Beppe was beginning to feel guilty about not being at the centre of this operation. The sooner the mushroom case was solved, the better, he thought.

He asked Oriana how she and Sonia had fared with the prostitutes and their contacts. Oriana said they had covered a lot of ground. He could find out from Sonia in more detail what the pair of them had achieved.

Beppe resisted the temptation to tell his team about his own investigation. He promised to fill them in as soon as it was all over – by the end of the week, he had rashly promised. However, Beppe was unable to resist the temptation to ask his gathered team, as they were about to disperse, the question that was uppermost in his mind.

"Can anyone here tell me where the *Vitello d'Oro* waterfall is – WITHOUT using the words *'Everybody in Abruzzo knows…'* Because, if you do, it will be a lie – since *I* don't know where it is!"

"FARINDOLA" came the reply in perfect unison. Beppe might have been irritated but for the fact that he was smacking his forehead smartly with his open palm. His feverish fingers fumbled in an inner pocket. He fished out the 'shopping list' that he had found at Salvatore Carlettini's house in Montebello. To his team's astonishment, their chief looked at the piece of paper and let out a cry of triumph. The badly scribbled letters which looked like the beginning of the Italian word for 'flour' now made perfect sense. The junior mushroom policeman had started to say a place name beginning with the letter 'f'. That clinched the matter.

Beppe was beaming at his team.

"Bravi, ragazzi! I couldn't do without you," was all he deigned to say. He passed the 'shopping list' round the team and asked them if they could suggest why the partial word 'Demi' also appeared on the piece of paper.

They each looked hard at the word, wanting to be the one who could enlighten their chief. With a sad shake of each head, they passed the paper on to the next member of the team. Beppe was about to close the meeting. Some officers had already stood up to leave. The piece of paper had arrived at its final destination – between the fingers of Oriana Salvati.

Her clear, bell-like voice rang out amidst the growing buzz of male conversation. The gathered officers fell silent in an instant. She had everyone's undivided attention.

"Capo," she said, "that's not an 'e'. Many Italians – me included – write the letter 'a' just like that…"

For the second time that day, Beppe kissed a member of his team on the forehead. The blush on Oriana's face was very apparent. The gathered team of officers held their collective breath in alarm. Had any other man in the world dared to make the same gesture – apart from her *fidanzato, Agente* Giovanni Palena – he would have been reduced to a quivering wreck within seconds by the scathing torrent of words that would have issued from Oriana's shapely mouth.

Beppe ran into his office where he kept an up-to-date Italian dictionary. The only word in the Italian language beginning with the letters, capital D. a. m. i. was the male name 'Damiano'.

With a feeling of elation, he drove to the television studio to be there for Sonia, only to discover that she had left in her car with the bar owner, Monica Barone. He phoned her and she told him to go home and wait for her there.

"I'm not letting you go back to Loreto Aprutino tonight, *amore,"* she said.

"I have no intention of going back tonight, *tesoro,"* he replied simply.

10: Ernesto Carlettini under siege...

With Sonia snuggled up to Beppe on their sofa, they studied the list of the names of licensed mushroom pickers which Remo Mastrodicasa had supplied him with the previous morning. There were only three names for the town of Farindola – and none of them went by the name of Damiano.

The sheer habit of refusing to be demoralised by set-backs came to his rescue. He shared the list with Sonia, who read out the names as if to fix them in her mind. To their surprise, one of the names was a woman called Silvia Guerra.

"A woman daring to break into the male dominated world of mushroom gatherers!" exclaimed Sonia. "Italy *must* be making progress!"

The other two names were Adolfo d'Angelo and Mauro Cecamore. *(chayka-MORey)*

"*Mauro Blind-Love* – what a surname to be lumbered with!" remarked Sonia.

"Enough to make someone resort to murder, I wonder? But no Damiano on the list," said Beppe concealing his disappointment bravely. "This means our man picks mushrooms without a licence, I guess..."

"That's very unlikely, Beppe. If the authorities didn't get wind of what he was doing, then the other mushroom pickers would probably lynch him before he got loam on his paws while tugging up their precious supply of *porcini* mushrooms. It's much more likely that 'Damiano' is his middle name. If your first name was Adolfo, wouldn't you prefer to be called something else?" reasoned Sonia. "As far as I know, nobody has been given the name Adolfo since 1943."

"Maybe his father was a secret Brown Shirt who supported the fascist regime?" suggested Beppe.

"Must have been something like that, Beppe. But I reckon this Adolfo d'Angelo – or Signor Cecamore – might well be your mushroom poisoner."

"Damiano – if I remember correctly – was the name of Satan's child in that horror movie called 'The Omen'. I'm not sure whether being called Damien is preferable to being called Adolf!" Beppe pointed out.

Whether this was true or not, Beppe reasoned, it should not be too hard to track down the culprit in a small town of little more than one thousand five hundred inhabitants.

Beppe looked at his watch. It was nearly ten past nine. The interview with Monica Barone was scheduled to go on air at quarter past nine.

The television was switched on to TV-Tavo and Beppe waited with bated breath to see if *his* Sonia appeared by Monica Barone's side, exposed to public viewing. He had not wanted to alert Sonia as to his paranoid fear, as he saw it, that she might become a target for reprisals if she came out so obviously in support of the forces of law and order.

Sonia sensed what was going through Beppe's mind and put a reassuring hand on his thigh.

"I wanted to appear next to Monica Barone, *amore,* but the *Questore* wouldn't let me," she said quietly.

"Remind me never to be unfaithful to you," said Beppe. "I wouldn't stand a chance of keeping it a secret."

"You'd do better never to try! I would deprive you of your manhood while you slept," she added – not at all playfully.

Beppe smiled and hugged her.

He was agreeably surprised to see Monica Barone flanked not only by their own chief, Dante Di Pasquale, but also by the *Carabinieri* Colonel, Riccardo Grimaldi, equally flamboyantly dressed in full regalia.

"Caspita!" exclaimed Beppe. "All stops out! Where were you sitting, Sonia?"

"Just out of sight, making encouraging faces in Monica's direction."

Monica Barone appeared calm and determined as she related what had happened to her in a tone of controlled anger to all the inhabitants of Pescara and beyond.

"Don't give way to them," she pleaded. "Be strong. If we stick together, there is nothing they can do."

She even managed to finish her passionate appeal with a humorous reference to the burnt door of the *Bar Galileo.*

I'm leaving it just as it is," she explained. "Everybody who passes by will see my own personal symbol of resistance."

"I hope her stance will treble the number of customers she gets," said Sonia.

"Viva la solidarietà!" added Beppe. "Long live mutual support!"

The programme finished with an equally strong and reassuring appeal from the two senior policemen.

"Don't hesitate to call 112 or 113 at any time of the day..."

"Or night," concluded the *Questore.* "This is, quite simply, a war that we cannot afford to lose."

* * *

"Let's go to bed, *amore,"* suggested Sonia seductively.

"I've just got one more phone call to make and I'll follow you..." replied Beppe as nonchalantly as possible. Sonia gave him a stern look.

"Not *that* kind of phone call, *tesoro"* he added quickly.

Beppe went into the kitchen and dialled the number which Bianca Bomba had given him earlier. Sure enough, the suspiciously resentful voice of Ernesto Carlettini was instantly recognisable.

From the bedroom, Sonia heard a voice from the kitchen which she did not recognise, speaking with a pronounced Milanese accent. She went into the kitchen to see who was talking – assuming that Beppe must have put his mobile phone into loud-speaker mode. She stood in the doorway with her mouth open in surprise. Her partner was holding a cheap-looking blue mobile device which she did not recognise. She was as fascinated by her partner's impeccable Milanese pronunciation as much as by the somewhat one-sided dialogue which ensued. Beppe switched to loudspeaker mode.

Pronto, chi parla?

Buonasera, Signor Carlettini. My name is Gianfranco Deluso. I am a reporter from the weekly Milanese publication, *Lo Specchio della Vita Italiana.* I'm sure you must have heard of us?

(A now very alert Sonia stifled a giggle at Beppe's choice of 'pseudonym' – Mr Deluded.)

Buonasera, Signor ehm…. Deluso?

Correct! An unfortunate surname, I grant you. According to that quiz programme on Rai Uno, there are only 17 families in the whole of Italy with that surname. A misnomer in my case, I can assure you, Signor Carlettini. May I call you Ernesto? So much less formal, don't you think?

You may call me what you think fit, signore. Would you mind telling me the purpose of this call?

(There was already a note of alarm in Ernesto's voice. Unfamiliar situations made him feel instantly ill-at-ease)

Of course, of course, Ernesto - I will come to the point immediately. You must be thinking of retiring for the night. But it was important for me to catch you at home – I know how busy you are during the daytime. We are carrying out a nationwide survey with a view to publishing a comprehensive report on those people who, like you, are engaged in significant careers in the medical world despite having had to overcome a certain ... shall we say, mental disability throughout your professional lives. All credit to you and those in the same situation as yourself who have prospered despite the setbacks.

(Ernesto Carlettini appeared to be having difficulty breathing and, clearly on the defensive, began stammering out his reply)

My... my disability, as you are kind enough to call it, has really not affected my career at all. I am beginning to resent your intrusion at this late hour...

I apologise, Ernesto. I understood that your... dyslexia - let us speak plainly – *did* cause a problem during a previous post you occupied. I do apologise if I have been misinformed.

I think I shall decline the offer of participating in your survey...

Of course, Ernesto - I quite understand. A shame! I'm certain your contribution would have been invaluable – and, needless to say, generously remunerated by our journal. But, I repeat, I do entirely sympathise with your misgivings...

(The word 'remuneration' had struck a chord in Ernesto's Carlettini's mercenary soul. He was hesitating. But Beppe had learnt all he wanted to know)

Never mind - you can always phone me back, Ernesto, should you have a change of heart. *Buona serata.* And good luck with your dental studio."

Beppe turned off the phone and grinned at his nonplussed partner. Only after the phone call had come to an end did Ernesto Carlettini begin to ask himself how the caller knew so much about his personal life.

"You're a wicked man, Beppe Stancato – when you have a mind to be. What on earth was all that about?" said Sonia gaspingly. She realised she had been holding her breath whilst listening to the phone conversation.

Beppe told her what Bianca Bomba had surmised after looking at Salvatore's brief e-mail.

"I needed to check that the number she extracted from Salvatore's mobile phone was really his brother's. I also wanted to confirm that Ernesto suffers from dyslexia – like his brother.

"He never admitted he did," Sonia pointed out.

"No, but he certainly didn't deny it. And I have a hunch that the Carlettini couple are covering up something that happened in the past. This is only surmise at present but Ernesto Carlettini said nothing just now to make me change my mind. I have a vague idea as to what it might be about. However, I need to…"

"But do you really think it has a bearing on Salvatore's death, Beppe?" interrupted Sonia.

"Yes, I believe there *is* a connection between some incident in Ernesto's past and the death of his brother. I don't suppose you noticed a faded photo of the two brothers in the Carlettini's living room when you were there, did you Sonia?"

"Yes, I did. I *always* look at family photos when I'm in other people's homes. It's a kind of investigator's habit, I suppose. They looked so alike - as if they could have been..."

Sonia's face lit up as she caught up with Beppe's tortuous line of reasoning. It had taken her longer than the *Questore* to make the mental leap, but she was there now.

"You mean this Damiano mistook Salvatore Carlettini for his brother?"

"It's mere guesswork at present. But it might well account for the Carlettini couple's discomfort and evasiveness."

"But how will you be able to find out without alerting Ernesto?"

"Ah well, Sonia. I'm hoping the *Guardia di Finanza* will do the spadework for me tomorrow," replied Beppe.

Sonia looked at Beppe in total mystification. It was time for Beppe to tell her how he had spent the earlier part of his day. They retired to bed – where other imperatives rapidly asserted themselves. By the following morning, there were still a number of gaps in their respective narrations.

Back at the police headquarters, Beppe deliberated whether he should return to Loreto Aprutino immediately. He was already one day later than he had promised his colleague, Enrico Nardini. But was there any point in going back inland until he had the information about Ernesto Carlettini that he hoped the *Guardia di Finanza* would be able to unearth? If he was lucky, their raid on Ernesto's studio might well be scheduled for that very day.

He contented himself with making a phone call to Enrico Nardini, assuring him that progress had been made.

"You're not the only one who's been busy, *capo*," the *carabiniere* officer informed him. "We've managed to track down Salvatore's housekeeper in Torino. The local police will go and see her later today."

"Bravo capitano! I'll be back very soon, I promise. And I hope we shall be in a position to wrap the matter up very quickly."

"You're not telling me you've found out who the mushroom poisoner is, are you, *commissario?"* asked Enrico Nardini in disbelief.

"Could be!" was all Beppe deigned to tell him before hanging up.

Good! Beppe was pleased to be staying one more day in Pescara – and one more night with Sonia. Being apart from her was proving to be harder than he cared to admit.

He shook himself free of his personal thoughts and went to look for Pippo Cafarelli.

"Come on, Pippo. Let's see whether we can forestall your old enemies from Foggia before they try to muscle in on the estate agents. Can you bring a copy of that photo of the two helmetless hoodlums with you? There's a particular estate agent I would like to make a start on."

The police car had to drive past Beppe and Sonia's apartment along the sea front. Just opposite their *palazzo*, he noticed a car which he did not recognise. There were two men wearing sunglasses sitting in the front seats. Beppe wore a deep frown as they drove past the stationary car. He made a mental note of the registration plate.

Pippo gave his chief a sidelong glance. He too had seen the occupants of the car and thought they seemed out of place. His sharper, younger eyes had spotted the two small letters on the right-hand side of the *targa* - NA for Naples. That did not bode well, thought Pippo darkly.

11: The dark night of Damiano's soul...

He simply could not go on like this. He had ventured out once only since his fatal encounter with that man who had arrived at his house out of the blue, clutching his pathetic little wicker basket full of poisonous mushrooms – not to mention Salvatore's two Labradors which had sniffed their way suspiciously round the ground floor of his rambling old house.

He had been forced to go shopping in the town's mini-market for some basic provisions to prevent the onset of starvation. He had walked past the *Bar Commercio* as nonchalantly as possible – convinced that the bar owner would challenge him as to why he had suddenly stopped frequenting her establishment for his daily dose of *grappa.*

"Ehi! Damiano!" It was inevitable, of course! One of the regulars had spotted him from inside the gloomy interior of the bar and had come out on to the pavement to hail the departing figure, clutching his plastic bag of meagre provisions.

"Are you avoiding us all of a sudden?" said Damiano's pursuer.

Inside the bar, the buxom, jovial bar owner was already pouring out a dose of *grappa* into the squat, fluted glass as a reluctant Damiano found himself being led to the counter.

"What happened to *you*, Damiano?" asked the bar owner with a mocking smile on her face. "Gone off the *grappa*, have we?"

"I had a stomach bug," muttered Damiano feebly.

"Just like that Salvatore Carlettini bloke the other week! He came in here asking if there was anyone who knew about mushrooms in the village. We sent him down to you, Damiano."

The inevitable, crudely expressed words that encapsulated Damiano's principle fear had been realised – it *was* the owner of the *Bar Commercio* who had directed Salvatore Carlettini to his house on that fatal morning. But the owner of the bar claimed to be knowledgeable about mushrooms herself.

"Why didn't *you* offer to advise him, Silvia?"

"Too risky, Damiano – and I was busy. I didn't want to get involved, I guess. Besides which, *you* are the real expert in these parts."

This was the moment Damiano had been dreading. He had rehearsed his two cover-up stories so many times that he was no longer able to assess which version of events was likely to sound the more plausible. Faced with the immediate dilemma of what to say, he opted for the simpler but riskier alternative. He hardened his heart at the last moment.

"Thank you for the compliment," he said to the bar owner with feigned surprise. "I saw the report of that Carlettini chap's death on the television – as I am sure you must have too. But nobody remotely resembling him ever showed up on *my* doorstep, I can assure you."

There! The words were out! Damiano had told the lie which he hoped would deflect the world's attention away from him.

When he was back behind the ramparts of his own solitary fortress, the inevitable guilt and doubts assailed him anew. His fragile alibi could be broken so readily by any one of his neighbours who might have spotted Salvatore Carlettini arriving that morning with his dogs in tow. He hadn't dared broach the subject with any of his neighbours – it could be interpreted all too easily as an admission of guilt.

Damiano opened the big wooden door that led down to the cellar beneath his house. It was gloomy down there – even with the three bare electric bulbs switched on. It was the only place where he felt protected from his own demons. The place was redolent with the loamy perfume emanating from the various species of mushrooms that he cultivated beneath his house. Apart from being near the waterfall, his cellar was the one place where he dared to allow himself to reflect on what had happened.

You haven't killed anyone, Damiano. It was the mushrooms that are responsible for that man's death. Not you! It felt as if he had some kind of intimate bond with his victim at moments like this – as if Salvatore wanted to absolve him of his heinous crime of omission. *Salvatore is at peace now – stop worrying.*

The insidious inner voice was so soothing... so convincing. He could almost come to believe it. Should Damiano really blame himself if he had got the wrong brother? His fear was that the customers of the *Bar Commercio* must have discussed his name in connection with Carlettini's visit to his house. What if some police detective turned up and began asking questions? He had dug an even deeper hole for himself by denying that the man had ever arrived on his doorstep.

The guilt and the fear about the ease with which his murderous deed could come to light sent him into a state of turmoil yet again. He was locked inside a labyrinth of conflicting arguments and terrifying images of punishment – earthly as well as Dantesque pictures of infernal torture.

He remembered vividly the occasion when he had visited that church in Loreto Aprutino with his wife Renata – all those years ago. They had held hands as they gazed at the frescos, laughing smugly at the images of the albino lizard-cum-humans scrambling across the Bridge of Hairs. Their emotional intimacy shielded them from the effect of the damning truth depicted by those plaintive figures. Now he knew that the figure which was portrayed falling through the bridge's flimsy structure into the torrent below was *HIM*.

At other times, Damiano would feel a sense of injustice and anger welling up inside him. He experienced an overwhelming desire to continue his mission in life; to track down the other Carlettini brother and exact vengeance where he had failed before. However, the sensation was quickly supplanted by the certainty that he would never be reunited with his Renata if he set about the killing of the real culprit.

How could he have been so precipitous on that fatal morning? Why hadn't he just stopped to think? He could just as easily have admitted that Salvatore *had* come to his house but that he, Damiano, had mistaken the poisonous mushrooms for the genuine ones. Why had he not thought of that third possible explanation this morning? Nobody could ever have proved anything to the contrary. He could have let himself off the hook with the greatest of ease.

"Pointless crying over spilt milk - in the eyes of God, you are already doomed to eternal damnation, Damiano," the deeply Catholic part of his psychological make-up reminded him. Thus, the unstoppable cycle of conflicting arguments began all over again.

It was Renata who came to his rescue in the end. In a dream, he heard her docile voice and saw her pitying face imploring him to confess his sin to Holy Mother Church – so that he would be able to be reunited with her in Paradise.

He woke up with the first feeling of calm he had experienced for many a day. But the sense of peace was short lived. He could not, he *dare* not, go to his local parish priest. It was not that he feared the old priest would betray him – the seal of the confessional was sacrosanct. But every time he passed the ageing cleric in the street, he would see that look of covert reprobation in his rheumy old eyes.

Then he remembered hearing somewhere that the Archbishop of Pescara – acting out his favourite role of humble parish priest – held confessions in the Cathedral of *San Cetteo*. He checked it out on the Cathedral's website. That was the only solution – short of obtaining an audience with Pope Francis himself.

Yes, he would go on a pilgrimage to Pescara to make his confession. There was no point in procrastinating. He would catch one of the few daily buses which wound its way through the countryside to Penne. A second bus would end up in Abruzzo's main coastal city some ninety minutes later. He let out an agonised sigh and went to pack a holdall with the few things he would need for his journey to 'salvation'.

On the bus to Pescara, Damiano started to formulate the words he would use in the confessional to express his deep remorse in the eyes of God the Father. He would have to guard against saying *anything* that might suggest he regretted killing the wrong man; best not to even mention Salvatore's brother. There was always the risk that the Archbishop might refuse him absolution. If that happened, he would be back where he started. No, it would be much worse! There would be no other way to go. He would let the rushing torrent of the *Cascata del Vitello d'Oro* engulf him once and for all...

Oh Damiano – che pasticcio che hai fatto! What a mess you've got yourself into!

12: The shadow of fear...

Beppe's fearful vision of the future was due to something far more tangible. He deliberately stopped himself from asking Pippo if he too had spotted the two swarthy individuals seated in the midnight blue Mercedes parked just opposite his *palazzo.* Apart from the giveaway factor of the designer sunglasses, the two men had been sitting unnaturally still. They weren't there to make conversation. They were waiting, spying, on the look-out.

The habit of stifling his personal anxieties rather than sharing them was second nature. He was not worried for himself. His apprehension was solely for Sonia – Sonia plus infant, maybe. It would be impossible to leave her even for one night if the underworld had their home under surveillance. He would say nothing to Pippo, who appeared not to have noticed anything amiss.

What he could not be sure of was the real shape of this threat. Were the two gangsters from Foggia – and therefore part of the SCU clan – or might they be from the Naples mob? If it was the latter, he should be far more worried. Since he had arrested Don Alfieri a few months ago, he was only too aware there might be repercussions from Don Alfieri's successor – the son, Stefano Alfieri. Beppe remembered the encounter with Alfieri Junior all too well from the night they had rescued Serena Vacri. A nasty piece of work, Beppe recalled, whose parting shot had been to spit on the ground behind Beppe's departing figure whilst uttering some nameless curse in his native dialect. The mafioso was hardly likely to let the snub of being humiliated in front of his family go 'unpunished'.

Pippo had pulled over and parked the police car in front of the estate agent's studio. Beppe sighed as he and Pippo entered the studio and spotted the shifty estate agent with whom Beppe had had dealings during the Serena Vacri case. Andrea Cataldo stood up with nervous haste, looking wildly from the uniformed police officer to *that* chief inspector with the penetrating gaze - which usually left his knees in a jelly-like state.

"*Buongiorno commissario,*" he said, holding out a limp right hand, which Beppe deliberately ignored. "How can we help you today?"

"Sit down again, please," said Beppe curtly, as he and Pippo occupied the two chairs facing inwards - as if to oblige clients to focus on the estate agent sitting on the opposite side of his desk.

A secretary, sitting in another part of the studio, was looking intently at a computer screen, obviously agog with curiosity at the arrival of the two police officers.

"I want you to look at this photo," began Pippo while his chief continued to stare unblinkingly at Andrea Cataldo's face, as if to catch the slightest twitch of discomfort.

The estate agent took one look at the photo of the two hoodlums clutching their crash helmets as they stepped into the jeweller's shop. He knew instantly that he had managed to end up on the wrong side of the *commissario* yet again. Beppe was gratified to notice that the estate agent was blushing to the roots of his hair.

"I see you recognise these two individuals, *signore,*" said Beppe menacingly. At least this part of his investigations was proceeding without a hitch. "You will be pleased to know that you have given invaluable help to the underworld by housing these two delinquents in Pescara."

"I told you they were up to no good, Andrea!" came an accusing female voice from the other side of the studio. If confirmation of Beppe's suspicions was needed, then he had it in double measure.

"I wasn't responsible for finding them a flat," stammered the estate agent. "I sent them to a...colleague who has a small agency in another part of Pescara."

"No doubt belonging to your uncle or some cousin," suggested the *commissario* sarcastically.

"My sister's *fidanzato*," replied Andrea Cataldo as if by way of apology. He hastily wrote down the address and phone number on a sheet of notepaper and handed it eagerly to Beppe, in the hope of redeeming himself.

"I expect you saw on the television the interview with the bar owner who had her door set fire to," stated Beppe in a venomously calm voice.

Andrea Cataldo nodded, looking down at his desk, unable to look Beppe in the eyes.

"*That* is the kind of low-life you have allowed to get a foothold in our city," said Pippo, adding to the estate agent's mortification.

"Now listen to me carefully," continued Beppe in the same tone of voice. "At some stage, you will almost certainly be contacted by a respectable-looking couple. They will make you an irresistible offer to buy you out of this business while allowing you to continue as a paid employee..."

The estate agent looked at the *commissario* with growing perturbation. How did this police inspector always know everything as if he had the power of clairvoyance?

"It's already happened, *commissario.*"

It was the helpful secretary who had spoken out. She was obviously not in awe of her employer.

"Did you accept the offer?" snapped Beppe.

"No...no, *commissario.* I said I would have to think about it," replied Andrea Cataldo, utterly defeated.

"I have news for you, *Signor* Cataldo. You have absolutely *nothing* to think about. When you are next approached by this couple, you will pick up the phone and

117

ring the *Questura* immediately – with them present, if possible.

"But they threatened to annul the deal if I contacted..." began Cataldo, looking terrified.

"No threat from that couple will come anywhere near what *I* will do to you, *Signor* Cataldo, if you so much as blink at them," said the *commissario* with total conviction.

"*I'll* phone you, *commissario,*" said the secretary throwing caution to the winds. "My name is Angela Petri, by the way."

Beppe and Pippo got up to leave. Beppe nodded in Angela's direction with a complicit smile on his face.

In the car, Pippo made a joke about the probable exchange of words that would be taking place between employer and employee.

"I can imagine who will come out on top," said Beppe.

Beppe and Pippo went immediately to the other estate agency owned by Cataldo's future brother-in-law - who received a similar dressing-down to Andrea Cataldo. At least, they found out where the two Mafioso stooges were living.

On leaving Andrea Cataldo's studio, Beppe had surreptitiously checked up on the dark blue Mercedes. He was disconcerted to see that the car was still parked in front of his block of flats. Of the occupants, there was no sign. Thank heavens he and Sonia had decided at the last minute to rent the flat on a six-month lease, thus leaving their options open.

The two police officers spent the rest of the morning doing the rounds of the smaller estate agents before driving back to the police headquarters. Beppe was anxious to catch Sonia before she took it into her head to return to their apartment. Pippo parked the car and turned off the engine in a deliberate fashion and said quietly:

"*Capo,* I know perfectly well you spotted those two men in the Mercedes outside your *palazzo.* Did you notice that the number plate was from Naples?"

It was the worst-case scenario.

"I'll get the license plate number checked out for you," said Pippo. "You know what this could mean, don't you, *capo?*"

Beppe merely nodded. It took him several seconds before he said:

"It means Sonia and I will be looking for somewhere else to live."

Why did this have to happen just at the moment when he needed to be away from Sonia's side?

As if reading his thoughts, Pippo said:

"We'll look after Sonia while you're away in Loreto Aprutino, Beppe."

"*Grazie mille,* Pippo – I'll talk to Sonia first. It's good to have you by my side. Thank you…for everything."

The fleeting instant in which Beppe and his junior colleague had become friends rather than compatible colleagues had just taken place. Pippo had called his chief by his first name and Beppe had not immediately registered this departure from accepted police etiquette. It was one those crucial moments in life when a seemingly trivial gesture, or word, steal up on you unawares, consequently altering the perception of a relationship. But now was not the moment to become philosophical, thought Beppe, getting out of the car and heading purposefully for the main entrance. He had to seek out Sonia.

* * *

The trouble was that Sonia was nowhere to be seen. Everybody whom Beppe asked assured him she was on the premises. He sent Oriana to see if she had got locked in the toilet – Sonia, Oriana and Bianca Bomba had all complained about a temperamental lock on one of the toilet doors that occasionally refused to let the occupants escape. It was one of those little maintenance jobs that no one had ever got round to sorting out. Oriana returned immediately, shaking her head. The officer on the reception desk remembered seeing Sonia taking a call on her mobile phone about ten minutes previously.

"It looked as if she was agitated by the call, *capo*. I'm sorry, I didn't see where she went afterwards," said the officer.

Beppe hurried to his office to retrieve his mobile phone. His office was the one place where nobody had thought of looking – simply because, in the normal scheme of things, she would have no cause to go there on her own unless Beppe had summoned her there on business. Beppe saw her sitting in front of his desk through the glass screen, her back turned to the door. This was unusual, thought Beppe. Maybe she had heard from her doctor? Maybe she had carried out a pregnancy test? As Beppe entered, Sonia turned round at the sound of the door latch. She looked very pale and anxious. It was not going to be good news.

She stood up as Beppe approached her and hugged him tightly. Hugging was something they never did in the *Questura* – it was an unspoken rule between the two of them.

"I've just had a phone call from our nosey neighbour, Beppe. You know – the little nun. She told me she heard someone knocking on our apartment door so, being her, she went out on to the landing to see who it was. She didn't like the look of them..."

"Two swarthy-looking *teppisti* wearing sunglasses," said Beppe, who knew the answer already. *(teppisti = crooks)*

"Yes, *amore,* but how did you...?"

She did not bother to finish the question. Her partner usually managed to be abreast of events before they had even happened, it seemed.

Beppe explained to Sonia how he knew and what conclusions he and Pippo had reluctantly drawn.

"Did our Little Nun tell them anything?" asked Beppe fearfully.

"She's not all that dotty, it seems. She told them that the place was unoccupied and then went back inside her flat and locked the door," replied Sonia with a half-smile returning to her face. "She told me she felt intimidated by their presence and thought she had done the right thing to put them off the scent."

"Our aged and reliable guardian angel!" said Beppe. "But guardian angel or not, Sonia, you can't go back there – especially not while I'm away…"

"It's not ME I'm worried about!" retorted Sonia indignantly.

Beppe had to point out to her that, in the likely event that the men had been sent by the Naples clan, she was just as liable to become the target as he was.

"They won't hesitate to use you as a means to get to me, *amore.* No, I'm sorry, I cannot allow you to go back there until this is cleared up."

He declined to tell her that they would both have to find somewhere else to live – just to keep one step ahead of the Naples mob.

"I don't want you to go away again, Beppe," she said bluntly. "I want you near me."

This was the first time that a potential conflict between his personal and professional life had arisen – at least in Abruzzo. He did not like the sensation.

"I wasn't going to go back to Loreto Aprutino tonight," he tried to reassure her. "I need to wait for the outcome of the

Guardia's raid on the Carlettini studio before I can go back to help Enrico Nardini."

They decided to wait until the *Carabinieri* had removed the immediate danger of the two men in the dark blue Mercedes. They would then go and collect what they would need by way of clothes and things for the next few days.

"Somebody will put you up while I'm away, Sonia. The others will jump at the occasion to help us out..."

"No, Beppe," replied Sonia quietly. "I'll go and stay with my parents in Atri."

Beppe knew that would be the best solution so he did not protest.

"I'll ask the *Questore* to give you time off, *amore.* I'm not going to be away for more than a day or two at the most. Then we'll work things out..."

Sonia obviously understood what 'working things out' stood for.

"But moving will mean we have to leave your boat behind!" exclaimed Sonia in genuine dismay. "It's your baby..." she began, but was stopped short by the intense look on her lover's face. He held her and kissed her openly – never mind who might be looking through the glass screen. But there was nobody there.

* * *

The remainder of the day passed busily. The *Questore* contacted his *Carabiniere* colleague, Colonel Riccardo Grimaldi. The *Carabinieri* brought the occupants of the blue Mercedes in for questioning. They discovered that the Mercedes was on lease from a car company in Naples – run by the mob. Pippo Cafarelli confirmed the mafia link by phoning up the *Polizia Statale* in Naples – where he had a second cousin who was a policeman – the family Network doing its job.

Despite vociferous protests from the two gangsters in the Mercedes, Riccardo Grimaldi kept them overnight in separate cells. They claimed that they were just on holiday in Pescara – they had heard it was as beautiful as their native *Napoli*. They denied ever having set foot in Beppe and Sonia's apartment block.

"You've got no right to keep us here. We want to phone our solicitors," said the gangster in charge. "You've got no grounds to..."

"Let's try intimidation of the old lady in flat 25," said the *Colonnello* smiling beguilingly.

"We never even spoke to the old crone, let alone..." began the other gangster, whose brain cell count did not match those of his companion.

Their fate was sealed for long enough to allow Beppe and Sonia to return to their apartment later that evening.

The rest of that long day kept everyone fully stretched at the police headquarters in Via Pesaro. It was a constant hive of activity – just the way Beppe had rashly wished for, he recalled. He had not foreseen in what manner his prophetic words would be played out in reality.

"It's a bit like Macbeth," he said to Pippo later on that afternoon.

"I don't believe I did Macbeth at school, *capo,*" he said.

"All of the prophetic utterances made to Macbeth turned out to be a two-edged sword," explained the *commissario* – and had to leave it at that. Officers Gino Martelli and Danilo Simone marched in with the two – helmetless and handcuffed – hoodlums belonging to the Foggia clan.

"*Eccoli!*" announced Gino as if he had been delivering his chief's lunch on a plate.

Beppe quickly made a mental calculation as to which of the two youths was the ring-leader out of these two low-ranking crooks. With a deliberately disdainful gesture in the direction of the more dominant member of the pair, he said to Gino and Danilo:

"Take this one back down to the cells, *ragazzi,* and lock him up – and ask Pippo to join me here," ordered Beppe. The 'dominant' one gave his partner a venomous, warning stare.

The remaining youth looked nervously at Beppe.

"I'm *Commissario* Stancato," said Beppe reassuringly. "And you are....?"

"Dario Fo," replied the youth in an attempt to be insolent. Beppe doubted whether this youth from the backstreets of Foggia bore the same name as the distinguished ninety-year-old Italian intellectual and playwright. He stared fixedly at the defiant youth, who began to look shifty. 'Dario Fo' reached into his anorak pocket and fished out a packet of cheap cigarettes. Beppe opened the draw of his desk and took out a lighter. He lent over the table, smiling at the youth, who leant forward to meet the flame, cigarette in mouth. With a sleight of hand that took the youth off his guard, Beppe whipped the cigarette out of his mouth and deftly slipped it inside a clear plastic evidence bag.

"Thank you, young man. Now we shall have your DNA on our records."

Beppe doubted whether it would be of any help but it was a tactic that inevitably impressed the minor criminals he had to deal with.

The youth looked sulky but tried to look aggressive at the same time.

"Your identity document, please, *giovanotto.*"

"Must have left it in the flat," said the thug petulantly.

"Fine! Offence number two!"

"Hey, wait a minute! What was offence number one?" He was used to being stitched up by the police, so he felt he should make an effort to stand up for himself.

"Entering a jeweller's shop, armed and exhibiting threatening behaviour, *Signor* Dario.

"That's a lie!" said the youth. "We never…"

Beppe slapped the flat of his hand sharply down on the desk, making the youth jump out of his skin.

"Would you like to see the video footage? Remember you made the mistake of taking off your helmets," said Beppe, speaking calmly and in total contrast to his previous gesture.

At that moment Pippo entered the room. He took one look at the youth in his early twenties – only a few years younger than Pippo himself.

"Mannaggia a te!" exclaimed Pippo to the youth. "If it isn't Dario Conte – *what* a surprise! Your mum's going to kill you once she finds out the trouble you've got yourself into."

The lad's attempts at defending his flimsy cover collapsed at the sight of the *sbirro* whose path he had already crossed in his native Foggia. Furthermore, it was a cop who knew his mother. The youth was looking crestfallen. *(sbirro = cop)*

Beppe laughed openly at the lad's discomfort. "That must have come as a shock to you, Dario! Now, let's see if you can make life easier for yourself by cooperating with us."

Beppe phoned down to the front desk and ordered someone to bring up the other culprit from the cells. He charged them both with violent behaviour, physical damage to property, association with *mafioso* activities, failure to carry any form of identification on their persons - and a long list of other minor offences which he concocted on the spot.

The 'thug-in-charge', Giorgio, felt he should deny setting fire to the door of the *Bar Galileo.* It was vital not to lose face in the eyes of his side-kick.

"Sorry, *commissario*. We've got witnesses. We was with our mates at the time of that fire."

"Ah, so you know at what time and what day the door was set alight, do you, Giorgio?" asked Beppe sweetly, "even though neither the time nor the date was ever made public. Take them away, *raggazi*. I've wasted enough time with these two for one day. Turning to the youths, he said: "We're holding you in custody overnight. You'll be in front of the magistrate tomorrow morning. Then we'll talk again to see if you've decided to cooperate with us. You can stay in the same cell together – that'll be nice and cosy for you both. Oh, just a warning – the cells are all wired for sound as well as having CCTV cameras…"

"We have a right to make a phone call, *commissario*. Our mobile phones have been confiscated."

"Certainly – but you can use our telephones. They are monitored, of course. Dario, you'd better let your mum know you're in a police cell in Pescara - just in case she's worried about you." Beppe knew that his final parting shot would create a wedge between the two culprits, which could be exploited the next day.

"Thank you, again, Pippo," said Beppe when they were alone. "I knew your local knowledge of Foggia might come in handy one day. Tomorrow, I want you to interrogate them and squeeze as much as you can out of them."

"Separately or together, *capo?*"

"I'll leave you to decide, *amico mio.*"

Pippo had a secret dread that his safety might well have been compromised by his confrontation with Dario. Word would get around. But then it was he who had decided to become a policeman – his own mother had endeavoured to deter him from such a hazardous career path. No, it had been his own choice to become a cop. *Non c'è scampo, Pippo!* No way out!

Beppe was contemplating his life in a brief moment of calm later on that afternoon. He really must make an effort to telephone his mother. Her constant and usually inopportune phone calls to her escapee son had been reduced to once or twice a week. Sometimes she would forget altogether. Now his sister, Valentina, had got married and was about to give birth, his mother had more immediate things on her mind. His reverie was interrupted by the phone on his desk ringing shrilly.

He was surprised to hear the *Questore's* voice telling him that the *colonnello* from the Finance Police wanted to talk to him. Beppe had forgotten all about the police raid by the *Guardia di Finanza* on Ernesto Carlettini's studio. He wasn't even sure that the raid was due to take place on that day. He went upstairs and took the call in the presence of his chief – as he had been ordered to do.

"*Pronto, colonnello,*" said Beppe, with a feeling of keen anticipation.

"*Buona sera, commissario.* I thought you might like to know how our little expedition to see *Signor* Carlettini turned out. I hope you're not too busy..." began the colonel.

Beppe assured him he had his undivided attention.

* * *

"Well," began the *Guardia* colonel, "there are three people who work there including our friend Ernesto. The other two are the technicians who do the real work of making the dental appliances. Ernesto Carlettini is the boss. He's responsible for dealing with the clients and the finances. It's quite a sophisticated set-up, *commissario,* including some very expensive equipment. Do you know what a three-dimensional photo-copier is? No? Neither did I. It's something to do with nanotechnology. This machine can apparently create dental plates and artificial teeth exactly to the specifications of an individual client by building up the plate, or whatever, molecule at a time. It cost a cool million euros or so to acquire..."

"Where did the capital for equipment like *that* come from, I wonder," interrupted Beppe in amazement.

"He says it was partly from money inherited from his parents – who had inherited from their parents. The rest was with a bank loan. We quickly got to the bottom of his VAT payments. It was a simple enough error. He seems to have reversed a couple of digits and moved the decimal place up the line a few columns. So he ended up with a figure long short of what he owed the State. He sounded convincing, *commissario.* But he might just as easily have been trying it on..."

"Ernesto Carlettini suffers from dyslexia, *colonnello.* I discovered that only yesterday. So it was probably a genuine error on his part. His mind plays tricks with his visual concepts. It makes you wonder if his problem was spotted during his education."

"That *is* interesting, Beppe," said the *colonnello.* Then on a more humorous note, he added: "I wonder if that was the reason why my colleague's mother ended up with a dental plate that was too large for her mouth? Maybe he fed the wrong algorithm into his amazing machine!"

"If my surmise is correct, his difficulty with figures and letters might have led him to make a far more serious blunder in the past. Did you by any chance discover anything about his previous career path?" asked Beppe as nonchalantly as possible.

"Not a great deal, I'm sorry to say. It all sounded very straightforward to me. He did a nursing degree at Bari University – where he met his wife. Then he held a couple of nursing posts – which didn't seem to last all that long. The last thing he told us about was a post in a private clinic just outside Teramo. He seemed very reluctant to talk about that part of his life, dismissing it as a short-lived and unimportant aspect of his career. Apparently, the clinic closed down suddenly about five years ago – just after Ernesto Carlettini left. I sensed the whiff of scandal, *commissario.* But it didn't seem to be particularly relevant to us – or even to you. So I let it go."

Unbeknown to the *Guardia* officer, Beppe was sitting on the edge of his swivel chair.

"Did you get the name of the clinic, *colonnello?*"

"Oh… something like *Il Clinico Salvavita* – some high-sounding name like that…"

Beppe was holding his breath, willing the *Guardia di Finanza* to continue talking.

"The clinic specialised in blood," added the *colonnello,* as an afterthought. "You know – transfusions and blood analyses. That kind of thing…"

The *Guardia* officer could not see the look of beatific self-satisfaction on the *commissario's* face.

"I'm sorry I haven't been more help to you, Beppe…"

"On the contrary, *mio caro colonnello* - you have just solved a murder enquiry for me."

"I'm happy to hear you say so, Beppe. Although, I can't for the life of me fathom out how…."

"I'll fill you in as soon as the investigation is over, I promise you," concluded Beppe, not wishing to waste precious time on lengthy explanations. A vain hope – since Beppe found his own chief, Dante Di Pasquale, looking intently at him with an eyebrow raised so high it seemed to reach his hairline.

"You can fill *me* in right now, *commissario*," he said categorically.

So Beppe did just that - in elaborate detail. He also told him about the threat from the Naples mob and asked if Sonia could have time off while he was away in Loreto Aprutino.

The *Questore* was looking deeply concerned.

"Of course she can, Beppe – absolutely with my blessing. Leave the rest to me until you get back."

Beppe thanked his chief and ran down the stairs in search of Remo.

"Remo, my indispensable colleague, I'm sorry to impose on your talents yet again, but I've got another job for you..."

13: Le difese di Ernesto Carlettini vanno in pezzi...
(Ernesto's defences in shreds)

Sonia was experiencing a mixture of fear tempered by a sense of outrage as she and Beppe loaded a couple of suitcases into her car, parked in the basement parking lot serving their block of apartments. Hers was the long-forgotten sensation of deep resentment at having her personal living space invaded by strangers. Her parents' house had been burgled while she and her family were away on holiday. The memory of the childhood feeling that her familiar surroundings had been violated came back vividly as Beppe edged the car out of the car park and headed northwards in the encroaching dusk towards the town of Atri, where her surprised but happy parents were awaiting the unexpected arrival of their only daughter.

But Sonia's fear was provoked by an intuitive sensation that Beppe was going to be exposed to danger without her by his side. She was reassured by the thought that they would be sleeping in intimacy that night. But the nebulous dread that something bad was about to happen to her partner lurked beneath the surface of her rational mind. How would she feel when Beppe left her alone the following morning and headed back towards Pescara?

Sensing her emotions, Beppe put his right hand on her thigh once they were heading up the main road towards Atri, managing to drive for several kilometres with only his left hand on the steering wheel, before she judiciously replaced the affectionate hand on the steering wheel.

They talked long into the night curled up tightly together before slumber stole up on them. Beppe was reassuring. He told her he had little fear for his own personal safety from the Naples clan.

"Our *Questore* and the *colonnello,* Riccardo Grimaldi, will be watching out for my back, Sonia. And as for the poisonous mushroom case, all I have to do is wait for Remo to check a few details tomorrow morning. Then I can go and confront Ernesto Carlettini to confirm my suspicions as to the circumstances surrounding his brother's death. After that, I shall go and join our friend Enrico Nardini. We'll go to Farindola together and find out where this Damiano character lives – and arrest him. Then I'll come back to be with you..."

"But we'll have to find somewhere else to live, Beppe," she said.

"Somewhere special, *amore* – a place where we can raise our children..."

"In the countryside..." she murmured drowsily.

In fact, they both had a secret yearning to escape from the city – a life-style choice dictated solely by the demands of their work. Driving up from Pescara, they had discussed how much of the past had been lost by the encroachment of twenty-first century 'civilisation' as they drove past hilltop towns and breathed in the scent of the night through the open car windows.

"Yes, let's look for a place out of town as soon as..." she murmured drowsily.

Beppe lost her final words to slumber, but he was sure he had heard her aright.

* * *

The following morning, Beppe returned to the police headquarters in Pescara. Pippo Cafarelli had driven up to Atri in a police car to pick his chief up, thereby leaving Sonia with the means to get about under her own steam.

As soon as Beppe stepped over the threshold of the *Questura* at about 11 o'clock that morning, he spotted Officer Remo Mastrodicasa hovering expectantly in the background. He was clutching a few sheets of paper and had a beatific look on his face as he waited for his chief to notice his presence. Beppe could not help noticing a vague similarity between Remo and the fictitious creation of the police officer called Catarella in the Montalbano stories by Andrea Camilleri. They shared the same desire to please, the same loyalty and gave the same impression of not being wholly cut out for police work. In the TV series, which he and Sonia watched avidly, you never found out where Catarella lived and rarely got a glimpse of his private life. Beppe realised that he was quite ignorant as to where Remo lived, although he assumed it was with his new-found partner, Marta. In the case of Catarella, it had to be assumed that he had no intimate partner. No, Beppe decided, Remo was more contained - not so gloriously and comically eccentric as Catarella – but then, Remo was from Abruzzo, far removed from Sicily, where emotions were often worn on the sleeve.

He smiled warmly at Remo as he approached the spot where his junior officer was standing waiting for his chief.

"You're looking pleased with yourself, Remo. What have you found out for me?"

Beppe was unaware of the fact that Remo had been up well into the small hours researching, combing the web and collating the information he had gathered – until his partner had protested and dragged him to bed. As soon as he had arrived at work, that morning, he had been on the telephone to the local newspaper and *TV-Tavo,* the local TV station. Remo looked tired, but triumphant.

"Come on, Remo! Let's get a cup of coffee and go to my office. Then you can tell me why you are looking so pleased with yourself."

Out of affection for his junior colleague, Beppe sat down on the second chair in front of his desk, adjacent to Remo.

"Well, *capo*... I managed to find out about the clinic where Carlettini worked for a while. The information on the internet was very scrappy indeed – there was a definite attempt at covering up the real reasons for its closure. It appears the *Clinico Salvavita* didn't quite live up to its name - at least for one of its patients! *(Salvavita = Life-saving)*

When I got in this morning, I contacted a person I know at *TV-Tavo* and a reporter on the local paper who has been working there for nearly fifteen years. That's how I found out that Ernesto Carlettini didn't just leave the clinic because it closed down all of a sudden – he was the main reason for its closure."

Despite his trust in his favourite *commissario,* Remo found the intensity of his stare marginally disconcerting. "Go on Remo," said Beppe encouragingly. Beppe was waiting to see if his half-formed surmise about this complex case had been correct.

"It appears that the clinic was treating two ladies in their late forties or early fifties for a serious blood deficiency - something to do with a lack of iron. They gave them blood transfusions but – this is the vital part of the story – it appears the patients were given the wrong blood type. One of the patients was 'O' type but, by accident, they administered 'A/B' type blood instead... with fatal consequences. The other patient was given a transfusion too, but it was compatible with her blood type – so she recovered.

There was a breakdown in communications due to the unexpected absence of one of the nurses on that day – she had to go to her grand-father's funeral. Apparently, there should always be two nurses checking the issue of the correct blood bag. On that particular day, there was only one nurse available. That nurse's name was Ernesto Carlettini. It seems the two patients being treated had similar names – a *Signora* Macrillo Renata and another patient whose surname was Macrino and her first name was Regina. I don't know how Ernesto Carlettini mixed up the names..." concluded Remo.

"Oh, I think *I* know how that happened, Remo," replied Beppe, keeping the note of triumph out of his voice. "Our friend Ernesto Carlettini suffers from slight – but professionally undeclared – dyslexia. He must have had an off-day. Somehow, he must have misinterpreted the names or the code on the blood bag. Maybe he was under too much stress and this triggered his state of mental confusion. Now that you tell me a second nurse was absent on that day, it all makes perfect sense. What was the name of the patient who was given the wrong blood type, did you say?"

"The first name I gave you, *capo* – Renata Macrillo."

Beppe stood up and just stopped himself hugging his colleague. He shook him warmly by the hand cupped in both of his.

"Is that all you wanted to know, *capo?*" asked Remo, who could not quite comprehend why his chief was looking so self-satisfied.

"You have confirmed my theory about the mushroom poisoning case, Remo. *Bravo! Bravissimo!* But if you are willing to do one more piece of research for me - that would make my interpretation of events doubly certain."

"Of course, *capo – con piacere!* What do you want to know?"

"If you could search through the records of marriages – going way back, I imagine – and find out the name of the man whom this lady, Renata Macrillo, was married to. They could have got married almost anywhere. Macrillo is a Calabrian surname – another emigrant from the Deep South, just like me! When you find out, just send me an SMS. I am going to see our friend Ernesto Carlettini and confront him with what you've told me. I knew he was concealing *something* from us. Now it all makes sense."

"But I don't quite see how…" began Remo, puzzled.

"Think about it, Remo. The two Carlettini brothers were sufficiently alike to be mistaken one for the other by someone who didn't know them well."

Beppe was already half way out of the door. He was impatient to confront Ernesto Carlettini and obtain the definitive truth about this case before he returned to Loreto Aprutino to meet up with Enrico Nardini again. He would phone Sonia later, when he had finished with Ernesto Carlettini. She was as safe as houses where she was. Sonia, for her part, was simply wishing they were geographically closer – never mind any threats from the outside world. She was aware that it was only a matter of hours, rather than days, before the hidden workings of her body would confirm what she instinctively knew to be true.

* * *

"It is a very inconvenient time, *commissario,*" said the petulant voice of Ernesto Carlettini over the phone. "Does it *really* have to be right now? We already had the *Guardia di Finanza* invading our studio yesterday. That set us back hours. A complete waste of time…"

"Really, *Signor* Carlettini? I understand they saved you the embarrassment of being faced with a hefty fine from the *Agenzia delle Entrate* for underpayment of your VAT returns. Besides which, I have news about your brother's untimely demise – as you so delicately expressed it."

"He ate poisonous mushrooms, *commissario.* Why do still insist that…?"

"Your brother was poisoned quite intentionally," interrupted Beppe abruptly. "Furthermore, *signore,* YOU were the intended victim - as I'm sure you suspected from the outset. I shall be round to visit you in thirty minutes along with one of my colleagues. Please make sure you are at home, unless you would prefer us to visit you at your studio, of course..."

Ernesto Carlettini inwardly admitted defeat from that moment. He hung up without a word, knowing his past life was about to be exposed like a cadaver being dissected under the pathologist's scalpel. He had turned very pale.

* * *

"It was your half-sister in Penne who first alerted us to the possibility that your brother, Salvatore's death was not accidental - as you would have had us believe, *Signor* Carlettini," Beppe began, "and I am quite certain she was not being over-imaginative."

Beppe and Pippo – seconded for the occasion - were sitting in the Carlettini living-room in the company of Ernesto and his wife. Lorenzo was once again nowhere to be seen. Maybe he had started back at his school. Luisa Arielli, the wife, wore an expression which was in conflict between resignation and defiance – holding herself in readiness to justify their reluctance to be open about their side of the story.

Beppe had made up his mind in advance to adopt a conciliatory approach. After all, his main objective in being here was to confirm the details of the events that had led to Salvatore's death.

"I began to suspect something as soon as I saw the photo of you and your brother – which I see you have removed. You look as alike as two drops of water. You could pass for twins. My guess is that the man responsible for telling Salvatore that the mushrooms he had picked were edible had some serious grievance which he was longing to avenge. How does that sound so far?"

Ernesto shrugged and his wife looked as if she wanted to speak. Beppe continued:

"I want to make it crystal clear to you both that I do not believe you have committed any crime. Therefore, you have absolutely no reason to be reticent about anything."

Ernesto was looking very uncomfortable but would still not open up. He appeared to be thinking hard. His expression had altered and there was a frown on his face.

"Was it *you, commissario,* who phoned me two nights ago pretending to be a journalist from Milan? This man had a Milanese accent – but his voice sounded a bit like yours..."

Beppe had to admit he was nearly caught out by the unexpected suddenness of the accusation. Pippo was the one who – apparently quite innocently – came to his chief's rescue.

"*Signor* Carlettini – the *commissario* has a strong Calabrese accent which is quite unmistakable. I cannot believe you have jumped to such an outlandish conclusion." Beppe always tried not to tell lies – but he would need to crush any suspicion on Ernesto's part that he was the perpetrator of such a prank – however well-intentioned his motives had been. No, he had to admit in the brief second of time he had in which to cover his tracks - his reasons for making the false phone call had been far from innocent or impartial. He had been motivated by a mischievous sense of fun.

"*Signor* Carlettini – Ernesto – such an accusation sounds as if you are doing your utmost to side-track me from the grave matter in hand. I may not be able to arrest you for any crime but I can most certainly charge you with wasting police time. Now... may we continue?"

Ernesto's wife, Luisa, was looking embarrassed and angry.

"You never told me about this phone call, Ernesto. Why on earth should the *commissario* indulge in such a childish prank?" She turned to the two policemen and said:

"We will be direct with you from now on, officers. I don't know how much you have already gleaned but..."

"We know about the serious incident at the clinic near Teramo. We suspect that Salvatore somehow met the man whose wife died as a result of your fatal error, Ernesto. I am sure you have had to live with the consequences of your mistake – and it must be very painful for you. I am waiting for confirmation of the name of the victim's husband. But we believe this man mistook Salvatore for *you.* Need I continue? We also know that you visited your brother's house days before he died and that your little boy, Lorenzo, found the mushrooms in the refrigerator. For his own childlike reasons, he had a nibble of those mushrooms. You were both, quite understandably, reluctant to admit your lack of supervision in view of his life-threatening illness, but..."

"How did you find that out?" asked Luisa ingenuously. She was simply intrigued.

Beppe allowed himself the briefest of smiles – and told her how he had discovered the Lego pieces in the fridge.

"But you were not to know that Lorenzo loves playing with his Lego. How did you find out about that?" Luisa asked.

Beppe merely pointed a finger in the direction of the hallway from where he was sitting in their living room.

"Mirrors!" he said mysteriously.

Ernesto and Luisa looked at this devious police detective with respect and something akin to awe.

"We are all so pleased for you both that your son was cured in such a miraculous manner. My partner Sonia and I were present at mass in the cathedral," said Beppe kindly.

Their resistance was broken. They could hardly wait to pour out their pent-up feelings of guilt to the two police officers. It was cathartic – more like a confession than an interview.

Beppe's mobile phone indicated that he had a message. He ignored it. He did not want to interrupt the Carlettini couple's rush of words.

When they had finally run out of steam, Beppe asked them why they had not answered Salvatore's final phone call. In the end, looking very sheepish, Ernesto admitted that they had taken the call.

"He was inarticulate, *commissario*. We couldn't understand what he was trying to tell us. He kept on repeating something about a housekeeper... saying we should look after her when he had gone. He sounded delirious. As we all know, my brother lived by himself in that big house. We both assumed he must have had too much to drink..."

"What a totally insensitive couple!" commented Pippo as they walked back to the police car. They must have realised he was in trouble!"

"I think they are quite oblivious to what is going on beyond the confines of their own little world. It seems they are quite unaware that Salvatore had a woman living with him. That will come as a big shock when they find out!" Beppe added maliciously.

There had been a number of other things that Beppe would like to have asked, but he had had enough. He had found out what he needed to know.

He remembered he had received an unchecked message while in the Carlettini's home. It was from Remo. The text simply said: 'His name is Adolfo D'Angelo' - the same name that was on the list of mushroom experts from Farindola. Sonia had been right - 'Damiano' must be his middle name – or a nickname he had acquired.

Everything was in place. Now Beppe could return to Loreto Aprutino. He and Enrico Nardini could proceed immediately to Farindola and close this investigation.

Pippo was smiling to himself as he drove them back to Pescara.

"What's amusing *you*, Pippo?" asked Beppe curtly.

"I didn't know you had a talent for imitating accents, *capo*," he said.

He got a hard look from his chief – who said simply: "No comment, *Agente* Cafarelli."

14: In which Commissario Stancato ignores correct procedure...

The road back to Loreto Aprutino was by now very familiar to Beppe. He picked up the first main turning into the town, passing once again in front of the church of *Santa Maria in Piano*. Even the exterior of the church was possessed of an imposing sanctity, he thought.

In a few hours' time at most, this Damiano character should be under lock and key and he could return to Pescara that evening. There might even be time to treat himself to another look at the frescos on the way home. But, he reminded himself, he would also have to make the time to go and visit that waterfall. Telling himself that it had nothing to do with the investigation in hand would, in all likelihood, not be a sufficient deterrent.

But even the best laid plans in life can go awry. As capricious fate would have it, Beppe's arrival at the *Carabiniere* police station coincided with the hasty departure of his colleague, Enrico Nardini, seated in the dark blue *Alfa Romeo* whose siren was switched on and its blue light flashing. Enrico braked the car with tyres screeching. He leant out of the window and shouted at Beppe:

"It's an emergency, *commissario* - somebody's just shot a hunter instead of a hare! I'll be back as soon as I can. Oh, and by the way, *commissario,* the Turin police interviewed Dinusha, the housekeeper - except she isn't Carlettini's housekeeper at all! Tell you all about it later! Sorry, must dash now..."

And with that, the police car shot out of the car park with another screech of tyres, leaving Beppe in a state of frustrated inactivity.

He continued to sit in the car for a period of five minutes or so, wondering how he could usefully fill the time before Enrico Nardini returned. He briefly considered the possibility of going to visit Ludovica Carlettini in Penne, but thought it might seem incorrect if he turned up on his own. "What the hell!" he thought and dialled her number.

"Pronto," she said in her usual animated way. Beppe explained where he was and said he was calling to keep his promise that he would keep her up to date on the investigation.

"Commissario! How good of you to call me! Unfortunately, I'm helping out at my daughter's little school today. I can't get away until later on this afternoon."

Beppe excused himself and said he would try to come round later on in the day. He felt a sense of relief as he realised the proposed visit would have been highly irregular. He was missing Sonia, he admitted to his inner self and this propelled him into seeking female company. There was nothing for it. He would have to drive up to Farindola under his own steam and meet Enrico Nardini there later on in the day to make the arrest. He could make preliminary enquiries as to where Damiano lived. That would save a lot of time when Enrico finally arrived at Farindola.

Beppe set his Satnav for the mountain village and drove off in the direction of Penne. He was feeling pleased that he wasn't going to be kicking his heels in Loreto Aprutino all morning waiting for the *Carabinieri* to return from the hunting accident.

The country road from Penne to Farindola climbed inexorably upwards along a winding trajectory. He must have encountered no more than half a dozen cars and one empty yellow *scuolabus* returning to Penne to pick up its infant charges. The middle-aged to elderly car drivers whom he encountered travelling downhill seemed to know every curve in the road like the back of their hand. They did not slow down at all, taking the bends in their stride in top gear. Beppe found the journey more unnerving than driving round Pescara during rush hour. This was the conclusion he came to at the moment when one of those perilous three-wheeled *Ape* contraptions, favoured by Italian small-holders all over the country, hurtled round a bend on his side of the road. The farmer swerved out of the way at the last minute with an angelic grin on his swarthy face. The *commissario's* heart remained in his mouth for several minutes after the near miss.

But it took him no more than an additional few minutes before he unexpectedly found himself entering the *comune* of Farindola, on rounding a bend in the road as it began its descent through the village down to the valley below.

The first thing which caught his attention was a well-worn signpost pointing like an imperious finger down the steep hillside. The words *Vitello d'Oro* were written in white letters on a brown background. The official signpost seemed to be telling Beppe in no uncertain terms that his inescapable fate that day was to pay a visit to the waterfall. He let out a sigh of resignation and parked his car in the *piazza* in front of the town hall. He wouldn't do *anything* until he had had an espresso coffee.

There was one bar above the *piazza,* whose neon light he could just see from where he stood. He must have passed it as he began his descent into the village. The only other visible bar was a few metres down the road just opposite where he had parked his car. It was called the *Bar Commercio* and was not in need of a neon sign to attract the local populace. He could hear the sound of male conversation and a burst of ribald laughter coming through the open door. He headed for this bar without any further debate, ready for the reaction to a stranger crossing the threshold.

There were about half a dozen men all standing at the bar and one or two others sitting at the tables reading the newspaper. There was a lively, but not very serious political debate going on about Italy's notorious Prime Minister, Sergio Balducci.

"All you can confidently say about *him* is that he is feeding on the fat of the land and having hair transplants as he prospers at our expense. He struts around Europe as if he owns the whole continent – making diplomatic gaffes all along the way," said someone.

"Just think of the alternatives," said another voice. "Balducci is at least trying to deal with Italy's problems – in his own sweet way."

"Let's give the new party, *Cinque Stelle* a chance," said another man who looked as weather-beaten as the signpost pointing downhill to the waterfalls. Another burst of ironic laughter from one or two of the group. The unanimous conclusion seemed to be that it wouldn't do any harm to let the new rebel party - led by the famous comedian turned politician, Beppe Grillo – have a go.

"Things can't get much worse than they are..." was someone's philosophical conclusion.

Beppe approached the bar with a reassuring smile on his face and said *'Buongiorno'* in the general direction of everybody present. As he had expected, all eyes were focussed on the newcomer – the 'outsider'.

The barkeeper was a middle-aged lady of generous proportions who smiled briefly at this stranger, whose eyes were darting round the place taking everything in with a single glance.

"Signore?" she asked enquiringly.

"*Un caffè salvavita, signora!* I need to recover from the several near misses I have just had on the road from Penne – including an *Ape* driven by a Michael Schumacher driving on the wrong side of the road."

Any tension in the bar was broken immediately.

"Sounds as if you've just had a close encounter with our Bruno Cellini!" said one man, laughing.

"He's got an unfulfilled death wish, *signore.* He's been driving like that for years without managing to hit anyone," said another, joining in enthusiastically.

"You deserve a *grappa* with your coffee to recover from an experience like that." added someone else.

"I actually came to see the waterfall, which all my colleagues in Pescara have been going on about." said Beppe, who had done his best to look amused by the banter. What he had no intention of doing just yet was to ask the whereabouts of one Adolfo Damiano D'Angelo for fear that these amicable-seeming locals would instantly close ranks. Beppe was wondering how he could broach the subject of mushrooms without seeming too obvious. He was saved the trouble by a fortuitous comment made by the lady bar owner, addressing the group at large as her glance encompassed the men standing at the bar.

"Just don't be tempted by the mushrooms up there near the waterfall, *signore.* The last stranger who came here a couple of weeks back made the mistake of eating them when he got home. He didn't live to tell the tale..." she said ominously.

"Oh yes," said Beppe with practised nonchalance. "Didn't I see something about him on the local TV news?"

There was a distinct atmosphere of caution in the bar. One of the group began a sentence with the words:

"Yeah, he made the mistake of asking..."

"He should have asked Silvia, here," interrupted the man who had dominated the conversation up to that point. He was indicating the barkeeper. "She knows all about mushrooms!"

The name Silvia rang a bell in Beppe's mind. The only woman on Remo's list of mushroom experts from this village had been a person called Silvia Guerra.

Beppe took his leave as soon as he could after paying for his coffee – the *grappa* was on the house, he was assured. He was followed by cheerful enough comments of '*Buona passeggiata, signore*' from the group of men – wishing him a good walk. A glance at the name over the entrance to the *Bar Commercio* confirmed that the proprietor was indeed called Silvia Guerra. He might pay her another visit later on. She was bound to know where Damiano lived. The bus from Penne had arrived and stopped just outside the town hall. A single passenger descended. Beppe stared in fascination at the white-haired man who was clutching a battered hold-all. His face was a cross between that of a cherub and the Wild Man of Borneo. He headed towards some steps with an odd lolling gait and disappeared out of sight. Mountain inhabitants can be weird, thought Beppe, recalling similar sightings in his native Calabria.

"It's about a five-kilometre trek up to the waterfall, you know," said a voice behind him, interrupting his reverie. It was the kind-looking man who had identified Bruno Cellini as the eccentric owner of the three-wheeler.

"I'll survive – as long as I don't meet any more mad *Ape* drivers," he said.

"My name's Gabriele, by the way," said his new companion. "You see that bright red house up there? The waterfall is just above that. I live up that way. If you like, I could give you a lift. It'll save you a bit of time."

"That's kind of you, Gabriele. My name is Giuseppe. I think I'll accept your offer. I can always walk back. The exercise will do me good." It would also help him kill a bit more time, thought Beppe.

Gabriele gestured to Beppe to get into an ancient grey Peugeot which coughed all the way down to the valley and then laboured up the mountain road towards the waterfall in second gear. The engine seemed to miss a beat every so often, as if in protest at having so many demands laid upon it.

The noise was such that conversation with Gabriele was difficult. Beppe learnt that Gabriele was a sheep farmer and that Farindola's main industry was the production of its own Pecorino cheese.

"You should try some before you go, Giuseppe. If you have time, you can come to my house and have a taste. I live down there," he said pointing to a track that led downhill to the river valley. "The path to the waterfall is just one hundred or so metres further up this road. You can't miss it. I'd come with you, but my lunch will be ready soon."

Ah, lunchtime! Beppe had not given food a thought up until that moment. He thanked his companion for his kindness and promised he would come down to his farm after visiting the *cascata.*

The din emanating from the engine of the ancient Peugeot had subsided now it was no longer expected to climb up the steep hill. Beppe shook Gabriele by the hand, looking into the warm face of this dignified man in his sixties.

"Damiano D'Angelo lives in that sprawling yellowish house we passed before coming up the mountain road," said Gabriele with a mischievous glint in his eyes. "I take it you *are* a policeman – even though you don't look or act like one!"

Beppe looked at the man sitting next to him in silent admiration. He was astounded at the incredible intellectual feat which lay behind the few simple words Gabriele had just uttered. Not only had he guessed that Beppe was from the police but had equally made a quantum leap of logic as to his fellow townsman's involvement in the Carlettini affair.

"Your powers of deduction are singularly impressive, Gabriele. You should have been a detective. My name is *Commissario* Stancato. I won't insult your intelligence by asking you to be discreet."

Acqua in bocca, commissario," said Gabriele simply. "My lips are sealed. But take care, won't you... Damiano is a strange man. He has never really recovered from the loss of his wife."

"Tell me, Gabriele. Doesn't Damiano have any children?"

"I believe he has a son but, if I remember correctly, he emigrated to Western Australia as soon as he finished his basic education. Ironically, he went to become a sheep farmer somewhere near a town called Albany."

Beppe was frowning in deep thought. Gabriele coughed politely as a hint that he needed to make a move homewards.

"A pity I don't know what he looks like," muttered Beppe as if to himself.

"Oh, you've already seen him!" replied Gabriele with a mischievous chuckle. "Now I really must leave you, *commissario* – or I'll be in trouble with my wife."

Beppe looked at his companion but realised he was not going to glean any further information.

"Thank you, Gabriele." He shook Gabriele's hand and got out of his car. He waved and smiled at this extraordinary maker of cheese as he drove off down the steep, tree-lined slope towards his house, leaving Beppe on his own to walk up the forest road towards the waterfall. The silence was broken only by the echo of bird-song and, progressively, by the sound of cascading water reverberating in the still air.

Who could Gabriele have meant? Was he telling him that Damiano was one of the drinkers standing at the bar? No, concluded Beppe, because somebody had nearly blurted out Damiano's name while they had been discussing mushrooms. Ah, but it could easily have been one of the customers sitting at a table reading the paper. Beppe had not paid enough attention to the others present in the room.

He shook his head to clear his mind from needless conjecture. A wide, grassy path had appeared on his left with a signpost pointing downwards at a crazy angle towards the *Cascata del Vitello d'Oro.* He had arrived at his self-imposed destination.

15: La cascata del Vitello d'Oro...

It was with a sense of growing awe that Beppe drew ever nearer the sound of the cascading water. He had paused to read the notice boards giving information about the waterfall on the way down the grassy slope leading to the river – the Tavo, of course! From whence the name of the local TV channel, he realised. Apart from the solitary wildness of the place, he had just read that "bears and wolves roam freely" in the surrounding national park. He felt a shiver of wonder and a brief stab of vulnerability as he realised that he was totally alone. It occurred to him that he had left his revolver locked away in his car boot, under the spare wheel. He read about the 'golden calf' that had purportedly appeared to two young women who had been washing their clothes in the waters of the Tavo – centuries previously - in the far-off magic times when people were free to dream and to have visions of the hidden wonders of creation.

He managed to dismiss any negative thoughts as he ambled down to the waterfall. The river ran between a deep, rocky gorge. The natural beauty and eternal tranquillity of the place finally overwhelmed all other emotions. A set of steep steps led down to a walkway. The sound of the waterfall drowned out all other sensations. And there it was – the *cascata* emerging from a hole bored in the cliff by the rushing torrent, some thirty metres above his head. It was magnificent. He stood there spellbound until he lost all sense of passing time.

He was summonsed back to the present by an almost imperceptible sound on a different wave-length to that of the relentless cascade of water above and around him. He finally identified it as the ringing of his mobile phone. A wave of guilt swept over him as he saw it was Sonia calling him. He had neglected her for hours on end.

"I can't hear you, *amore,*" he shouted at his phone.

Sonia said *she* could hear *him* and there was no need to shout.

"What are you doing?" she asked. "It sounds as if you are having a shower – or being battered by a hail storm."

Beppe said he would have to move away from where he was standing. He walked back along the concrete walkway and climbed the steps until he reached the grassy area which was sheltered from the full force of the waterfall by a wall of rock.

"I'm at the *Vitello d'Oro* waterfall," he explained to Sonia in something like his normal voice.

"I was under the impression that you were investigating a murder, *tesoro mio,*" said Sonia sarcastically, but she was unable to conceal the underlining anxiety in her voice. "Are you on your own?"

Beppe had to explain how Enrico Nardini had been called out to a hunting accident, leaving him to his own devices for the morning.

"Do you mean you have gone in search of a murderer without any back-up?" she asked angrily.

"I promise you I am just doing a little reconnoitre to while away the time, *amore mio.* I've found out where Damiano's house is..."

He went on to tell her all about his strange encounter with Gabriele, the remarkable maker of Pecorino cheese.

Sonia was unable to subdue her anxiety any longer.

"Beppe, you *must* wait for Enrico Nardini to arrive before you confront that man. He might well be mentally unstable. You *do* realise that, don't you? I have had a strange feeling of dread ever since you left my side this morning. I just couldn't bear anything to happen to you now..."

Her voice trailed off. She was close to tears.

"I'll go back to the village immediately and contact Enrico Nardini," he said reassuringly. "I won't do anything rash, Sonia, I promise you."

"And phone me later instead of keeping me in suspense!" she added, a hint of anger returning to her voice.

"*Un bacio, amore. Ti amo,*" he said as he brought the call to an end – before his resolve to continue the investigation evaporated altogether.

'*He might well be mentally unstable*' - Sonia's voice rang in his ears – echoing almost precisely the words used by Gabriele under an hour ago. They were both right, of course. He would return to the village of Farindola and rescue his car – and his revolver. Then he would sit tight and wait for Enrico to arrive. He was even beginning to feel peckish, he realised in surprise. He would go down and visit Gabriele and taste his Pecorino cheese on the way back to Farindola. Enrico would certainly be back in Loreto Aprutino by then.

He sighed, reluctant to leave the wild beauty of this spot. He found that his feet were retracing their previous path back to the waterfall. Just one last look, he promised himself. He did have the presence of mind to phone his *Carabinieri* colleague, who did not reply to the call, however. He composed a brief text message and sent it off into space in the hope that it would be read. The process of texting seemed so inappropriate in this wild setting. He had an image of the two girls, having visions of a golden calf whilst washing their clothes in the waters of the River Tavo two hundred years previously. And here he was sending an invisible message through space to someone miles away in another place altogether. However, the network signal was strong, so he had to assume that Enrico Nardini would receive his call for help before too many hours had elapsed.

He stood looking at the scene for some time, allowing the sound of the water and the spirit of the tall rocky cliffs –

the guardians of this secret place - to seep into his soul. As he resolutely turned round to walk back along the concrete promontory, a fleeting movement on the other side of the cascade caught his eye. He saw the figure of a man climbing up the precarious steps towards the platform at the top of the falls. He had no idea how the man had arrived at that spot. From where Beppe was standing, there seemed no way of reaching the stairway. He was reminded of the 'Bridge of Hairs' on the fresco – so flimsy did this steeply ascending flight of steps appear.

He watched the strange figure climbing ever higher up towards the summit of the waterfall. In a flash of revelation, Beppe knew who he was looking at without a shadow of doubt. Gabriele's words came back to him with a shock. Yes, he had already seen this eccentric-looking individual as he alighted from the bus about an hour or so ago. He was looking at Adolfo Damiano D'Angelo for the second time that day.

Beppe stared at the figure without moving a muscle. Damiano, the mushroom poisoner, had reached the top of the flight of steps and was contemplating the torrent of water cascading downwards with eyes that saw nothing else. His eerily puffy, baby-like cheeks were the predominant feature of his face, the whole being topped with a head of unruly white hair. He was obviously unaware of the presence of another human being. Was he about to throw himself over the rickety iron rail? There was something unsettlingly desperate about this not-quite-human figure perched high up above him. Beppe did the only thing he could think of on the spur of the moment.

"DAMIANO" he shouted after taking a deep lungful of air.

The effect on his adversary was immediate and unexpected. The look of shocked surprise that he was being observed by someone who was a complete stranger to him –

but a stranger who appeared to know who *he* was – galvanised Damiano into action. With an alacrity which left Beppe open-mouthed in wonder, Damiano descended the steps with the agility of a mountain goat. The stairway seemed, from Beppe's perspective, to come to an abrupt end as it reached its lower level. But to Beppe's astonishment, the figure disappeared behind the jutting rock. The stairway must lead down to the level of the River Tavo. After the space of a few seconds, Beppe spotted his quarry hurrying away from him as rapidly as the terrain allowed, with a strange lolloping gait. His head swung from side to side as he walked. 'Neanderthal Man' were the words which sprang to mind quite unbidden.

There was no point in attempting to follow him along the river – he wasn't dressed for such an undertaking. Besides which, Damiano had a good five-minute lead on him. He would have to return to the road and try to catch up with Damiano that way. He could safely assume that the man was going to return to his house which he should easily be able to identify from Gabriele's earlier description.

His encroaching hunger was momentarily forgotten as he strode back down the road towards Farindola. He briefly questioned what on earth he was hurrying for. He had found the man he was looking for and knew more or less where he lived. His next step *should* be to call Enrico Nardini and wait for back-up. But, as always, there was an overriding determination to pursue matters to the bitter end – preferably without any delay.

"You mean, you're impulsive!" he heard Sonia's accusing voice inside his head. She was right, of course. He would try to contact Enrico Nardini as soon as he reached Damiano's house. If he met Damiano, he would think of some excuse to talk to him – without letting him know he was a police officer. This seemed like an acceptable compromise.

The walk down the mountain road was rapid. He reached the house which he assumed must belong to Damiano D'Angelo and eyed it up and down. The word 'derelict' would be inaccurate to describe the building. 'Rambling' would be more apt – rather like the impression given by its owner. He tried to get through to his *Carabiniere* colleague but to no avail. Beppe came to the conclusion that Enrico must be in a zone where there was no signal. There were, he knew well, pockets of land all over Italy where mobile signals never reached – the so-called *digital divide.*

He was about to give up and follow his original plan of returning to the top end of the village where he had parked his car when he became aware that he was being covertly observed through one of the first-floor windows. It was like being scrutinised by an alien – a man from another era or another world. Beppe did the only thing which civilised convention seemed to dictate; he waved at the figure peering at him. The face vanished in a trice.

Mindful of his former resolve not to get involved without the presence of his fellow officer, Beppe began walking away from the house. It was, therefore, to his immense astonishment that he heard a gentle, courteous voice addressing his departing back with the words:

"Did you want to speak to me, *signore?*"

The whole tone of voice and demeanour of the man belied his wild appearance. Beppe was caught off guard. He found himself walking back towards the man standing expectantly at his front door.

Beppe walked up the steep stone steps which led up to Damiano's house. The man occupied most of the area immediately in front of the main entrance, obliging Beppe to stop one step short of the top. Damiano held out a hand to Beppe, who was left with the impression that his adversary was a good thirty centimetres taller than himself. He shook the proffered hand, which was firm, soft but quite cold. Damiano stepped back through the open double door and gestured to Beppe to set foot inside the house. The brief hesitation was noticed by Damiano who reacted by smiling – his baby cheeks puffing out to make room for the smile. His eyes, Beppe registered, remained grey and impassive.

"You have the advantage over me, *signore*," continued the gentle voice. "You seem to know who I am. Yet I remain in complete ignorance as to who *you* are. Does that seem fair to you?"

"Oh, the explanation is simple enough, Damiano. Somebody told me who you were as you got off the bus this morning. They told me you were an expert in counselling people on the subject of mushrooms."

Damiano's reaction was to draw in his breath sharply.

"I see," he said. "They are a little behind the times, however. I'm afraid I no longer give advice on mushrooms. Besides which, you still have not told me *your* name."

The gentle voice had an edge to it which did not go undetected.

"My name is Giuseppe. Giuseppe Stancato."

This time the face flinched momentarily – as rapid as a nervous tic before Damiano's face resumed its benign aspect.

"I'm sorry to say, Giuseppe, your name means nothing to me."

Beppe noticed that the voice was gentle again. He realised that Damiano was forcing himself to appear unruffled. But why? His name could not possibly mean anything to this man, surely?

"There is no reason why you should know me, *Signor* Damiano. I am a stranger here."

"I do not normally encourage strangers to come to my house, Giuseppe. But you seem to me to be a thoroughly pleasant person, so I'll make an exception in your case.

Please... do come inside. Why don't you join me for lunch? It will only be a simple affair."

The turn of phrase was disarming. Damiano had implied in some way that it was *he* who was taking the risk by inviting a *forestiero* into his home. Beppe noted with interest that Damiano had used the Italian word for an 'outsider'.

Damiano smiled his podgy smile and stood aside to usher his visitor into the house.

What was there to lose, Beppe considered. He was younger, fitter and physically able to overpower the man if need be. It would seem churlish to refuse the invitation.

Damiano set out bread, local pecorino cheese, a carafe of wine and an unopened bottle of mineral water on the rustic wooden table. He was eating the same food and sharing the same wine and water as his guest. Beppe felt too hungry to refuse after his prolonged exposure to the clear, oxygen-laden mountain air.

"I see you live on your own, Damiano. Have you always lived in this house?" It seemed an innocuous question which anyone would have asked a stranger.

"Yes, I have lived here on my own ever since my wife died. She left me some years ago now. A problem with her blood..."

Damiano's gentle tones were almost hypnotic, thought Beppe, but the deep sense of nostalgia in his voice was unmistakable.

"Nowadays, I just cultivate my mushrooms. I'm writing a book on the subject, you see..." he said, vaguely indicating an ancient desk-top computer on a bureau down the far end of the room. "It's nearly complete now – and I already have a publisher in Milano," he added with childlike pride. "I've given up advising people on mushrooms," he added unexpectedly. "They sometimes ignore one's advice completely and become ill as a consequence..."

Beppe's ears were alert in an instant. Was he listening to a confession or could it possibly be the case that he had advised Salvatore Carlettini not to eat the mushrooms? Beppe's face remained concentrated and neutral. No, he thought, there could be no mistake about his conclusions. Damiano was attempting to assuage his guilt by rationalising his crime. It must be weighing heavily on his conscience.

"Come, Beppe," said Damiano. "Oh, I'm sorry... How presumptuous of me! Please forgive me for my unforgivable familiarity. It's just that I have a son in Australia called Giuseppe. I'm so used to calling him Beppe."

It was skilfully done, thought Beppe, who was nevertheless cautious enough to be even more on his guard from that moment on.

"Please let me show you my cellar, Giuseppe. It's my pride and joy."

What could the *commissario* do? It would seem impolite to refuse after the man's gesture of hospitality. And Damiano could not possibly know the real reason for his visit. Beppe was thinking hard. He had never appeared on the local television and he was always careful to keep his name out of the press. Nevertheless - he should remain vigilant.

Damiano led his guest towards a thick oak-wood door set into the wall, He undid the single bolt and the door swung inwards. The damp air which wafted up from the cellar was redolent of the earthy perfume of wild mushrooms. Beppe was watchful, ready to react rapidly. But it was Damiano who stepped inside the cellar and began to descend the steep stairway. The cellar was lit by natural daylight coming through an iron grill set high up on the opposite side of the cellar, which must have stretched under the length and breadth of the house above. Nevertheless, after the bright daylight of the kitchen, the cellar seemed gloomy.

"I'm used to the twilight down here, Giuseppe. Mushrooms much prefer not being over-exposed to light," said the gentle voice. "Would you care to put the lights on before you come down the stairs? There's a switch just behind the door."

Beppe had to half close the door before he could reach the switch near the well-oiled iron hinges, feeling in the semi-darkness.

The alacrity with which Damiano leapt up the stairs and out into the kitchen was phenomenal. By pushing the door wide open, Damiano forced Beppe up against the wall. All traces of the lolloping gait had vanished. Damiano was strong and amazingly nimble. The door was slammed shut. Beppe heard the bolt being shot. He was Damiano's prisoner. 'Neanderthal Man' had outwitted the *commissario* – with consummate intelligence and skill.

16: La notte in bianco di Sonia...

(Sonia's sleepless night)

Capitano Enrico Nardini had spent an exhausting day. In the first place, it had taken him and his junior colleague nearly two hours to discover the location of the hunting accident, outside some remote hamlet in a deep valley up in the Maiella Mountains. He discovered that there was no telephone signal.

"So how did you manage to call out the *Carabinieri*?" he asked the group of huntsmen testily.

"One of us had to drive to Caramanico Terme," was the surly reply from one of the hunters.

"So why the hell didn't you call for an ambulance at the same time?" demanded Enrico, hardly managing to control his exasperation.

The group of hunters shrugged indifferently.

"There didn't seem much point," muttered one of them.

"So you set yourself up as medics and decided your colleague was already beyond help – does that about sum up the situation?" said Enrico coldly.

The group of hunters shifted guiltily from one foot to the other, studiously avoiding looking the *capitano* directly in the eye.

"I've a good mind to arrest you all," Enrico said sternly. "Where's the body?"

Enrico Nardini and his junior colleague followed a short track through the woods. He had to dragoon one of the hunters into showing them where the body was lying.

"He's been shot at close range," whispered Enrico's horrified junior officer.

The group of men had not moved when they retraced their steps back to where the group of surly men were standing in a close huddle.

"Your colleague couldn't have been more than twenty metres away from the person who shot him," began Enrico, no longer bothering to conceal his anger. "How come he got shot in broad daylight?"

"He got separated from us," replied one the other hunters. "He was concealed behind a bush. We saw something moving suddenly. We thought it was a wild boar."

"And that is your explanation?" shouted Enrico. "I'm seriously considering arresting you all for manslaughter. I shall want statements from all of you – separately. I shall need your identity documents, gun licences – the lot. Now... which of you drove to Caramanico Terme to call us out? Good. You're going back again. And this time you call for the forensics team on this number." Enrico Nardini handed him a piece of paper. "Say that *Capitano* Nardini needs them. Make sure you explain why I can't call in person. And this time, wait where you are so you can lead the forensic team back here. Do it now!" he barked. "And make sure you leave your gun here."

The youngest member of the group did not argue but shuffled off in the direction of his car with ill-concealed resentment. *Tenente* Mozzagrogna had never seen his *capo* so angry; he had never hidden his mistrust and dislike of the hunting fraternity, dismissing them as 'a bunch of lawless, trigger-happy bandits' on many occasions. The *tenente* was secretly forced to agree with his senior officer on this occasion – mindful nevertheless that his own father was an avid hunter - a fact which he preferred not to announce in public.

As there were only two officers present, it was necessary for both of them to check and photograph the hunters' documents, at the same time as trying to make sure the individual members of the 'tribe' were unable to collude. It was a very frustrating procedure, which tested the

Carabiniere captain's patience even further. It quickly became apparent that the six hunters had already had time to agree on what they should say to the police. They claimed that they had all shot at the same time.

"I don't believe a word of what you are saying, *signori*. I expect every one of you to present yourselves at the *Carabiniere* station the day after tomorrow – without fail. I shall decide whether to charge you with manslaughter when I have the forensics report. Now, leave ALL your guns here – one at a time so we can bag and label them – and get out of my sight!"

Enrico's junior officer had even ostentatiously unbuckled his revolver to emphasise the importance of his chief's order.

The huntsmen left muttering oaths under their breath. There would be no chance of expecting leniency from this young captain, they decided – not even with the offer of a suitable inducement. There was a muted discussion about whose lawyer should represent them 'if it gets to that point'.

Enrico and his colleague had then had to wait for well over two hours before the other hunter returned with the forensics team and ambulance in tow. The hunter was asked to identify his weapon, which had to be labelled and bagged, as had all the other guns. Enrico Nardini interrogated the last hunter, who, being the youngest member of the tribe – Enrico's word - was less well rehearsed than his mates. He looked terrified of this police officer. Enrico took full advantage of the man's inexperience and got him to admit that only one person had fired in the direction of the bush where their friend had been concealed. The hunter claimed he did not know which one of the men had fired the fatal shot. He insisted that it had not been him. Enrico believed him. It was one step in the right direction, thought Enrico Nardini resignedly as he handed over the shotguns to the forensics team – including a sample of the live cartridges used by every last man in that gaggle of huntsmen. A pity, thought Enrico, that there was no proper collective term in the Italian language to denote a group of irresponsible killers whose mentality bordered on the psychopathic. His insistence on the inclusion of a cartridge used by each hunter had really put the wind up them.

Enrico had felt obliged to wait for the forensics team to complete their task, by which time it was late afternoon and the autumn sky was darkening. He called in at the police station in Loreto Aprutino where he belatedly discovered that the *commissario* had called him and sent him a message. When he tried to phone Beppe, it appeared that his phone was switched off. He sent him a message apologising for his absence on that crucial day.

"I guess he got fed up with waiting for me and decided to give up for the day," he told his colleague, Officer Mozzagrogna. "Tomorrow morning, we must go to Farindola at first light as a matter of priority. I don't care how many bloody hunters take pot shots at each other."

It never occurred to Enrico that Beppe would have acted alone.

He went to see his girlfriend, the primary school teacher, and sought solace in her company to help him forget the frustrations of that long day.

"You really are very good at your job, *amore,*" she had told him with a look of intense admiration on her face.

* * *

Sonia was sitting at her parents' home in Atri, anxiously waiting for Beppe to call her. It was already six o'clock in the evening. Her anxiety was turning to dread as the minutes ticked by. In desperation, she tried calling him on his mobile. Now she was experiencing something close to panic – the automated voice told her repeatedly that the caller was 'unavailable'. He never left his phone switched off when they were apart. She had had an intuitive sense of impending danger as soon as Beppe had left her side. At the time, she had ignored the premonition, trying to convince herself that it was a normal reaction to him being absent. Now it was impossible to ignore the nagging conviction that something bad had happened to him.

To make matters worse, she was mindful that her period had been due that day. Instead of the usual discomfort prior to it starting, there had been a tranquil awareness that something had changed inside her. What should have provoked joyful anticipation was marred by fear for Beppe's safety. Without thinking what she was doing, she got into her car and headed resolutely for Pescara, She did not offer any explanation to either her mother or her father. They understood without words that she was deeply troubled. If she had questioned what she was intending to do, she would have simply turned the car round and returned home. The Lancia Ypsilon seemed to be taking her in the direction of the cathedral of San Cetteo.

She left her car precariously parked in front of the presbytery and rang on the bell. Don Emanuele opened the door, took one look at her face and said simply: *"Vieni con me, Sonia."*

He led the way to the cathedral through a passageway. As if by mutual consent, they both sat down side by side on the carpeted steps leading upwards to the raised altar.

"Tell me what's troubling you, Sonia."

The words poured out in a torrent. She told him all about the complex investigation which Beppe was involved in and the conclusions that it had led to.

"This morning he went to Farindola. He spoke to me while he was standing near the waterfall. I made him promise not to look for this man until Officer Nardini was with him. But I know what he's like when he's hot on the trail. He just cannot bear any delay. All I know is that the man he went to arrest is called…"

The archbishop had held up his hand to silence her.

"Damiano," he said quietly. "This is partly my fault, Sonia."

He ignored the look of absolute bewilderment on her face.

"I cannot tell you how I know about Damiano without betraying the sanctity of the confessional, but I can help you find your wonderful *fidanzato*. Go and pick up a couple of your team and meet me here at midnight. There is someone I have to go and visit first. Don't worry, Sonia. Beppe is not dead – but he might well have miscalculated the risk he was taking."

"How the devil do you know…?" Sonia began.

"*Appunto,* Sonia - it is quite assuredly my familiarity with the machinations of Satan that helped," he replied, his grey eyes smiling from within. "I'll see you outside the cathedral at midnight."

Her instinct, or her guardian angel, had guided her wisely along the path which had led to Pescara's cathedral.

She phoned Pippo and, after some careful thought, Oriana Salvati - perhaps simply because she felt the need for the presence of another woman. Or was it because, deep down inside her, she believed it was Oriana who had indirectly brought about Beppe's involvement in this case? If that was her unconscious motivation for depriving Oriana of a night's sleep, then it was an ignoble reason, she thought.

She had arranged to pick Oriana up in Loreto Aprutino, since she had already left the police station in Via

Pesaro. No doubt Officer Giovanni Palena, Oriana's other half, would accompany them. That would make another body to add weight to the proceedings.

"I'll tell you what's happened when we meet," she said stemming the inevitable tide of questions from Pippo and Oriana. "Beppe is in trouble. He needs our help. The archbishop is coming too," she added enigmatically. This revelation finally silenced their quest for further explanations. Just as well, she considered – she would have been hard put to explain what was behind Don Emanuele's insistence that he be present on this mission. All she needed was the deep sense of reassurance that his presence among them would bring her.

17: Nocturnal goings-on in Farindola…

Beppe's initial emotion was a profound feeling of anger directed against himself, followed a few seconds later by an inner cry of anguish for Sonia. How desperately anxious she would be when she discovered that he was not answering her calls – because the first thing he had checked was his mobile phone. The network signal did not stand a chance of penetrating the solid stone floor above his head.

The swiftness with which Beppe mastered his anger and conquered the fear of being at the mercy of the man he had come to arrest for murder was born of a long-standing professional patience. A latent sense of self-preservation, from the old days of evading capture at the hands of the *'ndrangheta* came to his rescue. Besides, he argued, several of his team knew where he was – not to mention the elusive Enrico Nardini. It would surely be only a matter of hours before they would come looking for him. Not that he had any intention of waiting passively for his rescuers to arrive.

He had not even moved from the spot where he was standing near the heavy wooden door at the top of the flight of steep steps leading downwards to the floor of the cellar when he heard his captor's voice addressing him through the solid door. He had abandoned the gentle, persuasive tone of voice. He sounded more like a peeved adolescent who had been thwarted in his attempt to conceal a serious misdemeanour. Nevertheless, Damiano's words astonished Beppe.

I've just come back from Pescara after meeting Don Emanuele in the cathedral. I made a full confession to him. And do you know what he said to me?

Beppe had already begun to outline how he should set about the task of outwitting his adversary. Beppe was no psychiatrist, but he intuited that the man's prolonged state of grief and guilt might have provoked a schizoid mental condition. At the very least, Damiano must be deeply emotionally disturbed.

Thus, Beppe deliberately did not react to the subtle form of torment to which Damiano – probably unintentionally – was subjecting him. He knew his tactic had hit the mark as soon as Damiano felt the need to raise his voice when no reply came from the other side of the door.

He refused to give me absolution – can you believe that, commissario? He told me I had to prove to God that I was truly repentant. I had to go to the Questura in Pescara and ask to see a police inspector called Beppe Stancato.

Silence from the cellar...

They told me at the Questura that Commissario Stancato was out investigating a case. Commissario – can you hear me?

Silence...

Can you imagine how I felt when you told me your name? Meeting you at the waterfall like that – I knew you were someone special, commissario.

An ever-deepening silence from the other side of the door...

The lack of response was profoundly troubling to Damiano. His fear was that he had somehow killed his unlooked-for guest, thereby adding to his list of mortal sins.

Commissario? Can you hear me?

The anxiety in Damiano's voice was apparent. Beppe debated whether he should try out one of his voices to alarm his captor even more. But he decided it would be more effective later on – maybe after dark when Damiano was more susceptible.

I'm not sure what to do with you. I can't kill you because I would have to go to confession again. But you're too dangerous. I can't let you go now, don't you see?

170

The psychological war of nerves had begun. Beppe heard Damiano's deceptively clumsy footsteps retreating into the kitchen. He could hear the man muttering to himself. The opening gambit had had the desired effect. From now on, he would have to devise a strategy to keep his quarry on tenterhooks. Above all, he must not allow Damiano time to think that a rescue attempt by the police was imminent. That might drive him to an act of desperation.

The three light bulbs in the cellar suddenly went out – he supposed that Damiano must have switched them off from the central control box. Beppe would have to make his preparations rapidly while there was still sufficient light coming through the grill, just above ground level.

He descended the steps to the floor of the basement. The smell of mushrooms was overpowering but, fortunately, Beppe found the scent of mushrooms pleasing – like the sweet smell of manure spread on farmland. The variety of mushrooms which Damiano cultivated was impressive. He thought he recognised porcini mushrooms in one huge trough filled with loamy soil. He wondered if one of the troughs contained *Amanita Muscaria* – they were a garish yellowy-orange in colour. Damiano had constructed a complex irrigation system; water dripped constantly from tiny holes in the plastic hose-pipes which ran all around the cellar. At least, he would have water to drink when thirst got the better of him. Where there were no mushrooms, up the far end of the vast underground cellar, there was a chaotic mass of tools, planks of wood, taps, a toilet bowl, balls of string, lengths of chain, spare cupboard door handles, saucepans, drawers full of screws and nails, a step-ladder that reached only half way up to the ventilation grill, a bike and bits of an old engine strewn around the floor. In one corner, it seemed that Damiano had stored a huge collection of toys, games and musical instruments which must have belonged to his son when he was a boy. Something that looked like an inverted metal funnel caught his attention. Of all things, it turned out to be a primitive megaphone. Maybe it had been used to call his son from the river or mountain slopes when it was time to come home for supper. It gave Beppe an idea. He picked it up and carried it like a prized possession placing it in the middle of an old wooden workbench that he had dragged into the empty space immediately under the ventilation grill. Bit by bit he carried all the items that he had earmarked and placed them in an orderly manner on or under the workbench.

He then found a bit of old material and tied it round his head like a blindfold. He spent the next exhausting two hours or so feeling his way round the cellar with both hands groping in the darkness until he was sure he could navigate his way round without bumping into anything. When he finally removed the blindfold, it was dark outside and no light came through the ventilation grill. He had found a decrepit deck chair, covered with cobwebs. He sat down on the chair and waited in a kind of trance-like state so as not to become impatient with the slowly passing minutes. He told himself stories and ran over the details of films he had seen and enjoyed. He dared not think of Sonia. He risked turning on his mobile phone every so often just to look briefly to see what time it was. Nearly half past ten. There was the distant sound of voices coming from upstairs – a continuous stream of alternating male and female voices. Beppe understood that Damiano had the television turned up loud. He must be watching Rai Uno's political programme with Bruno Vespa, *Porta a porta* -Door to door! Doors seemed to be playing an important part in his life that night. It was far too early to mount his theatrical performance just yet.

It must have been half past eleven when he heard the familiar footsteps approaching the cellar door. As Beppe had predicted, Damiano was feeling the need to check up on his imprisoned guest before he took himself off to bed. The note of anxiety in his voice was unmistakable.

I don't want to do this to you, you know! I'll talk to you tomorrow. Maybe we can work something out. Euh? What do you say?

The *commissario* said nothing. There was an eerie silence. Damiano's tone changed dramatically. He sniggered as he attempted what he considered to be a humorous contribution to his prisoner's discomfort.

I'll bring you some breakfast tomorrow morning. Meanwhile if you get hungry in the night, you can always nibble some mushrooms. Be careful though, commissario. Some of them are poisonous! If you pick the wrong ones, it won't be my fault, will it? Then I shan't have to confess to the Archbishop again...

His prisoner's silence was playing on his nerves. His intention had been to provoke some reaction from Beppe. But no reassuring words were forthcoming. Damiano banged on the door in panic.

Buona notte, commissario!

In the darkness, Beppe reached for the megaphone. Now was the moment to sow the seeds of real fear in his captor. He had only done this voice a couple of times in his life. The first time was when he had been a rebellious seventeen-year-old, tired of his devout Catholic mother's insistence that he go to confession every Saturday afternoon. It was the price he had to pay if he wanted to go out with the lads later on every Saturday night.

He had been astounded at how well it had worked in the middle of the night. It had alarmed his mother so much to hear the magnified voice of a woman who claimed to be the Blessed Virgin Mary announcing that he, Beppe, should never be made to go to confession again, because - the voice had proclaimed – he was a 'good boy' living entirely in a state of grace.

You must let the commissario go, Damiano. You must release him before dawn. Otherwise you will never see your beloved Renata again. She is waiting for you. Do not let her down, I beseech you...

The woman's voice seemed to be echoing round the old house, shaking it to its very foundations. Beppe was gratified to hear a kind of gurgling sound emanating from his captor's mouth – he was speechless with shock. The footsteps stumbled away. But the three dim light bulbs came on, illuminating the cellar in a sepulchral light. Ironic, thought Beppe. If the rest of his scheme were to work, it would require total darkness. He was going to 'disappear'.

Now Beppe's three hour vigil would begin. He was sure that sleep would get the better of him, so he decided to run the risk of leaving his mobile on with the alarm clock set for two in the morning. At two o'clock precisely, he was woken up by the insistent beeping noise from his phone. The house was silent, but through the ventilation grill, he could clearly hear the sound of Farindola's church bell ringing out across the valley. Beppe was thirsty and went to find the tap. When he had drunk his fill he set about the next stage of engineering his release. The church bell was still tolling solemnly. Surely it couldn't be...?

* * *

Sonia and Pippo arrived outside the cathedral of San Cetteo on the dot of midnight. They had taken a police car from the compound since this was "official business". Don Emanuele was not there waiting for them.

"He's not infallible, you know, Sonia," Pippo pointed out to his increasingly tense friend and colleague. Her nerves

174

were nearly at breaking point when the Archbishop arrived some thirty minutes later.

"I'm so sorry to have kept you waiting. I had to administer the last rites to a lady I've been visiting in hospital for months. I'm sorry, Sonia. You must be very anxious. But, you see, I have to take care of departing souls before I attend to the living. And I *am* talking about Beppe,"

Sonia felt gently admonished for her lack of faith.

They drove quickly along the empty roads towards Loreto Aprutino. Oriana and Giovanni Palena were waiting patiently for them outside their apartment. Introductions were made – since neither Oriana nor Giovanni had ever met this tall, shaven-headed priest with the piercing grey eyes. They seemed in awe of him.

"I am pleased to make your acquaintance," said Don Emanuele cupping each of their hands in both of his. "And, Oriana... Giovanni, there is no need to look so worried. I am not expecting you turn up for mass next Sunday – or any other Sunday, come to that."

Sonia shook her head in quiet disbelief. Yet again, he had understood the situation instantly – appearing thereby to be a mind-reader.

Giovanni and Oriana both smiled.

"It's amazing the residue of guilt that so many Italians feel when faced with the sight of a priest, after years of being made to attend mass as kids," he said gently. "Now, let's go and rescue your *commissario.* I suggest you take your own car – this one might have an extra passenger on the way back."

By just before two o'clock, the cortege of two police cars had pulled up in the silent piazza opposite the *Bar Commercio.*

"*Oh, dio mio!* There's Beppe's car. He must be somewhere nearby," exclaimed Sonia in alarm.

"*Mia cara* Sonia... that's why we came to Farindola, isn't it?" said Don Emanuele soothingly.

Sonia blushed.

"Just one problem," said Pippo. "We don't know where this guy Damiano lives."

"There must be plenty of people here in Farindola who know where his house is," said Don Emanuele with a humorous glint in his eyes. Once again, he was enjoying the sensation of holding back a secret that put him one strategic step ahead of his companions.

"But they are all quite self-evidently fast asleep," said Oriana sharply.

Giovanni looked alarmed at the sudden scathing tone of his *fidanzata's* words. Pippo smiled to himself. Apparently, even archbishops were not to be spared from the asperity of Oriana's tongue.

The Archbishop merely grinned impishly at Oriana.

"Not for long, they won't be, Oriana! Sonia, come with me. The rest of you, wait here. A large number of people will soon appear on the scene. Some of them are bound to know where Damiano's house is."

Don Emanuele strode off down the hill, followed by Sonia following a few steps behind him.

Pippo, Oriana and Giovanni remained rooted to the spot looking mystified.

"Where are we going, Don Emanuele?" asked Sonia breathlessly. She practically had to run to keep up with the Archbishop.

"To the church of course, Sonia."

"You mean, we're going to *pray* for Beppe? I thought you said he was safe."

"I didn't say he was safe. I said he was alive."

"But the church will be locked at this time of night."

"I *am* an archbishop, *carissima* Sonia. They can't possibly keep me out of a church – at *any* time of day or night."

Sonia should have known Don Emanuele better. He had already arranged for the incumbent parish priest to come and open the door. The said parish priest was about eighty years old, but he was waiting in the shadows for his archbishop to arrive.

The group of three uniformed police officers waiting in the *piazza,* were amazed to hear the church bell ringing out its summons across the sleepy village. In under three minutes, there was a small crowd of people, clad in various forms of nightwear, standing in amazement in the square.

"Is it an earthquake?" someone asked the police officers.

"No," replied Pippo." We are looking for the house of a man called Damiano. It's an emergency."

The church bell had finally fallen silent. Don Emanuele and Sonia reappeared, adding weight to the urgent request for information, which the townsfolk seemed reluctant to divulge. A well-built lady emerged from the *Bar Commercio.* She was wearing a pair of pink fluffy pyjamas which seemed quite inappropriate for her stocky build.

"My name is Silvia Guerra. What is this all about? It must be something serious, I assume."

Sonia instantly recognised the name from the list which Beppe had shown her.

"We are looking for the house of Adolfo Damiano D'Angelo. We have reason to believe that he is involved in the disappearance of our *commissario.*"

"Come inside the bar for a minute, officers and...?" She was looking quizzically at Don Emanuele. "And you too, *Monsignore.*"

Silvia Guerra shooed the other onlookers away as soon as they thought they might take advantage of the exceptionally early opening of their local bar.

"We don't want the whole village to know what's going on," she explained.

She offered them coffees and listened to the lengthy explanation given by the police officers.

"I thought there was something fishy going on," she commented. "It must have been your *commissario* who was in my bar yesterday. I'll take you to where Damiano's house is. Just give me five minutes to get dressed. May I just ask one obvious question – merely to satisfy my curiosity? How come an archbishop is involved in a police investigation?"

Such was the jovial, open manner in which she had expressed herself, Don Emanuele replied simply: "Damiano will definitely be in need of spiritual guidance, *Signora* Guerra."

She seemed perfectly satisfied with the answer and went off to change. She reappeared ten minutes later, wearing an army camouflage jacket and trousers. All the officers were smiling at her. But it was, as usual, Oriana Salvati who came out with what they were all thinking.

"I know your surname means 'war' *signora* – but do you really believe we are going into combat?"

"No – that's your job, my dear. But I couldn't be bothered to sort out my Sunday best clothes for this event," was her succinct reply.

The group hung around for another gruelling twenty minutes while they discussed how they should set about the task of approaching Damiano's house without alerting the owner. Sonia was growing increasingly desperate. The archbishop placed a gentle hand on her arm.

"It's alright Sonia. They are just being thorough."

"I shan't relax until I know he's safe," she burst out.

"Ah, I see!" said Silvia Guerra with genuine sympathy. "This is more than just a simple police operation, isn't it?"

* * *

Damiano was lying awake on his bed, still fully dressed. He no longer bothered changing into pyjamas these days. The problem of whether the *commissario* was alive or not was nagging away inside his head. Half of his mind was still earthbound, preoccupied with the problem of how he could avoid ending up in jail. Not being in his familiar surroundings would be physically and spiritually unbearable. He would not survive in prison.

But then there had been the manifestation earlier on. The supernatural voice of a woman – who could only have been the Blessed Virgin herself – pleading with him not to destroy his chances of rejoining Renata on the other side of the great divide between life on Earth and eternal life in Paradise.

As he lay sleepless, another inexplicable element intruded into his conscious mind. He could hear a bell tolling. It sounded very similar to the village church bell. What could it mean? But in that instant of time, his meditations were rendered superfluous by an almighty, earth-shattering din coming from the floors below. It was the end of the world, surely? It was as if a mighty hammer was dealing thunderous blows – one after the other. A pause - and then the hammering would begin all over again.

He became irritated and fearful all in one breath. Was it the imprisoned *commissario* or could it be his angry spirit wanting to escape from its earthly prison? Either way, the din ran the risk of alerting his nearest neighbours who might call out the police. Silence returned. But it was a disturbing, eerie silence. He thought he heard a woman sighing – a long, protracted moan of grief. Could it be the Blessed Virgin Mary trapped in his cellar with the dead *commissario?* There was no way out. He would have to go down to the cellar and face the truth of the consequences of his own desperate attempt at resolving his spiritual dilemma.

He took hold of the powerful torch by his bedside and made his way downstairs. It was a throwback to his innocent childhood. His parents always turned the electricity off at night time – to save spending money on this extravagant new method of avoiding the darkness which God had intended human beings to rejoice in.

He approached the cellar door cautiously and unbolted the door as quietly as he could. It did not matter about disturbing the *commissario.* He was more concerned about the mysterious woman who had taken residence in his cellar. Damiano was surprised, as he gingerly pushed open the door. In the first place, the door seemed to be even heavier than usual. The lights which he had reconnected did not seem to be working. He was about to reach behind the door to switch the lights on when he heard a clattering noise coming from the floor of the cellar. *Grazie a Dio!* The police inspector must still be alive. He shone his torch in the direction of the noise and began to descend the steps one by one. What was that piece of string doing trailing down the stairs? Then it came to him... the reason why the door had been so heavy. He swivelled round like lightning and for a split second caught sight of his quarry spread-eagled on the back of the cellar door in the beam of his torch. Damiano roared in anger. But Beppe was too quick for him this time. He was out of the cellar in two seconds. The door slammed shut and Damiano heard the bolt being shot to.

"Don't go away Damiano," said the friendly voice of the *commissario.* "We can have a proper talk in the morning.

Right now, I really need to use your bathroom, if that's OK with you."

* * *

Outside the house, the archbishop was standing on the landing in front of the main door. He was staring at the obstruction as if willing it to open of its own accord. The three police officers with Silvia Guerra were walking round the back of the rambling house, looking for any open window or an ill-secured back door. There was no other way in except through the front door.

"Pippo," whispered Sonia desperately, "have you got your 'spare keys' on you?"

Pippo's claim to fame – far less spectacular than his chief's ability to mimic voices – was that he could pick locks. But the ancient lock on Damiano's door stubbornly refused to give way.

"The key is in the lock on the inside," he said.

"What can we do?" wailed Sonia, her last shreds of self-control in tatters.

"*Knock and the door shall be opened unto you,*" proclaimed Don Emanuele – who did just that; three ponderous knocks which resonated all around them.

To everyone's surprise – except Don Emanuele's – they heard the key turn in the lock and the door opened.

"Ah, there you all are!" said Beppe, weary but beaming at them. "I was wondering when you would come and rescue me."

Beppe did not register any surprise at seeing Don Emanuele – but he was looking very grateful for his presence among his rescuers.

In his weakened state, Beppe was nearly knocked over by the force of Sonia's embrace as she ran into his arms. The other four figures stood rooted to the spot, unwilling to let go of this moment of sheer relief that Beppe was unharmed.

It was Oriana who broke the spell. She had been staring at Don Emanuele, realising belatedly that she was not in the presence of an average man of the cloth.

"Excuse me, Don Emanuele, but how did you know that the door would open?"

"Where is your faith, my dear Oriana? *Knock and the door shall be opened unto you.* Have you never heard those words before?"

Oriana was looking with deep respect at this holy man, whose reputation, it was beginning to dawn on her, was thoroughly justified.

"Besides which," he added with a self-satisfied grin, "didn't you hear the footsteps walking down the hallway towards the door?"

Oriana decided it might be worth her while going to church occasionally after all.

* * *

Sonia wanted to take Beppe home immediately. But it was not to be. Damiano had to be rescued from the cellar. It was Don Emanuele who opened the door to the cellar. Damiano was waiting in ambush and rushed upstairs like a madman.

"DAMIANO" intoned the Archbishop, holding up his right hand in command.

Damiano broke down as soon as he saw the admonishing figure standing before him like God on the Day of Judgement.

He allowed himself to be handcuffed before being led into the kitchen.

"Do not be afraid, Damiano," said Don Emanuele. "Everything will be alright from now on. I won't desert you."

Beppe phoned Enrico Nardini. He was ordered to drive over to Farindola without delay.

"He's *your* suspect, my dear Enrico. It was you who correctly suspected he was guilty. You should take the credit for arresting him."

Beppe was painfully aware that he was exacting a kind of unfair justice on the man who had abandoned him at such a crucial moment the previous day. No doubt he would apologise to his *Carabiniere* colleague in the days to come.

Enrico Nardini took his painful leave of his new girlfriend, after phoning his junior colleague with instructions to pick him up in the police car. Alessia was getting her first taste of what it would be like being married to a policeman.

* * *

As everybody was about to leave, Beppe noticed a new figure walking up to Damiano's house. Despite his encroaching physical exhaustion, he recognised Gabriele, his friend the cheese-maker.

"I heard the church bell ringing, *commissario*. I figured it must be something to do with you. I became worried about you when you didn't show up at my place, so I came along to see if I could help."

"You were right to warn me about poor old Damiano," said Beppe. "I should have listened to you."

Gabriele held out a small package.

"Here, *commissario* – take this with you as a souvenir of Farindola," he said with an ironic smile. The sweet smell of fresh Pecorino cheese seeped through the wrapping paper.

Beppe shook Gabriele by the hand. Then the whole group finally departed – Damiano in the *Carabiniere* police car with Enrico Nardini and his *tenente*.

Finally, Beppe and Sonia were alone in Beppe's car, which they had reclaimed from its space outside the *Bar Commercio*. Beppe had accepted the offer of a *grappa* from Silvia Guerra before they drove off into the nascent autumn dawn.

"What a pity that Salvatore Carlettini didn't come to *you* for advice about his mushrooms," Beppe told Silvia Guerra.

"It would have spared us a lot of anguish," said Silvia Guerra.

In the car, which Sonia was driving, they headed back towards Atri – and tumbled, almost unconscious with exhaustion, into bed.

"*Sono incinta,*" whispered Sonia reverently.

Those were the last words that Beppe heard – or dreamt he heard - before he fell into a deep sleep.

(incinta – pregnant. Pronounced 'inCHINta')

18: Ormai siamo in tre...

(Now there are three of us)

Beppe and Sonia stayed in bed until gone midday. Beppe hoped Pippo had not slept in as long as they had. Otherwise the *Questore* would fear he had lost three of his team of officers – rather than just one *commissario.*

"Don't worry," said Sonia's mother, when they appeared in pyjamas, begging for a belated cup of coffee. "We have already had a call from the *Questore.* I told him you didn't get back home until the early hours of this morning. He was very relieved to hear you were both safe and sound. The *Questore* said on no account were you to come in until tomorrow, Beppe," she added.

'Home', Sonia's mother had called the Leardi house. Strange how the word had sounded so soothing to Beppe's ears! He was mindful of the reason why Sonia and he had been forced to leave their apartment in Pescara so abruptly. The threat from the Naples mob had not been uppermost in his mind during the past twenty-four hours. But now they were, in reality, on the run from the Alfieri clan until further notice. That must have been the reason why Sonia's mother's words had sounded so reassuring, thought Beppe.

Beppe, still shaking off the effects of slumber, was wondering whether he had imagined the final words that Sonia had uttered earlier that day - just as the rim of the rising sun had edged its way over the distant horizon of the Adriatic Sea like a razor of golden light.

After their coffee in the kitchen, they had returned upstairs to the bedroom and promised themselves another few minutes of intimacy before getting ready for the rest of the day.

"Sonia...?" he asked simply when they were lying side by side on the bed.

"I'll do a proper test in a couple of days' time, but, yes... I know something has changed inside me. *Ormai siamo in tre.*"

Those four simple words were forged in steel. Even the quality of the sunlight illuminating the familiar objects in the bedroom had undergone some subtle transformation. Nothing in life would ever be the same again.

"And so, if you dare to attempt a stunt like yesterday's ever again, we shall *both* abandon you to your own well-deserved fate!"

The iron in Sonia's voice was unmistakable – and the threat truly formidable.

Beppe pulled her towards him and held her tightly.

"Never again, *giurin giurello,*" he said teasingly.

"*Cross my heart and hope to die, amore mio,* is precisely what I used to say to my dad when I was a capricious seven-year-old with pigtails. It usually meant I had no intention of keeping my promise for longer than it took my dad to be out of sight. You may have to do better than that," she warned.

"I swear to you, Sonia, that I will never be so stupid again," he said and held her even closer.

"Now, will you please satisfy my curiosity and tell me what happened in Damiano's house, Beppe? You will never know how surprised and full of joy I was when it was *you* who opened that door to us."

Beppe related the whole episode from start to finish. Despite her former anger that he had put his life at risk, she doubled up when he told her about 'the voice of the Blessed Virgin Mary', magnified through the loud-hailer. Sonia lay in her *fidanzato's* arms, listening with rapt attention to how he had nailed a plank of wood onto the back of the cellar door just above floor level and two cupboard handles to grip on to.

186

"I was worried that Damiano would try and switch the lights on when he entered the cellar, so I attached a string to an old watering can and some flower pots stacked precariously on the table. I just tugged the string as soon as he pushed open the cellar door – and that distracted him for long enough to let me escape..." concluded Beppe. Sonia decided that it was time to forgive him for his severe error of judgement.

"Tutto bene ciò che finisce bene", she thought, but did not say out loud because the phrase sounded too trite – and she did not want to let him off the hook quite so readily.
(All's well that ends well)

* * *

About an hour later, Sonia's mother announced that lunch was ready.

"It's so lovely to have family around the house again," said Irene – Sonia's mum. "You can both stay here as long as you wish."

Beppe instinctively looked at Sonia's father, Roberto, to gauge what his reaction was to this sincere but spur-of-the moment invitation. Beppe must have unconsciously raised an interrogative eyebrow in his direction, which he detected.

The father was busy devouring his plate of pasta with *vongole* sauce. With a concentrated look on his face, he finished the mouthful, wiped his mouth on a napkin and said without any alteration of facial expression:

"Va da sè."

To be told so simply that they should take his agreement for granted was heart-warming. His response reminded Beppe of the way his own long-suffering father would have expressed his secret pleasure – without any unnecessary flamboyance.

"*Grazie. Mille grazie,*" replied Beppe quietly.

Sonia looked at Beppe as if asking permission to forewarn them that the invitation might well include a third party. Beppe made an unobtrusive gesture to Sonia to say it was up to her to choose the moment when she should inform her parents.

Irene intercepted the rapid exchange and twigged immediately. She beamed at them both, but the expression on her face also held a question mark in suspension. Sonia read her mother's mind.

"*Sì, mamma,* we *are* going to get married – in the Cathedral of San Cetteo. The Archbishop is going to do the honours."

Alarmingly, Sonia's father stood up suddenly and left the table, still chewing a mouthful of pasta. He headed for the cellar and returned with a bottle of *Prosecco*. He was a man of few words – especially when eating, Beppe decided. The fact that Sonia only had a sip from Beppe's glass of sparkling wine was confirmation enough for her mother, knowing her daughter's propensity for enjoying wine with her food.

"*Auguri!*" Irene said to all present, as they raised their glasses – Sonia and Beppe both clutching the stem of the same fluted champagne glass.

"To our future together!" announced the *commissario* – intending that his words should encompass his new-found family in Abruzzo too.

Later on, Irene turned to her husband and said:

"You do realise your daughter is expecting a child, don't you, *mio caro?*"

"Of course, I do! Do you imagine I'm slow-witted or something? *Era ora!* It was high time," added Roberto, as if stating the obvious. "Why do think I went to fetch a bottle of *Prosecco* up from the cellar?"

There was no suitable answer to that question, reckoned his wife.

* * *

Beppe and Sonia grew restless after lunch and felt an overwhelming urge to get back into the swing of things. Ignoring the *Questore's* injunction not to return to work that day, they drove down to Pescara in the middle of the afternoon.

Pippo and Oriana had evidently been spreading the word about Beppe's escapade of the previous day, which explained why their chief was greeted as if he had been a refugee escaped from captivity at the hands of an army of terrorists.

"I thought I told you not to come in to the *Questura* today, *commissario,*" said Beppe's chief, Dante Di Pasquale, who nevertheless did not look at all surprised by his presence.

"Was it an order, *capo?*" asked Beppe casually.

The *Questore* simply shook his head with a gesture of mock despair.

"I suppose you had better come upstairs and tell me how it came about that four police officers had to miss a whole night's sleep yesterday because of you," he said pointedly.

"Because I made a very bad error of judgement, *Signor Questore,*" admitted Beppe contritely.

He was in the middle of explaining the outcome of the unusual investigation, which the *Questore* had originally assigned him simply to give his senior officer a purpose in life, when the reception desk phoned upstairs to say that a certain *Capitano* Enrico Nardini was downstairs. He was eager to talk to *Commissario* Stancato.

The *Questore* sighed. He had been entirely engrossed in the details of Beppe's 'adventure' as he chose to call it.

"I'll let Beppe know, Officer Remo. He'll be downstairs in ten minutes." The *Questore* was determined not to miss the ending of the story. When Beppe had finished his account, as rapidly as he could, the *Questore* ordered Beppe to come upstairs again after he had finished with Enrico Nardini.

"I need to fill you in on the *mafia* situation, Beppe. I mean the two Naples gangsters who turned up at your flat. I think we've made some progress."

* * *

By the time Enrico had finished explaining the arduous day he had spent with the hunters the day before, Beppe was regretting the authoritative manner in which he had summoned the *Carabiniere* captain to Damiano's house early that same morning.

"Where is Damiano, at present?" he asked Enrico.

"In Pescara jail, for now, but Don Emanuele has promised to go and see him as often as time allows."

"My guess is he'll end up in an institution for the mentally ill," said Beppe. "I hope so – for his sake. That is the line I shall take when he appears in court."

Enrico changed the subject. He was mindful of the fact that the following day he would have to interrogate the seven hunters. He was feeling out of his depth again and wished to enlist Beppe's help.

"Ah, *capitano*, I'm afraid I cannot desert my post here another time. We have the Puglian *mafia* to deal with – it's a very touchy situation."

Enrico Nardini looked crestfallen but was trying to put a brave face on things. Beppe took pity on him.

"But I will tell you how I think you might conduct the interrogation. What line of defence do you believe that group of legalised killers is going to adopt?"

"They will claim they all pointed their guns at the bush where the victim was in hiding. They'll close ranks, I'm sure."

"Have you got the forensics report back yet?" asked Beppe.

"Just an initial report for now; the pellets extracted could have been fired from any one of three guns judging by the number of pellets found in the man's body. But the shot pellets were nearly all in the left side of his chest – which would mean that the victim, Gregorio Cardone, was probably in the act of standing up but facing in the opposite direction to the rest of the hunters."

"So, they will want you to believe that all three of them shot at once."

"Yes, but I got the youngest hunter, who I sent back to Caramanico Terme to phone the forensics team, to admit that only one person let off the fatal shot. He didn't say – or was too scared of the others – to tell me who it was. Maybe he truly didn't know."

Beppe was thinking deeply. He remained silent for all of sixty long seconds.

"Alright, Enrico," he said finally. "This is how you should set about interrogating them..."

By the time Beppe had finished, Enrico Nardini was looking in admiration at his colleague.

"Don't worry, Enrico. You'll handle it perfectly. They'll be eating out of your hand by the time you've finished. *In bocca al lupo!*"

"Don't you want to hear about Salvatore's housekeeper, Dinusha?" asked Enrico.

Beppe had forgotten completely about the words that Enrico had shouted out from the departing *Carabinieri* police car just as he was setting off to deal with the hunting accident.

"Of course I do, *capitano!* It had completely slipped my mind."

"As we surmised, there was more to their relationship than met the eye. But we didn't guess they were man and wife. That's what the police in Torino found out. She broke down completely when she heard about his death. It's a good thing she is with her family up there."

Beppe looked taken-aback at the unexpected discovery that Salvatore had had a wife.

"That means she's got a claim on the house in Montebello. That will put the cat among the pigeons when his brother Ernesto finds out!" exclaimed Beppe, who was disturbed to discover the news struck a chord of malicious glee in his heart. "I don't envy the lawyer who has to sort *that* one out."

* * *

Stefano Alfieri, in Naples, was feeling angry and frustrated. He had been visited by the *Carabinieri* in the sanctity of his own fortified home and threatened with dire consequences by a senior officer. The two men, whom he had despatched off to Pescara, had been returned under escort to Naples. The police had confiscated his company's luxury hire car and he had been obliged to send someone all the way to the east coast to retrieve it.

His two henchmen had been under orders to 'take out' that *commissario* who had humiliated him in the presence of his family during his father's arrest on the occasion of his seventieth birthday party. His reaction, when faced with the *Carabinieri,* had been to sneer at them and deny all knowledge of what he was being accused of.

"They were taking a break from work, *Colonnello.* It's still a free country, isn't it?"

"You are forgetting one little detail in your desire to avenge your wounded pride, *Stefano,*" the condescending officer had stated. "Your father has been granted the privilege of being detained under house arrest, in view of his advanced years, in comfortable surroundings and in the presence of his wife. Only we know where he is being detained."

"So what?" Stefano Alfieri had replied aggressively.

"Quite simply, young man, if there is any further attempt to pursue *Commissario* Stancato by you or anyone else in your entourage, we shall instantly put your father in jail – and he can share his cell with some minor gangster or rapist until his dying day. At least, you will be able to visit him! But he is hardly likely to thank you for your pains. Do I make myself abundantly clear?"

After the departure of the *Carabinieri,* Stefano Alfieri seethed for hours. He would have to forego the pleasure of exacting his personal revenge. But there was a way round the problem.

He made a phone call, the following day, to a contact in Foggia...

What the hell! *Commissario* Stancato would be out of action for the rest of his life.

* * *

"So, you should be safe from the *Camorra* at least, Beppe," the *Questore* was telling him. "But stay vigilant – you never know what is just round the corner."

Beppe explained his new living arrangements. He still could not bring himself to tell his *capo* that he was sure he was going to be a father. That could wait for calmer times.

"Sonia and I are going to get married as soon as we can, chief. We've arranged to see the Archbishop later on this evening. In fact, in about an hour's time... if that's alright with you."

"As I gave you the day off, *commissario,* I can hardly object," he said smiling. "And my warmest congratulations to you both," he added, standing up to shake his colleague's hand.

* * *

"But how did you know I was expecting a child – that Sunday after mass?" Sonia asked Don Emanuele. The question had been niggling away in her mind, just waiting to be asked as soon as the opportunity arose.

"I didn't *know,* Sonia. The words just came out. If I guessed right, then it was pure intuition. Do you believe in telepathy?"

The Archbishop was surprised that Sonia and Beppe looked at each other and laughed. They explained to him how they had both asked the same question to each other simultaneously a few months previously.

"You're obviously very close to each other - so you shouldn't be surprised at my wild guesses," smiled Don Emanuele, evidently pleased with himself. "We take it for granted that text messages are transmitted as if by magic through the ether. I imagine that God has given us a similar power to do the same thing, directly from one human being to another - if we care to put our minds to it. I read somewhere that, before telephones were invented, certain races of people developed the ability to communicate mentally with each other over long distances – Eskimos did it on a regular basis, I believe."

His two guests, sitting in the presbytery, were looking very thoughtful. Beppe was remembering the extraordinary moment when the archbishop had appeared to foretell the road accident suffered by the Mafioso lawyer driving back to Naples – an accident that had prevented the lawyer from passing on the names of three innocent people who would assuredly have been 'silenced' by the clans.

"So, shall we fix a day in November for your marriage? Or do you need more time to plan that precious day?"

"No, Don Emanuele, we want it to be as soon as possible," replied Beppe. He had amazed Sonia because, just for once, he had spoken without a single second's internal deliberation.

"Amore!" she said, beaming at her partner.

And so the date was fixed.

"You are supposed to come and see me while I lecture you on your duties as good Catholic souls to bring up your children strictly according to the teachings of Holy Mother Church. But, I think I know you well enough to dispense with that formality."

Beppe looked gratefully at Don Emanuele.

"Besides which, Beppe," the Archbishop continued, "I feel I owe you a special favour as it was largely due to my indiscretion that you ended up in the clutches of a certain sorrowful individual called Damiano."

Any further discussion on the subject seemed superfluous – and Beppe's mobile phone was ringing.

"I apologise, Don Emanuele. It's my official phone."

His face tightened as he listened to the voice of Pippo Cafarelli.

"We'll meet you there in a few minutes, Pippo," he said. "I'm so sorry," he explained to the archbishop, "they've found a body on the beach up towards Montesilvano.

Beppe did not even question the fact that the Archbishop donned his cloak and came with them.

* * *

Beppe and Sonia found the spot on the long, sandy beach only because Pippo had posted Gino Martelli on the coastal road with a flashing torch in his hand to flag them down. The forensics team had not yet arrived on the scene, so Pippo and *Agente* Danilo Simone were standing some distance away from the motionless heap lying face down in the wet sand. A suspicious stray dog was trying to approach the corpse whilst performing an elaborate series of circles which brought it ever closer to its goal. Danilo chased it away as best he could but the animal instinctively began its manoeuvres again as if drawn by a magnet. The archbishop had put on a stole round his neck and was murmuring words to himself to send the unknown soul on the way to its final destination.

It was twenty minutes before the forensics team arrived, driving along the deserted beach from the direction of Pescara in a four-wheel drive vehicle. The dismal scene was soon illuminated and three efficient, white-coated figures carried out the last rites.

"Male, white Caucasian, about thirty," shouted out one of the team for the benefit of the gathered police officers and one archbishop. "Single shot through the back of the head," added the voice. "His hands are tied behind his back."

Pippo started and looked at Beppe. They both had the same thought. The nightmare was not yet over.

When finally the little group was allowed to approach, the forensics team performed the gruesome task of lifting the body into a body bag.

As Don Emanuele anointed the victim's forehead with oil, Sonia let out a gasp.

"I know who that is, Beppe. His name is Benedetto Gentile. He's got two girls who work out of an apartment in town. I spoke to him only a couple of days ago about the risk of being approached by the mob. Poor guy…"

"Far from being the girls' protector, he needed protection himself," said Beppe.

"Those bastards from Foggia," muttered Pippo under his breath.

"I don't think our work for the night is done just yet, *ragazzi,*" announced the *commissario,* thanking the forensics team as they took their leave. The Archbishop and the little team of policemen followed the torch beam back to the road. Gino was assigned the task of taking a saddened Don Emanuele back to the presbytery and Sonia gave Gino the address of the apartment where the victim's two girls worked from.

* * *

A moment of grim comedy was played out, as a well-known city dignitary, wearing a deeply embarrassed blush of shame and a pair of purple underpants, was summarily dismissed as the team of police officers arrived at the apartment from which the girls carried out their trade.

"Make sure you pay the girl before you leave," said Beppe cruelly, as the local councillor hurriedly wrestled with his clothes and stumbled out into the night, his shoe laces still undone.

"Put some clothes on, Eva," said Sonia kindly to the scantily dressed girl. "We need to talk to you. Where's… your companion?"

Eva dismally indicated the other bedroom door.

"Bella wasn't feeling very well, tonight," said Eva with a heavy Eastern European accent.

"We need to talk to both of you," said Beppe. "Please go and fetch her."

The team of police officers gasped in shock as they saw Bella's swollen jaw line, bruised by a vicious blow to her face. Her cheek had been cut by something sharp like a ring.

Beppe took one look at her and said they would take her to hospital. He pulled up a chair and sat down opposite the two girls.

"You need to tell us what happened, *signorine.*" Beppe spoke in a gentle voice.

"It happened just like you said, Sonia," began Eva. Bella could only nod her head and even that motion was painful for her.

"This guy phoned us up as if he was a client and we fixed an appointment for him. He said he wanted to come at eleven at night. Well, a lot of punters come at that hour but they don't book it, like, hours ahead..."

Beppe and Sonia looked at her to encourage her to continue.

"We thought he was trouble as soon as he stepped through the door, 'cos he said he wanted both of us at once. You know... But he was aggressive about it..."

"But where was your... minder when all this was happening?"

"He leaves us alone a lot 'cos he trusts us – more or less. He usually looks in about midnight to check up what business has been like..."

"Go on, Eva," said Sonia.

"Well, he said he wasn't interested in having sex, but he had a business proposition for us. But he made it sound like we didn't have any choice. It was Bella who told him where he could stuff his business proposition. She's a lot more… She's tougher than I am. But he just laid into her with a vicious slap round her face… really hard. And he left. He said he'd be back later on and if we told anyone, I'd get the same treatment. He made us give him a key to the door, too," Eva's voice trailed off.

"We tried to call Benedetto, but his phone was off…" Bella manged to say, but the pain was too great and her voice was almost unintelligible.

Sonia looked at Beppe as if to ask whether she should tell them about the fate of their 'protector'. He nodded.

Rather than being upset, their faces became rigid with fear. Beppe thought quickly. He would leave Danilo and Gino behind in the flat to await the return of the man 'with the weird accent' – as Eva had described him. Sonia and he would take both girls to the hospital, so they would not have to remain on their own, he explained to them.

"Don't come back here till we tell you it's all clear. *D'accordo?*"

They did not argue.

Pippo Cafarelli, mindful of the last occasion when Gino and Danilo had been left to capture whoever turned up – and subsequently let him escape - volunteered to stay with the two junior officers.

"This guy might not come back on his own," Pippo pointed out. "Besides if it's the Foggia mob involved, I want to know about it."

"*Va bene, ragazzi,* don't worry in what state you bring this man to the police station. I've had more than enough of this mob by now," were Beppe's parting words, as he and Sonia left with the two cowed girls. He was in no mood to be tolerant towards anyone who could so viciously strike a woman without any compunction – however lowly her social status might be.

19: The stuff of heroes – and heroines...

Beppe and Sonia decided to take the minimal risk of sleeping in their apartment that night, since they could not face the drive back to Atri. Besides which, they could begin to cart their other belongings to the parents' house in Atri. They had been assigned a whole floor on the upper storey of the Leardi household, which included a recently refurbished bathroom and kitchen for their exclusive use, two spare rooms for any new arrivals – and an attic.

"What about your boat, *amore?*" asked Sonia as they lay in bed. "We can't leave it here all on its own."

Beppe did not have an answer but merely reiterated that other more important factors had taken over their lives.

"It'll be winter soon. Our boat will be safe enough in the harbour for now," he said unconvincingly. But he knew Sonia was right - a solution would have to be found...

The following morning, when they arrived at the *Questura* in Via Pesaro, they were greeted by Pippo Caferelli, looking preoccupied.

"Did everything go off alright, Pippo?" asked Beppe, concerned.

"I guess so, *capo*. Two of them turned up just after midnight. We took them completely by surprise. One of them was armed with a revolver – which we've sent down to the technicians in the basement. They tried to convince us they were the girls' clients, would you believe, despite letting themselves in with the key. They're locked up in separate cells in the basement for now – protesting their innocence, of course. When I asked the ringleader precisely what he thought he was innocent of, he decided not to say anything else. By the way, I'm pretty sure I've seen him before in the backstreets of Foggia. The name of the clan he works for escapes me for the moment..."

"*Bravo* Pippo! We'll get the two girls to come in and identify their aggressor. That way, we can hold at least one of them for grievous bodily harm while we're waiting for the forensics' report on Benedetto Gentile."

Pippo nodded distractedly.

"Come on Pippo! What's bothering you?" asked Beppe.

"You know I've got a friend who's on Pescara's local council, don't you?"

Beppe and Sonia shook their heads. Pippo wore an expression of mild guilt.

"It's not a crime to be friends with a politician, Pippo," said Beppe. "It can even be useful at times."

Pippo grinned. "It's OK – he's a member of Le Cinque Stelle!" he assured them, as if belonging to the up-and-coming protest party justified the friendship. "There's a storm brewing up in the town hall because they think they've found a link between the *assessore* in charge of building contracts and the contractor who is building all those new apartments which are springing up like mushrooms in Tagliamonte, the village just outside the city. *(assessore = local councillor)*

Beppe winced at the simile which his colleague had used.

"Oh, sorry, *capo* - I wasn't thinking. They reckon the *assessore* took a massive back-hander to allow that particular contractor to begin building."

Beppe knew what was coming.

"And they've traced the source of the capital back to what appears to be one of the clans in Foggia – right, Pippo?" said Beppe, supplying the punch line.

"Yes, *capo* - I think all this stuff about intimidating prostitutes and shopkeepers is just a red herring, meant to distract our attention from what is really going on. We've also had a tip-off that the disco-club in down-town Pescara – the one called *The Night Owl* – has suddenly got a new supplier of drugs on a massive scale."

"Well done, Pippo. At least we shall all be busy for the foreseeable future. Let's nail that thug who beat up the girl – Bella – before we start worrying about the rest. We shall need to involve the *Guardia di Finanza* again to look into your *tangente* scam." *(tangente = bribe/ back-hander)*

Sonia was nudging Beppe.

"Ah yes, Pippo... we had an idea last night, Sonia and I. How would you like a little boat trip up the coast tomorrow? We would be very grateful if you could take my boat up to Silvi Marina, with some of our belongings, and sort out a new mooring for us. Does that appeal to you?"

Pippo was grinning broadly, flattered that his *capo* trusted him with his prized possession.

"Can I bring my girl-friend with me?" asked Pippo tentatively, fearing he might be overstepping the mark. The reaction he got was predictable.

"Since when have you...?" asked Sonia in surprise, but did not finish the sentence.

"She's only just come into my life," explained Pippo.

"What's her name, Pippo?" asked Sonia, curiosity getting the better of her.

"Mariangela," said Pippo defensively, as if he wished to avoid further interrogation. Beppe had that knowing glint in his eyes which Pippo knew too well.

"Bring her round to the 'Sleeping Beauty' apartment at about seven this evening. We'll meet you both there," said Beppe. "Tomorrow you'll be on boat duty – as long as the sea remains calm enough for the trip. Now let's get on with the day's work. Pippo can you go and fetch Eva and Bella and bring them here, please? We need them to identify the one who set himself up as their pimp. He's almost certainly our candidate for the beach murder too."

Back in Loreto Aprutino, *Capitano* Enrico Nardini was sitting behind the desk in his office. In front of him, the hunters – all bar one – were perched in nervous expectation on a row of plastic chairs facing the *Carabiniere* captain. Enrico's subordinate, *Tenente* Ludo Mozzagrogna, was standing stiffly behind his chief, looking embarrassed and ill-at-ease. His father had drummed it into his head that hunters had inherited centuries' worth of privileges which should never be taken away. Their ancestors had been the hunter-gatherers who supplied food and protection for their vulnerable women-folk and children. "Nothing has fundamentally changed over time," Ludo's father had brain-washed his son into believing.

"Where's Giancarlo?" asked Enrico Nardini affably. "We can't really begin without him, can we?" Nobody present was aware of the deception being practised on them. It had been Enrico himself who had rung Giancarlo up to inform him the interrogation had been reconvened for the following day.

"It will add to their sense of insecurity," Beppe had told him the day before.

The six hunters shifted on their chairs and looked at each other, waiting for one of them to break the silence. The *Capitano's* relaxed, amicable attitude towards them was making them wonder what was going on. This was precisely the reaction which Beppe Stancato had advised his colleague to create. The youngest hunter present was looking more than anxious. He was petrified with guilt that he had, in that moment of panic, revealed to the *Capitano* that only one gun had been fired in the direction of the victim. He tried to console himself that he could always plead that his memory of the accident must have been confused. But he knew this

Carabiniere officer would not be readily fooled. Enrico Nardini had even taken the precaution of confiscating all their mobile phones, which lay neatly side by side on his desk.

Enrico Nardini looked at his watch and sighed.

"We'll just have to begin without your... colleague, *signori*. But I shall have to detain you until he arrives... I am sure you can understand why from my point of view."

The *capitano* was still smiling affably at all of them. He stood up so abruptly that all six of the hunters nearly jumped out of their chairs. But all Enrico did was to walk round his desk. He began talking in soothing tones as he quite deliberately walked in a circle round the six seated hunters. They were unsure as to whether they should swivel their heads round to follow the *capitano* with their eyes. After two revolutions they grew tired of trying and sat facing the empty desk behind which Ludo Mozzagrogna was still standing rigidly to attention. Enrico was just beginning to enjoy himself.

"Well, *signori*," he was saying. "I am sure you will be relieved to know that we have decided not to press charges of manslaughter against you. I intend to take a written statement from all of you before you leave today and this sad matter can be put behind us..."

The sight of six bodies each sinking back into their uncomfortable plastic chairs was almost comical. Enrico could sense them mentally wiping the sweat from their brows.

"All, that is, apart from *one* of you."

Their relief was short-lived. They twisted their necks round to look at Enrico, who had deliberately waited until he was behind the row of chairs before delivering these words:

"Needless to say," continued the *capitano* as he resumed walking in circles round them, "you will be banned from hunting for three years to come. Your guns will remain in police custody and your hunting licences will be revoked. I am sure you will be prepared to make this sacrifice in memory of the victim. Your friend Gregorio Cardone was, by all accounts, a happy, good-looking man who enjoyed life to the full..." Enrico's voice continued to sound so reasonable. It was deeply disconcerting.

"That's not fair," said one the hunters. "We can't all take the blame for..."

He was nudged into silence by the man sitting next to him.

"Shut it, Guido!" he hissed under his breath.

"Now I'm going to ask you to go to our canteen downstairs," continued the *capitano*, as if he had failed to register the brief exchange between the two hunters. "*Tenente* Mozzagrogna will bring you coffee and sandwiches before we get you to write your statements in private. I really can't imagine what is holding up your colleague," Enrico lied smoothly. He was feeling an absurd sense of gratitude towards his mentor, *Commissario* Stancato. What insight he had gained in the space of a few minutes! But the task was not quite finished – and the rest of the charade involved his *tenente,* who, Enrico knew, was suffering from torn loyalties.

Tenente Mozzagrogna entered the canteen and placed sandwiches and plastic cups full of coffee from the neighbouring bar on the table in front of his 'prisoners'. He was looking even more embarrassed than before. To the surprise of the six hunters, the *tenente* sat down at the table and began eating a sandwich in their company. They had wanted to discuss strategy in light of the *capitano's* unexpected *volta face.* It was obvious that the *tenente* had something to say which he was reluctant to get off his chest. They were unaware that this junior policeman was more embarrassed about laying a trap for his 'fellow' hunters than being disloyal to his superior officer. One way or the other,

Tenente Mozzagrogna did not have too much trouble acting out his role in a convincing manner.

"Listen to me, *ragazzi*. I shouldn't be telling you this, but you ought to know that the *capitano* already knows that Gregorio Cardone was killed by a shot from one single gun. I'm sorry, lads, but...just be careful what you say."

The youngest member of the group breathed a sigh of relief. The *capitano* had not revealed him as the snake in the grass who had supplied this piece of information. Out of gratitude, he resolved to write his statement according to the truth – at least as close to the facts as gang loyalty allowed.

Tenente Mozzagrogna stood up to leave just as *Capitano* Nardini entered, giving the hunters no time to discuss what they should write. Enrico got them all to sit apart from one and other – like high school students sitting their *maturità* exams. Thus isolated and under the watchful eye of the *capitano,* they all gave variations of the same account. The victim, Gregorio Cardone, had disappeared into the undergrowth – a call of nature, most of the six hunters supposed – and one of their group had followed him at a distance saying he was just going to check if Gregorio was alright. They had all jumped when they heard the shot. The man in question came running back looking wild with horror, saying his gun had accidently gone off when he saw a movement in the undergrowth.

"Help me, *ragazzi!*" he had appealed to his fellow-hunters. He knew he could rely on the *solidarietà* of his comrades. Not one of the six men writing their statement had mentioned any names. But the threat of having their precious guns confiscated and their 'licence to kill' being revoked was enough to loosen the bonds of allegiance.

Enrico Nardini did not mind at all that the guilty man had not been named. He was certain that his name was Giancarlo Teatina, whom he had called earlier to say the interrogation had been postponed. Enrico had been round to see Gregorio Cardone's widow the day before. She was upset but pointed out with tightly repressed anger that her husband had been having an affair with Giancarlo Teatina's wife. Beppe knew too that the shot pellets found in the body matched the cartridges used by Teatina.

"Thank you for your help today," Enrico said to his colleague. "I think we might have a case of murder to deal with."

"*Bravo, capo!*" replied Ludo Mozzagrogna with reluctant admiration.

Back with his *fidanzata* at the end of another long working day, Enrico had related the details of the whole tragic mess.

"*Bravo, amore!* You're brilliant at your job!" Alessia had complimented him.

He had to admit, sheepishly, that he had *Commissario* Stancato to thank for the strategy he had employed.

"But you are the one who put it into practice," she pointed out loyally. She was not going to allow her partner to be anything less than a hero in her eyes.

At least publicly, Enrico considered, it might be preferable for the *Carabinieri* to be able to take the credit. It was better for the status of the supposedly grander body of the *Carabinieri* not to admit that they had been helped by the local police force. Privately, he would find some way of thanking Beppe Stancato for the invaluable insight he had provided when it came to handling complex interrogations.

"Deceit is the keyword, Enrico," Beppe had said to him half-jokingly. "Hoodwink them into believing what you want them to think…" It had worked like a charm.

* * *

"Yes, *commissario,* that's him. He's the one who came to our apartment and laid into Bella," stated Eva without a second's hesitation.

Bella just looked at the image on the internal television monitor and nodded. She had tears in her eyes. Beppe, in the company of Pippo, charged him with assault and grievous bodily harm, ignoring his predictable denials of guilt. His sidekick was arrested too on a lesser charge of intimidation. Pippo recognised the aggressor as Luciano Schiavone, a local Foggia 'enforcer' with an unpredictable and violent reputation. Pippo also identified the clan he worked for – the clan led by a *boss* whose surname was Luzzi.

"That is something positive we've achieved today," commented Beppe wearily. He was feeling the delayed effect of having lost a night's sleep in Damiano's cellar. The two mobsters were put into holding cells pending the result of the ballistics tests on the bullet found in Benedetto's brain and the pistol confiscated by Pippo, Gino and Danilo.

At half past seven that evening, Beppe and Sonia returned to the sea-front apartment where they met with Pippo and his newly acquired *fidanzata,* Mariangela. Pippo introduced her to Beppe and Sonia, hoping that his chief would not remember where he had seen Mariangela before. It was a vain hope.

"I'm so pleased for you and Pippo, Mariangela," said Beppe sincerely. "But I'm surprised that your father can spare you from your busy restaurant."

She smiled at Beppe. "Oh, there are plenty of cousins who can take my place at *La Vestina, commissario.* I think my dad is just pleased at the prospect of no longer having me under his feet."

Sonia cottoned on quickly – as soon as she realised where Beppe must have seen Mariangela before.

"Well, congratulations, Pippo! You certainly don't hang about," added Beppe. "You did well, *amico mio.*"

"I'll take that as a compliment, *commissario* – even if it is bordering on the sexist!" said Mariangela.

Beppe looked sternly at her, but his eyes acknowledged her barbed comment appreciatively.

Introductions were over. It was time to get down to making arrangements for Pippo and his *fidanzata* to take charge of the boat.

Beppe led them to the quay where his boat, *L'Angelo Custode* was moored.

Mariangela had an engaging, rippling laugh. "I don't suppose anybody else in Italy has come up with a name like *The Guardian Angel* for their boat," she said to Beppe.

Beppe explained every little quirky characteristic of his vessel that might manifest itself during their short journey up the coast to Silvi Marina. He fussed over each and every detail of the working of the engine until he was satisfied that Pippo and Mariangela would cope. Sonia was reminded of a father worrying about the welfare of a son or daughter about to venture on their first holiday uncluttered by parents. She smiled knowingly at Beppe who read the clear message in her eyes. He grinned back at her and shrugged his shoulders in acknowledgement of their wordless exchange. It took ten minutes to load up the boat with suitcases and boxes of basic cooking gear.

Pippo Cafarelli and girlfriend were standing on the pavement outside the apartment, ready to wave the couple off as they surfaced from the garage below. Sonia was driving her own car, laden with the remainder of their possessions, while an exhausted Beppe slumped in the passenger seat.

Suddenly, Pippo was alert. A black Audi had pulled out a few metres down the road and was following Sonia's Ypsilon. He could not identify why this should make him uneasy. He had nothing to go on but the instinct of a good policeman – added to the suspicion aroused by the appearance of the two men inside the Audi.

"*Oh Dio!*" he muttered under his breath as Mariangela lowered her arm from waving a final 'goodbye' in the direction of the departing car.

"Mariangela – go back to the flat. I'm going to follow them. I think there might be trouble ahead."

Mariangela sensed the dread in his voice without understanding exactly why.

"No way, Pippo! I'm coming too."

There was no time to argue as they both ran for the police car and set off at a fast pace along the route which Pippo knew they would be taking. Nevertheless, it took Pippo a good five minutes, driving over the speed limit, before he realised that he must have taken a different turning on to the main road to Atri and ended up ahead of Sonia's Ypsilon and the black Audi hot on their tail. Pippo and Mariangela waited in a side turning for a tense couple of minutes before Mariangela shouted out: "There they go!"

Pippo got his girlfriend to dial Beppe's number four or five times, the tension increasing exponentially as they failed each time to get a response. It was likely that his chief, not suspecting any trouble, had switched off his mobile phone and dozed off while Sonia drove him home. "Scroll down and find Sonia on the list, Mariangela. Try ringing her..."

They were only a few minutes' drive from Atri. The occupants of the black Audi would soon learn where their quarry was heading. Pippo needed to take drastic action.
"Hang on tight," he told his bewildered new girlfriend, who wasn't sure whether she was excited by this abrupt change from waitress to flying squad cop – or merely scared.

Pippo switched the siren and the flashing blue light on and closed the gap between the police car and the black Audi.

210

Some five hundred metres or so ahead, Sonia looked at her dozing partner and decided to put her foot down to take her Ypsilon out of range of the pursuit, which she could just make out in her rear-view mirror. She was distracted by the shrill ringing of her own phone, but decided that whoever was phoning her could wait until she had reached the outskirts of Atri – and home.

As the Audi occupants, unwilling to be distracted from their deadly mission, tried to ignore the pursuing police car, Pippo carried out the only manoeuvre possible. He overtook the Audi, headlights flashing and signalled the Audi to pull over to the side of the deserted A-road.

"Stay where you are, Mariangela," he ordered as he stepped out of the car, revolver holster already unbuckled in readiness.

"Will you step out of your car, *signore,*" he ordered the driver peremptorily, "Hands behind your head."

The passenger, on the nearside of the Audi, had his hand on the door handle. Pippo knew that he had got himself – and his new *fidanzata* – into a dangerous situation.

Instead of getting out of the car, the driver simply leered at Pippo and spoke a few words in the accent of his native Foggia. Pippo had to stifle his surprise. He had assumed that the two characters in the car would be from Naples, carrying out a second attempt at eliminating his chief. Why was he being pursued by the *Sacra Corona Unita?*

"Show us some ID first," snarled the driver. "We keep hearing about roaming gangs of highway bandits dressed up as cops."

"My name is *Commissario* Stancato," he said in a moment of rash bravado, instinctively wishing to protect the identity of his *capo* in the car somewhere ahead of them. It was dark apart from the torch which Pippo was shining in the two gangsters' faces. They could not clearly see Pippo's face – nor make out his rank.

"I would like to know why you were following my junior colleagues' car," stated Pippo with an authority which he did not feel. He had been dreading this moment for ages – the moment when he would have to confront members of the SCU clan face-to-face; the moment when the shadows from his past would inexorably catch up with him.

The two gangsters in the car looked at each other in surprise. They had assumed that the cop whose life they were supposed to mess up was in the car they had been chasing." How had the *sbirri* managed to make the switch?" their glance clearly implied. *(i sbirri = cops : pigs – slang)*

The rapidity of their reaction took Pippo by surprise. The driver swung open the door violently, knocking Pippo off balance. His torch rolled away somewhere into the darkness.

Simultaneously, Mariangela, looking in the rear view mirror and realising Pippo was in deep trouble, decided it was not the moment to ponder upon the wisdom of her actions. She used the only weapon at her disposal – a state police car with flashing blue lights. "It must drive like a normal car," she found herself thinking irrelevantly, as she shifted across into the driver's seat in one graceful, athletic movement. Pippo had not removed the keys from the ignition and the engine was running.

The gangster was holding a revolver in his hand aimed at Pippo's midriff. His intended victim was lying vulnerable on the tarmac in the certain knowledge that his end was nigh.

"Well, *commissario,* this looks like the end of your career," the mobster sneered. With a ruthlessness that only a habitual killer could muster, the mobster fired at Pippo's left kneecap without warning. Pippo could not imagine that such searing agony was possible in life. Now the man was pointing his revolver at Pippo's right knee. Mariangela swung the police car round with squealing tyres and aimed the car directly at the mobster, who was distracted by the headlights bearing down on him at speed. The blue flashing light dazzled him for an instant. Pippo, seizing this last minute reprieve, pulled out his police revolver from his prone position and shot the Mafioso in the heart. His sidekick just wanted to make a dash for freedom, but Pippo let off a second shot that struck the man in his right shoulder as he was getting back into the car. A third shot punctured the Audi's front tyre. Pippo had managed to ignore the agonising pain for those precious five seconds. Now he was conscious only of the excruciating pain which seemed to be tearing his whole body apart.

There was a screech of brakes as Mariangela brought the police car to a standstill, just centimetres away from where the dead mobster was lying. Pippo no longer needed to keep the pain to himself. He screamed out a lungful of air and wailed in agony, clutching his shattered knee.

Mariangela was phoning for an ambulance, shouting urgent directions into the phone. "And send the police too – my boyfriend's been shot in the knee by the mob!" she cried. She cradled Pippo's head in her lap and uttered a deluge of comforting words until his body's natural anaesthetic began to numb the pain.

There was a car coming towards them at speed from the direction of Atri. A frantic Mariangela wanted to flag the car down – just to have someone with her until the ambulance or the police arrived. The approaching car drew to a halt. With a cry of utter joy and relief, Mariangela recognised Sonia and Beppe leaping out of the Ypsilon and running towards them with a look of unabated horror on their faces.

Beppe took in the whole situation within seconds as he gripped his colleague's hand.

"Oh, Pippo! What have I let you in for?" Pippo looked as if he was about to pass out.

"It was my own fault, Beppe," he said, his speech slurred. "I pretended to be you."

"Impersonating a senior police officer, eh?" he added, trying to make light of the words he had just heard. Sonia had rushed to her car and returned with a first aid kit. She cut the leg off Pippo's trousers above the knee.

"*Oh, mio Dio!*" was all she said. Mariangela nearly fainted.

Beppe got through to a special emergency number to ensure that an ambulance and police back-up would arrive quickly.

He took one look at the dead mobster and turned his attention to the surviving thug sitting bleeding from his shoulder all over the car's upholstery. Beppe fetched a pair of handcuffs from the police car and quite mercilessly attached the mobster's left arm to the steering wheel.

"Now talk!" ordered the *commissario*.

"I gotta have a doctor," moaned his prisoner.

Beppe, like Pippo before him, was taken aback by the Pugliese accent.

"Your injuries are the least of your worries, *bastardo!*" snapped Beppe. "Tell me who put you up to this?"

"Who *are* you?" asked the injured mobster.

"I am *Commissario* Stancato."

"But that other cop told us *he* was the *commissario*. How many of you are there?"

The mobster earned himself a quick slap round the face from Beppe.

"Whose orders are you acting under, you piece of low-life shit?" snarled Beppe.

"I can't tell you that, *commissario*... They'd kill me."

214

"Fine, I'll just let you bleed to death here and now." Beppe squeezed the gangster's shoulder hard where his wound was.

"Alright," he yelled out in excruciating pain. "I was under orders from Arturo Luzzi in Foggia. We were told to maim the *commissario* for life – not kill him. We were doing a favour for a colleague in Napoli..."

Beppe slapped him hard round the face again.

"I want a name, you bastard – not his social status!"

"Alfieri... Stefano Alfieri..." screamed the mobster, knowing from that moment onwards, he had signed his own death warrant - or at best be on the run for the rest of his life.

Ten minutes later, the whole crew, with ambulances in tow, arrived on the scene and set about clearing up the mess.

"What made you both come back, Sonia?" asked Mariangela while Beppe was busy supervising operations. The thought had been puzzling her for the last few minutes, as soon as the pressure on them eased a little.

"Well, when Beppe woke up as we drew up outside my parents' home, he noticed Pippo had been trying to call him. And when I saw his number on my phone too, we realised that something must be wrong. We suddenly realised that the police car we saw coming up behind us must be something to do with you two."

"*Grazie a Dio,* Sonia," said Mariangela.

"I'm so sorry you have had such a violent baptism of fire," said Sonia gently. "I hope it won't ..."

"No, Sonia! Pippo is going to need me more than ever," replied Mariangela in a decisive tone of voice.

Mariangela insisted that she would stay with Pippo for as long as was necessary. She left in the ambulance holding Pippo's hand while the crew did their best to alleviate his immediate suffering. It was gone eleven o'clock before a desperately weary pair of police officers headed back in silence towards their new home in Atri. They simply could not face unloading the car that night.

The following morning, round a late breakfast table, Beppe told Sonia's parents that they intended to find somewhere else to live so as not to endanger the lives of their hosts.

Once again, Sonia's father stood up without a word. He returned with a hunting rifle in his hands.

"We are well equipped to protect ourselves, thank you, Beppe - and able to protect our family as well. You are as safe as you'll ever be in this house," said Sonia's father simply.

Beppe looked in gratitude at this doughty sixty-eight-year old, valiantly gripping his rifle.

"Grazie signore - I won't waste my breath giving you my opinion on private citizens who set themselves up as law-enforcers."

"Just as well," said Sonia's father, almost smiling for once. "That's settled, then," he concluded, "No more talk of you moving out."

Beppe and Sonia set off for Pescara much later that morning.

"Now we shall go and reprimand Officer Cafarelli for his misplaced act of heroism," said Beppe to Sonia, wondering if he could ever find a way to thank his colleague adequately for the sacrifice he had made the previous night. "That's *two* of you I shall have to keep out of trouble from now on."

"Three of us, in point of fact," Sonia corrected him. "Do you think Pippo will ever be able to walk normally again, Beppe?"

"They can work wonders these days - even with injuries like Pippo's," replied Beppe after a pause which lasted several seconds. He could not face the thought that Pippo might never be fit for police work again – nor ignore the fact that it should have been him who received such a crippling injury.

Pippo was lying sedated in a private room in Pescara's main hospital. Mariangela was fast asleep, curled up in foetal position on an armchair.

"I owe my life to her, Beppe, Sonia," Pippo said huskily. "And I've only known her a few days. I'm sorry, *capo* – your boat is still moored in Pescara."

"That is the least of my concerns at the moment, Pippo. But for goodness sake, make sure you are on at least one leg by November 20th. You've got to be my best man."

Pippo managed a fleeting grin of pleasure in their direction before his eyes closed in slumber as nervous exhaustion and the sedatives took hold again. Mariangela stirred in her sleep but did not wake up...

20: Of wedding bells and bombshells...

The news of Pippo's heroic intervention to protect his chief from the mafia and his subsequent injury were very soon common knowledge, from Bianca Bomba and Marco Pollutri, the technicians in the basement, up to the top floor where the *Questore* himself registered his horror at this violent turn of events which had struck his police force in Pescara overnight. Beppe had convened a general meeting as soon as he arrived at the *Questura*. The usual banter during such proceedings was absent as the shell-shocked gathering were told that one of their most popular colleagues was lying sedated and possibly suffering from an injury that might permanently exclude him from active police work.

"Concerning that aspect of this tragic incident," said Beppe, "we must hope and pray that modern surgery can restore him to his former state of physical glory. At the moment, we must be thankful that his life has been spared. I understand his injuries could have been much more serious had it not been for the courageous intervention of his new *fidanzata*. I'm sure Pippo will happily fill in the details when you go and visit him."

Beppe's announcement that he and Sonia were to be married the following month was met with a sober, but protracted round of applause.

"Naturally, you will all be invited to be present for the ceremony at the Cathedral of San Cetteo on the twentieth of November – and somewhere afterwards too. I'll ask one of you to organise that side of things."

It was Giacomo D'Amico, Beppe's longest serving officer, who offered to take on the task: "With the greatest of pleasure, *capo...* and Sonia." he stated simply.

The team left the meeting room in sombre mood. The news of Pippo's fate appeared to have hit *Agente* Remo

Mastrodicasa harder than most. Out of the corner of his eye, Beppe noticed Remo shaking his head while in deep thought. Beppe assumed that Pippo's injury had aroused his colleague's latent aversion to shooting people – or being shot at.

Beppe had to force himself physically and mentally to continue with routine police work after their meeting. He was saved from having to make a decision as to what his priorities should be by a summons from the *Questore*. While he and his *commissario* were discussing events and what action to take, the *Questore* became aware of a face peering in through the little square of glass set in the door to his office. Beppe, with his back to the door, became aware that his chief's eyes kept looking at something behind him. It was unheard of for Dante Di Pasquale not to give his interlocutors his undivided attention. Beppe raised a quizzical eyebrow.

"I believe Remo Mastrodicasa, is hovering outside the door, Beppe. He's obviously in a quandary as to whether to knock on the door or not. He must have something on his mind. Maybe we should put him out of his misery."

Remo stood to attention, stiff-backed and red with embarrassment. The *Questore* offered him a seat, which was declined.

"I couldn't do that, chief... chiefs," he announced.

"Tell us what's on your mind, Remo," said Beppe encouragingly.

"I...I just wanted to say... what's happened to Pippo left me deeply shocked."

"We all feel the same way, Remo," said Beppe, intuiting what his nervous colleague was about to say. There was another even longer pause while Remo continued to stand to attention, his eyes seemingly fixed on some point somewhere outside the window. Beppe and the *Questore* waited patiently.

"You remember, *capo,* they were going to convert Don Alfieri's house into a cookery school? Well, they're advertising for a couple, a man and a woman, to run the school and they want to appoint someone immediately to set it up. Marta and me, well, we would like to apply for the job. I'm so sorry, *capo,* but I really feel I would be better out of the police force..." The fifty or so words had been delivered at great speed without, as far as Beppe could ascertain, a pause for breath.

"I'm sorry, *signori...*" concluded Remo.

With a nod from the *Questore,* Beppe stood up and held Remo's shaking arms at the elbow.

"Whatever you feel would make you and your *fidanzata,* Marta, happy, Remo, we will support you totally."

There were tears of relief and gratitude in the corner of Remo's eyes. Beppe was reminded yet again of Catarella. Remo, however, saluted the two senior officers smartly.

"Mille grazie signori," he said, turned round and marched smartly towards the door, too proud to show his emotions.

The two senior officers remained speechless for some time before they could continue their detailed analysis of the events which had transpired over the last few days and what actions needed to be set in motion.

"Don't take it too hard, Beppe," said Dante Di Pasquale as an afterthought – referring to Remo's resignation. "It was bound to happen sooner or later. What happened to Pippo triggered the inevitable reaction."

Beppe nodded. "I guess you're right, *capo.* But Remo will be missed by more people than he realises."

* * *

The ballistics report on the bullet extracted from Benedetto Gentile's head confirmed that the shot had been fired from the pistol confiscated from the two mobsters who had attacked Bella and Eva. Beppe had to summon up his reserves of energy to deal with the mobsters. He added the charge of murder to that of grievous bodily harm. He got *Agenti* Simone and Martelli to fetch the mobsters from the local jail and harangued them for thirty minutes before charging them. Beppe's spirits revived somewhat as he took pleasure in seeing their faces collapse when he thanked them for their invaluable role in bringing their clan boss, Arturo Luzzi, to justice. It had been a bit of a shot in the dark, based on the confession of the wounded accomplice of the mobster who had shot off Pippo Caferelli's left knee – but it was obvious that his words had hit the mark.

"*Al fresco* for you two for the rest of your manhood. I trust you will enjoy the food and hospitality of an Italian State prison until you are both middle-aged," he concluded with sadistic pleasure. *(Al fresco = out in the countryside. An Italian reference to 'out-of-town' jails)*

He would deal with the mobster whom Pippo had shot in the shoulder later on. He had been transferred to the prison hospital outside Pescara earlier on that afternoon.

Beppe was happy to leave his chief, Dante di Pasquale, to contact the *Carabiniere* colonel, Ricardo Grimaldi about the Pescara night club called *The Night Owl* and the *Guardia di Finanza* chief concerning the suspected *tangente* paid to the corrupt local counsellor.

"Ah," said the *Colonnello* with ironic humour, "Please thank your *commissario* for making sure we remain fully employed."

"Yes, *colonnello*, there is no time to get bored when my senior officer is around. Remind me to tell you the story about his encounter with mushrooms when we next meet up. That will keep you spellbound," concluded the *Questore*.

* * *

It was nearly four in the afternoon. Nobody had phoned the police station to report a crime for at least three hours. Beppe wanted to call it a day and drive with Sonia to the hospital to visit his injured colleague. He went in search of Sonia but found Oriana instead by the reception desk.

"Sonia just popped out for a few minutes, *capo.*"

Her chief must have displayed a moment's anxiety so Oriana continued with an overly conspiratorial light in her eyes, thought Beppe: "She went to the chemist's just down the road. She'll only be a few minutes."

By the look on Oriana's face, Beppe assumed that Sonia must have let Oriana in on their secret. He put on his sternest and most menacing glare, which would have left anyone but Oriana quavering in their police boots. She raised both hands, fingers splayed, in a deprecating gesture.

"*Acqua in bocca, capo!*" she said smiling disarmingly at him.

"Let me know when she gets back, please Oriana," he said relenting.

Back in his office, the internal phone rang unexpectedly. It was the *Questore* again, requesting his presence upstairs.

"I have just initiated the process by which our Pippo Cafarelli will receive a *Medaglia al merito di servizio della Polizia di Stato* in recognition of his act of great courage yesterday. I hope you approve, *commissario.*"

"Thank heavens for police chiefs like you, *capo*. He deserves such an honour – even if it was in defence of an officer who was blithely returning home with nothing other than sleep on his mind! My lack of vigilance was…"

The *Questore* held up a hand to stem the flow of words.

"Rest assured. I don't suppose Pippo saw it that way, Beppe. But I'm glad you approve of my idea."

Back in his office, the phone rang again.

"A call for you, *commissario* – a gentleman called Ernesto Carlettini," said the officer on front desk duty.

"*Sì? Pronto signor Carlettini,*" began Beppe repressing his instant feeling of antagonism.

We were just wondering, commissario, if it might be possible to go and sort out my brother's house? We believe that it is no longer a crime scene.

One of my best officers is lying in hospital with a shattered knee-cap and his own brother's body has not even been released for burial, and he's thinking about his precious financial status, thought Beppe. Without fully analysing his own reaction – exacerbated by the feeling of guilt he was harbouring about Pippo's plight – the *commissario* took an inordinate delight in winding up this *piccolo borghese* of a man.

"Naturally you can go and visit your brother's house," he began ingratiatingly. "Do you have a front door key?"

Yes, of course I do, commissario.

"I only ask because you might not realise the lock had to be changed after the *Carabinieri* broke the door down."

I didn't realise that, commiss…

"Captain Nardini probably has the new keys. All you have to do is go to the *Carabiniere* station in Loreto Aprutino. I'm quite certain he will give you a cautious go-ahead."

Why 'cautious', commissario?

The note of petulance had crept back into *fratello* Carlettini's voice. Beppe prepared himself to deliver the *coup de grâce.*

"Oh, I suppose you haven't heard the news, *dottore*. Your brother was married to his Sri-Lankan housekeeper, Dinusha. Technically, the house does not belong to *you*."

Beppe noted with sadistic glee the gagging sound that was emitted on the other end of the line as he hung up. He looked up and saw Sonia regarding him with a mixture of disapproval and amusement on her face. "No comment!" her eyes said. Now they could go to visit Pippo in the hospital.

* * *

Pippo looked more like an invalid than he had on the day before in the immediate aftermath of the shooting. Neither Beppe nor Sonia were able to disguise the momentary shock on their faces as they stepped into the hospital room. Pippo managed a wan smile.

"It's the effect of the operation and the sedatives," he said. "Don't worry, I feel comfortable enough. I just hate being dependent on other people to make even the smallest movement."

"Where's Mariangela?" asked Sonia, secretly hoping that she had not abandoned Pippo to his fate and returned home to her father's restaurant in Penne.

"She's been here all night and most of today," Pippo reassured them. "The doctor had practically to force her to go and get some proper sleep. She's gone to my flat. She insists that I was the one who rescued her from the prospect of serving up *porchetta* for the rest of her life and she's not going to walk out on me now..."

The three discussed the forthcoming wedding just to focus on something more optimistic for all of them.

"The cathedral is ours for the day on the twentieth of next month," said Beppe. "All we need to do is decide where to hold the reception afterwards..."

"I know just the place!" announced Pippo and Sonia as if their response had been rehearsed.

"*Da Pipè,*" said Sonia.

"Just the place I was going to suggest," said Pippo.

"Where on earth is *Da Pipè?*" asked Beppe and instantly wished he hadn't.

"Oh, *everybody* in Pescara knows where..."

Beppe blocked his ears and started singing *Fratelli d'Italia* to drown out their words. *(The Italian national anthem)*

Thus, their visit ended in good spirits.

When they left Pippo to rest, Sonia and Beppe went in search of the surgeon charged with Pippo's welfare. He introduced himself as Daniele Orsini.

"I'm afraid we shall have to send him to Rome, *commissario...*" he said including Sonia in his glance. "Don't worry - they can work miracles these days. We've already sent the X-rays of his good knee to the Rome clinic. They will make a replica kneecap on one of those 3D nano-copiers and fit it to the thigh and calf bones. The muscles will then need to be repaired so that he should be able to walk normally again."

"And how long will all that take?" asked Sonia fearfully.

"Oh not long – eighteen months at the most," stated Daniele Orsini.

They both gasped in horror. The second bombshell of the day - after Remo had unexpectedly announced his resignation.

"Does Pippo know this kind of time-scale is involved in his recovery?" Beppe asked the surgeon.

"No, we shall break that news to him gently, when he's got more used to the situation. It's not all bad, *commissario.* Don't forget he'll be able to get around easily enough on crutches with his right leg - as soon as we are certain his wound is not infected."

On the way home, both Sonia and Beppe said very little.

"We shall know tonight, *amore*..."

"Of course, Sonia - your secret visit to the pharmacist! Haven't you...?"

"No, I was waiting until we were on our own. This is a moment that has to be shared, don't you think?"

Beppe placed his right hand on Sonia's thigh for a few seconds as they drove rapidly home towards Atri. Beppe constantly checked his rear view mirror.

* * *

The neglected *Angelo Custode,* still loaded with their belongings, bobbed gently up and down in its moorings in the marina back in Pescara. A fresh, cleansing north-easterly wind was beginning to pick up – the first harbinger of the change of season ahead.

* * *

A phone call as they were preparing happily for bed, with the good news tucked up soundly within Sonia's belly. Beppe knew instinctively that it would be his mother in Calabria, sensing when the least opportune moment for a conversation with her son was ripe.

This is your mother speaking, Giuseppe...

"I know that, *mamma.* We were just preparing for bed."

You should go to bed earlier – with the busy life you lead. So busy, it seems, that it is always your own mother who has to phone YOU.

"We have been literally rushed off our feet, *mamma.* We've moved house, by the way. I was going to tell you, but..."

How come I can still get through to you on this number, Giuseppe? Are you sure you've moved house? Or is this just another of your unconvincing excuses for leaving your mother in the lurch...?

Sonia was beginning to feel the need to giggle out loud – her usual reaction to phone conversations between Beppe and his overly doting mother.

"It's a mobile phone, *mamma.* It tends to follow me around wherever I go."

Who's this 'we' you keep on referring to?

Evidently, his mother had belatedly picked up on the plural pronoun.

"Sonia and me, *mamma.* Surely you can't have forgotten....?"

Oh, your nice police woman friend. Isn't it about time you got married to her?

"We *are* getting married, *mamma.* I was going to phone you tomorrow. We're getting married next month on the..."

I suppose you will expect us all to come up to that strange foreign city you've decided to live in? Now you've rejected the town of your birth!

"Mamma, you *know* why I left Catanzaro. Besides which, you can hardly expect the whole police force of Pescara to relocate to Catanzaro just for our wedding, now can you?"

Sonia was gesticulating to Beppe to let her speak to his mother.

"Here's Sonia, *mamma.* She would like a word with you..."

"Buona sera, Imelda..." began Sonia soothingly. "How are you keeping? I'm so looking forward to meeting you again..."

Beppe was praying she would not mention she was expecting a child. He need not have been concerned. Sonia understood her future mother-in-law perfectly. By the end of the conversation, *'mamma'* was purring like a cat.

Grazie a Dio, Sonia, that my son has someone like you to keep him on the straight and narrow.

They fell asleep immediately after the phone call – all three of them.

* * *

The main event over the intervening weeks before the marriage was due to take place was the arrival of two new recruits to the police headquarters in *Via Pesaro*. The move was precipitated by Beppe telling the *Questore* about Sonia expecting a child, the news that Pippo Cafarelli's absence would be protracted and the pending resignation of Remo Mastrodicasa.

"Misfortunes come in threes, Beppe," the *Questore* had stated with an ironic grin on his face, before congratulating Beppe warmly.

The first recruit to arrive, Luigi Rocco, had the stature and aspect of a Sumo wrestler. He looked as if he could halt a charging rhino in its tracks. He was soon nicknamed *l'Orso Bruno* by the team, in honour of the brown bears which roamed the upper reaches of the Appennine mountain ranges in Abruzzo. He did not once smile until three months had elapsed. The second recruit was in her forties – a fearsome-looking lady called Lina Rapino who had been a prison warden in Pescara's young offenders' penitentiary. "I want to help young people before they get that far," she had stated. Later on, she acquired the nickname of *L'Angelo Vendicatore (The Avenging Angel)* – a sobriquet coined, not by the police officers with whom she worked, but by a group of head teachers whose schools she regularly visited to warn

228

students of the perils of drug abuse. It was often the stressed-out teaching staff who took more notice of her warnings than the students themselves, the Avenging Angel had ironically claimed one day.

Fortunately, a far-sighted *Questore* had spotted the virtues of the two new recruits from the outset - which were not immediately apparent to the other officers. Beppe knew instinctively that his chief's assessment of the newcomers was bound to have been sound.

Nevertheless, a hard-pushed Giacomo D'Amico had leapt at the opportunity to assign the new officers to the reserve team who would have to man the police headquarters on the 20th November while the rest of them attended the wedding. The new recruits seemed quite happy to fulfil this role.

* * *

In the magnificent interior of the packed cathedral of *San Cetteo,* the sunlight, filtered by the warm autumn colours of the stained-glass windows high above the nave, shone down on the expectant figures of a uniformed *commissario,* a lofty archbishop – and a wheel-chair-bound best man. Pippo was wearing the top half of his police uniform; they had given up trying to insert his tightly bandaged left leg into his police trousers. Instead, his good leg was covered by half a pair of old jeans whose left leg had been sheared with scissors along its length.

Beppe's family could easily be distinguished in the front rows of joined-up chairs – they were the only members of the congregation to be wearing warm winter clothes before winter had properly arrived.

"Why did you elect to live in this polar region of Italy, Giuseppe?" his mother had complained almost as soon as they

had stepped off the aeroplane which had deposited them on the tarmac of Pescara airport.

"Just be thankful, *mamma,* we didn't get married in January!"

"Why couldn't you have waited until May?" she suggested in the scornful tone of voice she reserved for those she loved most.

There was no way Beppe could reveal to his deeply traditional mother that his future wife was already carrying their first child.

"We just didn't want to delay being married any longer, *mamma.* You know Sonia. Surely you can understand my haste."

The answer seemed to mollify his mother. Beppe's quiet and deeply-loved father had intuited the true answer. Beppe intercepted the knowing twinkle in his father's eyes and nodded at him.

Without preamble, the cathedral's remarkable organist-cum-university music professor began playing Bach; a soothing piece at first to settle the congregation down.

"Just leave the choice of music to me," he had told Sonia and Beppe beforehand. "You won't be sorry, I promise you."

In the next instance, the strains of Mendelssohn's Wedding March announced the arrival of the bride. Before anyone could register that the music smacked too much of tradition, the organist seemed, without any noticeable transition, to be playing a melodious version of The Triumphal March from Aida with strains of *Fratelli d'Italia* audible from the deep base notes of the pedals.

A smiling bride was flanked by Pippo's Mariangela plus a cousin and two of Sonia's nieces whose sizes graduated evenly downwards from the tallest to the shortest niece who was only seven years old. They were all five adorned in mint green dresses – Sonia's choice of colour. "I can hardly go to the altar in white – even if God and the Archbishop are just about the only ones who know what condition I am in!" she had argued.

"Not forgetting Oriana Salvati, your own parents and, I suspect, my father too," Beppe had added, quite surprised that so many people were already privy to their 'secret'.

It was certainly not going to be an ordinary ceremony. As Sonia and her cortège walked slowly and anything but solemnly up the aisle to the sound of the rousing organ music, a spontaneous clapping of hands burst out from the congregation as the procession drew level with each row of chairs.

The Archbishop had mounted the steps of the altar alone – with a beatific look on his face – and knelt down briefly in prayer. The filtered amber light from the stained glass shone on his bald head like a halo. As the procession approached the bottom steps below the raised altar, Beppe's family and those nearby were treated to a tut of disapproval from Beppe's mother. *"Why isn't she wearing white?"* she asked in a voice which the organ music failed to drown out completely. Beppe's sister, Valentina, sitting next to her mother and clutching a sleeping infant, whispered something into her ear. To amused titters from those in the vicinity, Beppe's mother uttered the words *"Oh Holy Virgin, mother of God!"* while she collapsed heavily onto her chair, crossing herself busily and muttering words which those nearby swore afterwards included the words *'devil's child'.* Whether this was true or not, Beppe's father silenced her with an authoritative finger raised in warning. Nobody had ever witnessed such a thing in public. The effect on Beppe's mother was instant.

On the opposite side of the aisle, Sonia's extended family – including her two elder brothers and their partners and offspring – remained blissfully unaware of the spiritual crisis being played out within the Calabrian contingent of the congregation.

The Archbishop was standing facing the congregation – an imposing spiritual giant whom the congregation saw as a silhouette against the light, his two arms raised in welcome.

Please be seated. Ladies and gentlemen, boys and girls, Children of God... he intoned in his warm voice which echoed round the cathedral. *On this holy day, we are gathered together to celebrate many miracles of life. Before we proceed to the point where we shall be uniting Beppe, Sonia and their future child (A suppressed groan from one member of the congregation) to be as one in the eyes of God, we have a very unusual and delightful duty to perform, in honour of a very brave man. He is quite unprepared for this event, so we must forgive his reaction of surprise. I will now ask our Questore, Dante Di Pasquale to step forward.*

To his initial surprise and shock, Pippo became the centre of attention for the next five minutes as his chief made a speech in praise of his courage in saving the life of his *commissario* and announced the award of the *Croce d'Oro* for bravery beyond the call of duty. As the *Questore* pinned the gold medal on to Pippo's jacket, a smiling Mariangela came and stood behind Pippo, her hands on his shoulders.

"If there was such an award for members of the public," added the *Questore*, "it would certainly be awarded to Pippo's *fidanzata*, Mariangela, who played a vital part in saving his life. I hope that you will both accept this award in spirit – even if the medal happens to be pinned on to a policeman's jacket."

The organist began playing his own version of the national anthem as the whole congregation rose to its feet in applause.

Pippo felt embarrassed despite his joy at the honour bestowed on him. Afterwards he would apologise to both Beppe and Sonia for upstaging them on what was, after all, their special day. His protest was dismissed. "Without you, Pippo, we might not even have been here," said Beppe.

The unconventional Archbishop had one more surprise in store for the congregation. After he had delivered his brief homily in honour of a couple in whose life he had become intimately involved over recent weeks, he asked Beppe and Sonia to turn to face the congregation while he proclaimed the most solemn words on Earth with his back to the congregation. "These two are the ones you should be looking at – not me," he had stated simply. His voice echoed round the cathedral of San Cetteo like the very voice of God himself: *I pronounce you Man and Wife.*

Nearly everybody left the cathedral wondering why nobody else had thought of this obvious reversal of the accepted custom. In what seemed like a twinkling of an eye, Beppe and Sonia were walking proudly down the aisle arm in arm. Sonia's tears were born of joy at the occasion. Her emotions were heightened by the choice of procession music. Not organ music at all – but a recording of Gianni Morandi singing one of his most haunting creations; *Solo insieme saremo felici. (Only together will we be happy)* "How did he know that's my favourite song?" asked Sonia. Beppe was genuinely unable to provide an answer.

Beppe and Sonia had to undergo a further brief ceremony in the vestry in the presence of a representative of the State before their union was legal. Outside the Cathedral, the representatives of the *Carabinieri* and the *Guardia di Finanza* shook the couple by the hand before taking their leave. Even the *Questore* felt he could not desert his official post any longer.

"See you all in an hour's time at *Da Pipè*," called out Beppe. Sonia and he were driven off to change their clothes. Sonia had proclaimed that there was no way she was going to be able to enjoy her food wearing her wedding garb. Beppe felt the same about his official uniform, in which he always felt ill at ease. Besides which, the first unannounced step in their joint lives was to be a short boat trip up the Adriatic to Silvi Marina, where a new berth had been arranged for the *Angelo Custode.*

The logistics of getting their respective family members to the restaurant had been organised meticulously by Giacomo D'Amico.

* * *

At the reception, the speeches and the witty audience participation were over. Don Emanuele had said grace. The copious fish antipasti had given way to three kinds of sea-food pasta. The Pecorino – and Trebbiano - white wine was flowing freely – after the Prosecco. A pause between courses had been agreed with the owner.

Beppe had given a moving talk about his new wife – extolling virtues and graces that she did not know she possessed, or so she claimed. He talked happily about a life-long commitment and the hope of at least three children. Beppe and Sonia were toasted warmly and applauded at length.

"Try to keep away from mushrooms, Beppe," the hospital toxicologist, Bruno Esposito, had interjected when Beppe had dwelt briefly on recent events.

Pippo had delivered a scintillating talk about his *capo,* displaying a dry sense of humour whose existence most of the people present had not previously suspected. Pippo went as near the mark as he dared with his chief.

"And it is now time to reveal a hidden talent that very few people know about. Our *capo* is a remarkable mimic. He can change his voice from a man's to a woman's at will and can imitate almost any regional accent that you care to mention. In fact, his rendition of the voice of the Blessed Virgin Mary is, I believe, well known to his family. *(Nods and smirks from father and sister, a cross look from mamma who remembered being hoodwinked by the 'confession' incident only too well)* It is quite possible that this particular talent saved his life during his most recent escapade. So if you receive a phone call at work from a person you don't recognise, think twice before you dismiss the caller – it may be our much loved and respected leader in disguise. *Commissario,* you have been a strength and an inspiration to us all. *Signori, un brindisi a Beppe e Sonia!"*

The Archbishop had taken the opportunity during the 'inter-course' break in the food to circulate, spending a long time with Beppe's and Sonia's parents – reassuring Beppe's mother that her son was not risking eternal damnation because their child had not been conceived in wedlock. "God, as far as I know, is always ready to bend the rules a bit for the righteous and deserving, don't you agree, *signora?"*

Remo Mastrodicasa, looking relaxed for the first time during his brief career as a policeman, was engaged in earnest conversation with the oldest member of the team, Giacomo D'Amico. He shook Remo warmly by the hand. Obviously, Remo has imparted his own bit of good news to Giacomo, thought Beppe sadly.

On the table furthest away from the bride and groom, the tone of conversation had degenerated somewhat, thanks largely to a generous supply of wine. Danilo Simone and Gino Martelli – no longer the newcomers to the team – were ragging Pippo, his knee bound up tightly, and his *fidanzata,* Mariangela, about the difficulties they must be experiencing in enjoying an intimate relationship whilst his left leg was stretched out horizontally. Gino had made some vulgar comment about the wrong member being rigid. Oriana had, with her usual biting candour, poured scorn on Danilo and Gino's naivety. "You two boys are just too sexually inexperienced to know you can have perfectly good sex even with a man who is lying flat on his back!" she was saying. "Although I doubt whether you two have the imagination to figure it out!" Mariangela was in stitches.

Pippo, from his remote position, since his leg would not fit under the table, could see that the Archbishop was sitting directly behind Oriana. He made a gesture with his head. Oriana looked horrified when she realised that her words must have been overheard by Don Emanuele.

The cleric in question turned round to look at Oriana and with absolutely no change of expression, said to her: "My dear Oriana, when you next go to confession, I hope you will spare some poor priest the more graphic details of your adventures."

He received a round of applause, a burst of unrestrained laughter – and their undying respect. The proceedings did not flag until the last person had downed the last coffee and the last *genziana.*

The team were to be picked up at six o'clock by the new recruit – *l'Orso Bruno.* He arrived in a khaki-coloured people carrier equipped with wire grills over the doors and windows. It had been borrowed for the occasion from the prison transport police.

"Get in you miscreants!" the Brown Bear had growled – without a smile. For the first time, they realised that this seeming misfit in their midst might have a sense of humour.

"Anything interesting happen today, Luigi?" asked Gino.

"Just a hold-up by a couple of mobsters from down south - a local restaurant near the police station."

The Brown Bear was never very forthcoming.

"So, I guess the delinquents got away?" said Danilo.

"*Nonsì, ragazzi.* I arrived in time."

"Where are they now? Wandering round the police station?" taunted another member of the team.

The Brown Bear was looking sheepish. "In hospital with concussion - I shouldn't have smacked their heads together quite so hard, *ragazzi.*"

It became a legend in Via Pesaro that, from that day onwards, the mob from Foggia gave up all attempts at amateur hold-ups in the city of Pescara. Rumours spread amongst clan members that the "Incredible Hulk" had been deployed by the local police force.

* * *

Beppe and Sonia waited patiently until the last people had left. Beppe's family had said their fond farewells; even *mamma* looked content with life. Promises were made that he and Sonia would visit Catanzaro as soon as possible. Sonia's parents merely said: "See you two later on tomorrow." Pippo, with Mariangela by his side, was carted off back to hospital. He would soon be transferred to Rome for the major operation to replace his kneecap. Giacomo D'Amico took Beppe and Sonia down to the boat, where they would spend their first post-wedding night being rocked by the gentle rise and fall of the boat.

"I never really thought about it before," confessed Beppe. "But what happens to the baby if we want to...?"

"I don't suppose he – or she – will notice at this stage, *amore.*"

But to Beppe's mind, it suddenly seemed like an invasion of another human being's territory, an illegal break-in. It was a strange sensation which he would have to come to terms with when he was on his own.

"We don't mind if it's a boy or a girl, do we, Sonia?" he asked instead.

She shook her head.

"No, we don't mind at all. All I would say is I was very happy to have two older brothers in my life. But I don't want to know until the time comes."

After the turbulence of the last few days, they lay awake soothed by the gentle motion of the boat, disinclined to think about what was going on at the *Questura.*

"How would you feel if we had twins, *amore?*"

Beppe smiled in the intimacy of that gentle darkness.

"*Due piccioni con una fava,* so to speak," he replied philosophically.

(Beppe's closing, tongue-in-cheek words: "Two birds with one stone" 'Two pigeons with one broad bean.' I am told that pigeons used to be 'culled' by putting out a poisoned bean to tempt the birds to their fate.)

Epilogue

The crime committed by Damiano is put into perspective when compared to the violent and brutal acts committed by the mafia gangs. Nevertheless, the court judged him to be entirely sound in mind and body. Thus, he was subject to the usual legal procedure of the law and found guilty of *omicidio colposo* – manslaughter. The mitigating circumstances put forward by Damiano's lawyer were taken into consideration. He was imprisoned in a single cell in Pescara's jail, where Don Emanuele visited him on a weekly basis. The Archbishop spent patient hours talking to the prisoner. He gently but firmly declined to hear Damiano's confession again – on the grounds that he had refused to grant this sinner absolution in the first place.

"*Mio caro Damiano,*" he would repeat patiently, "when I am convinced you are truly repentant for what you have done, I shall joyfully grant you absolution. Until that time comes, we must both pray fervently that you will recognise that you have taken one man's life from him – without just cause. At present, most of your anger and guilt seem to stem from the fact you killed the wrong man!"

"I think it would help me, *padre,* if I spoke to that *commissario.* Do you think he would be willing to see me?" asked Damiano. "I feel really bad about the way I treated him."

"I will ask him. The *commissario* is a good man. But he has recently got married and his wife is expecting a child. You must be patient, *amico mio.*"

"Well, I've got seven years to be patient...that should be long enough for him!"

Don Emanuele was always reminded that his decision not to grant absolution was based on his perception of some character flaw in this strange, wild man.

Damiano went on writing his book on mushrooms with a paranoid intensity – as if his sin could be absolved through this sheer act of dogged determination.

Don Emanuele would have to go on praying for several months.

* * *

The *assessore* accused of corruption and collusion with the mafia was duly brought to trial in Rome by the *Guardia di Finanza* and the DIA. Beppe, after their few days' rest and their boat trip to Silvi Marina, was treated to a description by the Finance Police in Pescara of the tortuous electronic paths they had been forced to tread in order to trace the blame back to the Luzzi clan boss in Foggia.

"*Un labirinto di conti segreti,*" said the Colonel, "finishing up in Morocco of all places."

Beppe was always fascinated and full of admiration for their colleagues in the *Guardia di Finanza*. "*Che bravi!*" he complimented them when he was shown the web of secret bank accounts which they had painstakingly revealed.

The Foggia clan boss was unable to extricate himself from the accusation of fraudulently acquiring building contracts in the public domain. He was given a fifteen-year jail sentence, which included incitation to murder and grievous bodily harm. His own underlings had turned State evidence against him. His collusion with Arturo Alfieri from the Naples clan led to the arrest of the Naples gangster, accused of inciting grievous bodily harm – Pippo's kneecap. The Alfieri clan were probably glad to be rid of Don Alfieri's eldest son, who had turned out to be too impetuous and a vindictive time-waster. That left the immediate threat to *Commissario* Beppe Stancato considerably diminished. The Alfieri clan quickly reconstituted itself.

"For every success story we can boast about, the monster manages to grow two more heads," complained the *Questore.*

The club in Pescara called *The Night Owl* was regularly invaded by the *Carabinieri* in search of drugs. All they managed to achieve was to thwart the traffickers and render their lives less predictable. It was difficult to stem the tide of drugs, simply because the public demand was ever present, Beppe's new recruit constantly pointed out. Apart from that, the obvious presence of the mafia clan from Foggia had been, at least temporarily, quashed.

As soon as the media – especially *TV-Tavo* - broke the story about the apartments under construction in Tagliamonte having been mafia financed, some of the the home-seeking inhabitants in Abruzzo looked elsewhere. Estate agents to the north of Pescara sprang up in droves, advertising the apartments as holiday homes for 'foreigners' – which included Italians from the north of the peninsula.

At a meeting with his newly constituted team, Beppe congratulated everybody on their efforts to foil the mafia invasion of their city.

"This has not been achieved without sacrifice," pointed out the *commissario.*

* * *

Beppe decided that the routine of police work was an aspect of his life which was to be welcomed. If he ever showed signs of *ennui,* he was quickly brought to heel again by Sonia. Comic relief from normal police matters was occasioned by a phone call from Enrico Nardini several months after the wedding – when snow still covered the upper reaches of the Gran Sasso and La Maiella mountain ranges - and Sonia's motherhood was becoming apparent.

"Just after your wedding, I was called out to a domestic disturbance in Montebello di Bertona. It was your friend Ernesto Carlettini who was publicly rowing with Salvatore's Sri-Lankan wife in the garden about who the house belonged to. It became very heated – at least on Ernesto's part. The woman, Dinusha, remained very calm as soon as I arrived. She's a real beauty, by the way, *commissario...*"

Enrico Nardini had had to ask Ernesto to leave the property. The house deeds were clearly and legally in her name. Ernesto Carlettini had hired a lawyer to sort out whether or not he had a rightful claim to the property. In the end, the wife, Dinusha, grew weary of the legal hassle and decided to return to her family in Turin – as long as she was duly compensated.

"Poor old Ernesto had to fork out nearly a million euros in legal fees and compensation to the girl before he could lay hands on his brother's property," Enrico informed Beppe at a later date.

Beppe was delighted to hear that the outcome of the dispute had left Ernesto Carlettini chastised and humbled – even if not cured of his petty-mindedness.

"I could never quite work out how Ernesto Carlettini had so much cash at his disposal," said Beppe. "Oh, and by the way, I want to thank you again for the case of wine you sent me, Enrico. If I wasn't so already, I am a complete convert to the wines of Loreto Aprutino now."

* * *

It took Pippo well beyond the confines of the events described in this book before he could walk again - Remo Mastrodicasa and his partner Marta were already running the countryside *agriturismo* outside L'Aquila before Pippo was released from hospital. This restaurant-cum-bed-and-

242

breakfast, owned by the city of Pescara, employed over forty youngsters who might otherwise have ended up *disoccupati.* Remo Mastrodicasa looked relaxed and in his element.

Pippo had had to learn to use his left leg again as if he had been a baby becoming a toddler. His *fidanzata,* Mariangela, had remained with him throughout the time of his convalescence. She had elected to stay with cousins in Rome and had found a job as a waitress in a very up-market restaurant – a far cry from the simple, homely *trattoria* run by her father in Penne.

"I will ask you to marry me, Mariangela, as soon as I am no longer walking around on crutches," he had rashly stated.

"I may not be able to wait that long, Pippo," she had replied tartly. Pippo had on several occasions noticed a similarity between her way of talking and that of his colleague, Oriana Salvati – who kept in regular touch by mobile phone.

Pippo sighed and tried to concentrate on walking along the rubberised track between the hand rails needed to support his weight. "At least my arms are strong," he said bitterly to his therapist.

Pippo wondered on many occasions who was paying for his treatment during his slow and painful return to normality.

"If I have understood correctly from colleagues in Naples, Pippo," Beppe told him during one of their frequent telephone calls, "I believe the Alfieri clan have made a very generous contribution to your private clinic."

"How obliging of them, *capo,*" observed Pippo. He was not sure how he felt about his slow cure being financed even indirectly by the mafia.

* * *

"I hope you don't think I'm becoming over-protective, *amore?*

"Telepathy again - I was just going to ask *you* the same question."

"I suppose it's quite natural in the circumstances. We both have a physically demanding and sometimes risky job."

"Let's just say that we have both become more dependent on one another."

"That sounds a good way of saying *I don't want to let you out of my sight.*"

"By the way, *tesoro,* I'm sorry to say it isn't going to be twins…"

Italian glossary and cultural notes:

Prologue

La Cascata del Vitello d'Oro:
The Golden Calf Waterfall *(All explained in the story)*

La Guardia Forestale:
The arm of the police charged with protecting the forests.

È la guerra:
It's war

amico mio:
my friend (m)

Buon appetito:
Enjoy your meal.

Chapter 1

amore mio:
my dear : my love

commissario:
the rank of chief inspector – cf Montalbano.

fidanzato (m) fidanzata (f)
fiancé(e) boyfriend : girlfriend (considered the same status in Italy, since it is assumed that if you date someone, it is a serious commitment. An interesting cultural difference when compared to the Anglo-Saxon world.)

San Cetteo:
The cathedral in Pescara built in the 1930s.

agente:
officer / agent

Questore:
Chief Commissioner i/c of a Questura

Chapter 2

capo:
chief : boss

dunque:
so : therefore

Carabinieri:
The national police force under the Ministry of Defence

In bocca al lupo:
Best of luck (lit. In the mouth of the wolf)

La Bilancia:
'The Weighing Scales' - A real-life restaurant near Loreto Aprutino.

La Chiesa di Santa Maria in Piano
The Church of Our Lady in the Plain – famous for its outstanding frescos.

porchetta:
hog roast

offre la casa:
It's on the house

genziana:
a liqueur from Abruzzo.

ragazzi:
guys : lads (and lasses if there are girls present)

che schifo:
How disgusting! *(kay SKI – fo)*

Non ci posso credere:
I can't believe it! *(credere – like the word 'creed')*

Chapter 3

Gianluca Alfieri:
The mafia *boss* from Beppe Stancato's previous investigation – 'The Case of the Sleeping Beauty'

salumiere:
The owner of a 'delicatessen' shop, selling cold meats and cheeses etc.

pugliese:
the adjective meaning 'from Puglia'

Sacra Corona Unita – la SCU:
the Puglia-based mafia clans – The Sacred United Crown

bravo (m)   brava (f)
Well done!

le ragazze squillo:
lit: call girls – uno squillo is a phone call

appunto:
precisely : exactly

Chapter 4

A domani alle undici:
See you tomorrow at 11 o'clock

un bacio:
a kiss on the cheek

A presto!
See you soon!

Piacere, commissario...
It's a pleasure, inspector...

osteria:
an inn : a simple eating place with limited menu

Chapter 6

d'accordo:
OK : I agree

Trenitalia:
The company that runs the state railway network – 50% State controlled!

La Freccia Bianca:

The White Arrow – the Intercity trains which run northwards to Milan or Turin

palazzo:
a block of flats : lit: a palace

zio:
uncle

Hotel Castello Chiolo:
Loreto Aprutino's magnificent castle hotel – with a moderately priced restaurant.

Chapter 7

the frescos:
The magnificent and perfectly preserved frescos in the church of Santa Maria in Piano - see them on the internet.

La Guardia di Finanza:
The financial police.

Chapter 8

un cornetto:
'a little horn' The Italian word for a 'croissant'.

the charred wooden door:
This episode is borrowed from a 'real life' event in Lecce, where the bar owner defied the local SCU clan by refusing to pay her *pizzo* – protection money.

la padrona:

a lady owner

simpatici:
plural of 'simpatico' = friendly *(simPA- tee chee)*

Chapter 9

Coraggio giovanotto!
A bit of courage, young man!

commercianti:
shopkeepers

Salento:
The southernmost region of Puglia whose capital is Lecce.

Farindola – pronounced with the stress on the second syllable: *fa-RIN-do-la*

tesoro
treasure – a common term of endearment

Chapter 10

112 and 113:
112 is the emergency number for the Carabinieri. 113 is the same for the ordinary police. Both numbers appear clearly on all police cars.

Pronto, chi parla?
What you say when you pick up the phone. 'Pronto' means 'ready'

Lo specchio della vita italiana:

An invented name for an imaginary publication - 'The mirror of Italian life'

targa
number plate on a car

Chapter 11

grappa:
a strong liqueur made from distilled grapes

Chapter 12

Serena Vacri:
The 'sleeping beauty' from the previous novel, kidnapped and held by the mob. Her dramatic rescue by Beppe and his team form the climax of the novel.

eccoli:
here they are

mannaggia:
a mild expletive indicating surprise

non c'è scampo:
no escape : no way out

Il Clinico Salvavita:
'salvavita' = life-saving

Chapter 13

their only daughter:

Sonia has two elder brothers who no longer live with the parents – see previous novel.

Catarella / Montalbano:
A reference to the fictional character created by the famous Italian author, Andrea Camilleri, now in his nineties. The 'Montalbano' series regularly features on BBC 4. The Montalbano books are written in Sicilian dialect – so the English version is essential if you want to delve into this author's highly entertaining stories. Andrea Camilleri has claimed that he himself prefers the TV film versions to his own books. Commissario Montalbano is played by the actor Luca Zingaretti.

con piacere
with pleasure

l'Agenzia delle Entrate:
the Tax Office

As alike as two drops of water:
'As alike as two peas in a pod' I used the English translation of the equivalent Italian expression – *assomigliarsi come due goccie di acqua.*

Chapter 14

Ape:
Anyone who has driven in Italy will have come across those chugging three-wheeled contraptions, propelled by a lawn-mower engine. The word 'Ape' means 'bee' – because of the buzzing sound these vehicles make.

Sergio Balducci:
My fictitious name for the Prime Minister at the time of this novel (2010). The clue is in the initials!

Cinque Stelle:
The '5 Stars' party was a fledgling affair in those days. This party, founded by the comedian Beppe Grillo, is now a force to be reckoned with. It represents a rebellion against traditional politics.

Pecorino:
In Farindola, they make their own delicious version of this sheep's milk cheese. 'Pecorino' is, confusingly, also a white wine producing grape variety – native to Abruzzo – as is the grape called 'Trebbiano'.

acqua in bocca!
'My lips are sealed'. Interestingly, the Italian equivalent means 'water in the mouth' – presumably because opening your mouth would cause the water to spill out.

Chapter 15
La Cascata del Vitello d'Oro:
The waterfall is real. I know, because I visited it in 2016. The description is authentic. I was given a lift from Farindola by the town hall handyman; his name was Gabriele.

Chapter 18

There are a number of references in this chapter which hark back to incidents from Beppe and his team's previous investigation in 'The Case of the Sleeping Beauty'. However, this should not impede your grasp of current events.

giurin giurello!
Beppe is teasingly making a promise of future good behaviour with a phrase used by very young children. Like 'Cross my heart and hope to die'. Sonia is not impressed.

Va da sè
It goes without saying. Lit: It goes by itself.

Chapter 19

The Sleeping Beauty flat:
Occupied by Beppe and Sonia. The drugged girl, Serena Vacri, was first discovered in this flat. See *The Case of the Sleeping Beauty.*

Maturità exams:
the Italian equivalent of our 'A' Levels

Chapter 20

Medaglia al merito di servizio:
A medal for bravery reserved for the State Police – can be gold, silver or bronze.

piccolo borghese:
Un petit bourgeois. A petty middle-class individual.

Fratelli d'Italia:
The national anthem: 'Brothers and Sisters of Italy'

croce d'oro:
golden cross

Gianni Morandi:
A very popular singer, actor and song-writer. I have allowed myself one anachronism – with apologies to GM. His song "Solo insieme saremo felici" was only issued in 2016. A touching, lyrical song by this great popular artist.

un brindisi

a toast

nonsì:
Luigi, the *Orso Bruno,* reveals his southern Italian origins. It's a cross between saying 'yes' and 'no' - but interchangeable at will, so that the speaker's attitude remains suitably ambiguous.

genziana
A liqueur – flavoured with the flower of the same name - peculiar to the Abruzzo region, as well as in parts of France, *la gentiane.*

Epilogue

D.I.A.
Direzione Investigativa Antimafia. The Antimafia police.

un labirinto di conti segreti:
a maze of secret accounts

disoccupato:
unemployed

About the author

You have probably already read in previous novels that the author has lived, loved and worked in Italy for eight life-changing years – and don't need to hear it again. The author would just like to say that recent disastrous events in the United Kingdom, brought about by politicians with no vision of the future, have scuppered the ambitions of many of us whose life has been enriched by sharing our common cultural heritage with our European neighbours.
I feel I have been robbed of my European status in the eyes of the world.
Amen.

Acknowledgements

My thanks to Dr. Andrew Webber and Dr. Kathleen Thompson – author of "From Both Ends of the Stethoscope" – for their help and guidance about blood groups and the illness, nephritis – from which I was "miraculously" cured when I was eleven years old.

Postscripts

I visited the little town of Farindola in May 2016. My main purpose was to visit the waterfall – La Cascata del Vitello d'Oro. I was struck by the kindness of all those who worked in the Town Hall of Farindola. Without their help, I may never have reached the waterfall. I was offered a lift up to the waterfall and back again by the Town Hall's handyman – whose name was Gabriele.

It was a huge shock to me in January 2017 to learn that it was in this remote mountain township where a tourist hotel, Il Rigopiano, had been devastated by an avalanche, resulting in twenty-nine people losing their life. My sympathies go out to all those affected by this tragedy. Such a tight-knit community as Farindola did not deserve such a fate.

The invasion of Pescara by the mafia is a purely fictionalised account of a phenomenon which could occur anywhere. I am assured by Italian readers that my version is, sadly, not too far removed from reality. The episode of the burnt door of the Bar Galileo was borrowed from a real-life incident which took place in the city of Lecce in Puglia – exactly for the motives described in this story.

Mafia involvement in the construction industries is well documented. After twenty years in the making, a new highway - running from Naples to Reggio Calabria – was completed in 2016. It was proudly proclaimed by the State that this engineering feat had been accomplished without interference from the mafia clans. QED.

RW February 2017 – up-dated version of the story.

Made in United States
North Haven, CT
15 July 2022

21422497R00143